PRAISE FOR *THE CATALAIN BOOK OF SECRETS*

"Life-affirming, thought-provoking, heartwarming, it's one of those books which—if you happen to read it exactly when you need to—will heal your wounds as you turn the pages."
—Catriona McPherson, Agatha, Anthony, Macavity, and Bruce Alexander–winning author

"Prolific mystery writer Lourey tells of a matriarchal clan of witches joining forces against age-old evil . . . The novel is tightly plotted, and Lourey shines when depicting relationships—romantic ones as well as tangled links between Catalains . . . Lourey emphasizes the ties that bind in spite of secrets and resentment."
—*Kirkus Reviews*

"Lourey expertly concocts a Gothic fusion of long-held secrets, melancholy, and resolve . . . Exquisitely written in naturally flowing, expressive language, the book delves into the special relationships between sisters, and mothers and daughters."
—*Publishers Weekly*

PRAISE FOR *SALEM'S CIPHER*

"A fast-paced, sometimes brutal thriller reminiscent of Dan Brown's *The Da Vinci Code*."
—*Booklist* (starred review)

"[A] hair-raising thrill ride."
—*Library Journal* (starred review)

"The fascinating historical information combined with a story line ripped from the headlines will hook conspiracy theorists and action addicts alike."

—Kirkus Reviews

"Fans of *The Da Vinci Code* are going to love this book . . . one of my favorite reads of 2016."

—Crimespree Magazine

"This suspenseful tale has something for absolutely everyone to enjoy."

—Suspense Magazine

PRAISE FOR *MERCY'S CHASE*

"An immersive voice, an intriguing story, a wonderful character—highly recommended!"

—Lee Child, #1 *New York Times* bestselling author

"Both a sweeping adventure and race-against-time thriller, *Mercy's Chase* is fascinating, fierce, and brimming with heart—just like its heroine, Salem Wiley."

—Meg Gardiner, author of *Into the Black Nowhere*

"Action-packed, great writing taut with suspense, an appealing main character to root for—who could ask for anything more?"

—Buried Under Books

PRAISE FOR *MAY DAY*

"Jess Lourey writes about a small-town assistant librarian, but this is no genteel traditional mystery. Mira James likes guys in a big way, likes booze, and isn't afraid of motorcycles. She flees a dead-end job and a dead-end boyfriend in Minneapolis and ends up in Battle Lake, a little town with plenty of dirty secrets. The first-person narrative in *May Day* is fresh, the characters quirky. Minnesota has many fine crime writers, and Jess Lourey has just entered their ranks!"
—Ellen Hart, award-winning author of the Jane Lawless and Sophie Greenway series

"This trade paperback packed a punch . . . I loved it from the get-go!"
—*Tulsa World*

"What a romp this is! I found myself laughing out loud . . ."
—*Crimespree Magazine*

"Mira digs up a closetful of dirty secrets, including sex parties, cross-dressing, and blackmail, on her way to exposing the killer. Lourey's debut has a likeable heroine and surfeit of sass."
—*Kirkus Reviews*

UNSPEAKABLE
THINGS

UNSPEAKABLE THINGS

THINGS

JESS LOUREY

Text copyright © 2020 by Jess Lourey
All rights reserved.

Published by Thomas & Mercer, Seattle

www.apub.com

Amazon, the Amazon logo, and Thomas & Mercer are trademarks of Amazon.com, Inc., or its affiliates.

ISBN-13: 9781542008785
ISBN-10: 1542008786

Cover design by Caroline Teagle Johnson

Illustrations by Tony VanDenEinde of Little Elephant Interactive

Printed in the United States of America

To Patrick, who showed me the way out.

AUTHOR'S NOTE

I was one of a few hundred kids to come of age in Paynesville, Minnesota, in the 1980s. I grew up thinking that every small town had a curfew siren that warned the children indoors at 9:00 p.m., that Chester the Molester was a common nickname for the bogeyman, that Peeping Toms were not unusual. I had my own problems at home, some childish, others much more serious, but the rumors of a man hunting children became the backbeat of my preteen and teen years.

I graduated high school in 1988 and moved to Minneapolis.

When Jacob Wetterling was abducted on October 22, 1989, from St. Joseph, Minnesota, thirty miles up the road from Paynesville, I was preparing to drop out of my second year of college. Those rumors from my early years (*don't go out at night or Chester will get you!*) rushed back into focus. Pictures of Jacob were everywhere. People came together to search for that sweet-faced eleven-year-old who'd been abducted by a masked man with a gun. Days passed into weeks into years, and Jacob was never found. Not until a local blogger began writing about the potential connection between Jacob's disappearance and the abduction and release of eight boys in and around Paynesville in the '80s was Jacob's abductor arrested, twenty-seven years later. He led authorities to Jacob's remains.

The experience has haunted me. It's haunted many of us in the Midwest, upending what we thought we knew about rural communities and the safety of children. The true version of events has been told well in other places, most notably in season one of the *In the Dark* podcast. It was the emotional repercussions of those events that I needed to give voice to. I needed to create coherence out of my memories of growing up in chronic fear. When Cassie McDowell, the fictional heroine of this story, came to me and begged for her story to be told, I saw my chance.

While the story is inspired by real people and events, it is entirely fictional. However, it's my hope that the character of Gabriel honors the goodness in all nine of those boys.

Thank you for reading.

PROLOGUE

The lonely-scream smell of that dirt basement lived inside me.

Mostly it kept to a shadow corner of my brain, but the second I'd think *Lilydale*, it'd scuttle over and smother me. The smell was a predatory cave stink, the suffocating funk of a great somnolent monster that was all mouth and hunger. It had canning jars for teeth, a single string hanging off a light bulb its uvula. It waited placidly, eternally, for country kids to stumble down its backbone stairs.

It let us swing blindly for that uvula string.

Our fingers would brush against it.

light!

The relief was candy and sun and silver dollars and the last good thing we felt before the beast swallowed us whole, digesting us for a thousand years.

But that's not right.

My imagination, I'd been told, was quite a thing.

The *basement* wasn't the monster.

The man was.

And he wasn't passive. He hunted.

I hadn't returned to Lilydale since that evening. The police and then Mom had asked if I wanted anything from my bedroom, and I'd said no. I'd been thirteen, not stupid, though a lot of people confuse the two.

Now that his funeral had called me home, that cellar stink doubled back with a vengeance, settling like a fishhook way deep in my face where my nose met my brain. The smell crept into my sleep, even, convinced me that I was trapped in that gravedirt basement all over again. I'd thrash and yell, wake up my husband.

He'd hold me. He knew the story.

At least he thought he did.

I'd made it famous in my first novel, shared its inspiration on my cross-country book tour. Except somehow I'd never mentioned the necklace, not to anyone, not even Noah. Maybe that piece felt too precious.

Or maybe it just made me look dumb.

I could close my eyes and picture it. The chain would be considered too heavy now but was the height of fashion in 1983, gold, same metal as the paper airplane charm hanging off it.

I'd believed that airplane necklace was my ticket out of Lilydale.

I didn't actually think I could fly it. *Big duh*, as we said back then. But the boy who wore the necklace? Gabriel? I was convinced he would change everything.

And I guess he did.

CHAPTER 1

"Fifteen two, fifteen four, and a pair for six." Sephie beamed.

Dad matched her smile across the table. "Nice hand. Cass?"

I laid down my cards, trying to keep the gloat off my face and failing. "Fifteen two, fifteen four, fifteen six, and a run for ten!"

Mom moved our peg. "We win."

I shoulder-danced. "I can give you lessons if you want, Sephie."

She rolled her eyes. "In being a poor sport?"

I laughed and dug into the popcorn. Mom had made a huge batch, super salty and doused in brewer's yeast. That had been an hour earlier, when we'd started game night. The bowl was getting down to the old maids. I dug around for the ones showing a peek of white. Part-popped old maids are worth their weight in gold, taste-wise.

"Need a refill?" Dad stood, pointing at Mom's half-full glass sweating in the sticky May air. Summer was coming early this year—at least that's what my biology teacher, Mr. Patterson, had said. Was really going to mess with crops.

He'd seemed bothered by this, but I bet I wasn't the only kid looking forward to a hot break. Sephie and I planned to turn as brown as baked beans and bleach our dark hair blonde. She'd heard from a friend of a friend that baby oil on our skin and vinegar water spritzed in our hair would work as well as those expensive coconut-scented tanning oils and Sun In. We'd even whispered about finding a spot at the edge of our property, where the woods broke for the drainage ditch, to lay out naked. The thought made me shiver. Boys liked no tan lines. I'd learned that watching *Little Darlings*.

Mom lifted her drink and emptied it before offering it to Dad. "Thanks, love."

He strode over to her side of the table, leaning in for a deep kiss before taking her glass. Now I was rolling my eyes right along with Sephie. Mom and Dad, mostly Dad, regularly tried to convince us that we were lucky they were still so in love, but *gross*.

Dad pulled away from kissing Mom and caught our expressions. He laughed his air-only *heh heh* laugh, setting down both glasses so he was free to massage Mom's shoulders. They were an attractive couple, people said it all the time. Mom had been beautiful, every cloudy picture taken of her proved that, and she still had the glossy brown hair and wide eyes, though incubating Sephie and me had padded her hips and belly. Dad was handsome, too, with a Charles Bronson thing going on. You could see how they'd ended up together, especially after Mom downed a glass of wine, and she'd let spill how she'd always been drawn to the bad boys, even back in high school.

My immediate family was small: just Mom and Aunt Jin; my big sister, Persephone (my parents had a thing for Greek names); and Dad. I didn't know my dad's side of the family. They wouldn't be worth sweeping into a dustpan, at least that's what my grandpa on Mom's side swore to my grandma the winter he died of a massive heart attack. My grandma hadn't argued. She'd been a docile lady who always smelled of fresh-baked bread no matter the season. A few weeks after Grandpa passed, she died of a stroke, which sounds like a swim move but is not.

They'd lost a son, my mom's parents, when I was three years old. He'd been a wild one, I guess. Died playing chicken in a '79 Camaro, probably drinking, people said. I could only remember one thing about Uncle Richard. It was at his funeral. Jin was crying, but Mom was crying louder, and she went up to Grandpa for a hug. He turned away from her, and she stood there, looking sadder than a lost baby.

I asked her about it once, about why Grandpa wouldn't hug her. She said I was too young to remember anything from Rich's funeral, and besides, the past should stay in the past.

"I think your mother is the most beautiful woman in the world," Dad said in the here and now, rubbing Mom's shoulders while she closed her eyes and made a dreamy face.

"Fine by me," I said. "Just get a room."

Dad swept his arm in a wide arc, his smile tipped sideways. "I have a whole house. Maybe *you* should learn to relax. I'll rub your shoulders next."

My eyes cut to Sephie. She was flicking a bent corner of a playing card.

"I'm okay," I said.

"Sephie? Your neck tense?"

She shrugged.

"That's my girl!" He moved to her, laying his hands on her bony shoulders. She was two years older than me but skinny no matter what she ate, all buckeroo teeth and dimples, a dead ringer for Kristy McNichol, though I'd eat my own hair before I'd tell her.

Dad started in on Sephie. "It's good to feel good," he murmured to her.

That made me itch inside. "Can we play another game of cribbage?"

"Soon," Dad said. "First, I want to hear everyone's summer dreams."

I groaned. Dad was big on dreams. He believed you could be whatever you wanted, but you had to "see it" first. Hippie-dippie, but I suppose a person got used to it. Both Sephie and I swapped a look. We knew without saying it that Dad would not approve of our plan to transform ourselves into blondes. *Girls should not try to be anything for anyone,* he'd tell us. We needed to command our own minds and bodies.

Again, *gross.*

"I want to visit Aunt Jin," I offered.

Mom had been going half-lidded, but her eyes popped open at the mention of her sister. "That's a great plan! We can drive to Canada for a week."

"Excellent," Dad agreed.

My heart soared. We hardly ever traveled farther than up the highway to St. Cloud for co-op groceries, but now that Mom had her full-time teaching job, there'd been talk of road-tripping this summer. Still, I'd been afraid to suggest we visit Aunt Jin. If Mom and Dad were in the wrong mood, they'd kill that idea for eternity, and I really needed some Aunt Jin time. I loved her to death.

She was the only one who didn't pretend I was normal.

She was there when I was born, stayed on for a few weeks after that to help out Mom, but my first actual memory of her was from right after Uncle Richard's funeral. Aunt Jin was a decade younger than Mom, which put her at no more than seventeen at the time. I'd caught her staring at my throat, something a lot of people do.

Rather than look away, she'd smiled and said, "If you'd been born two hundred years ago, they'd have drowned you."

She was referring to the red, ropy scar that circled where my neck met my shoulders, thick as one of Mr. T's gold chains. Apparently, I'd shot out of Mom with the umbilical cord coiled around my throat, my body blue as a Berry Punch Fla-Vor-Ice, eyes wide even though I wasn't breathing. I exited so fast that the doctor dropped me.

Or at least that's the story I was told.

There I hung, a human dingleberry, until one of the nurses swooped in and unwound the cord, uncovering an amniotic band strangling me beneath that. The quick-thinking nurse cut it, then slapped me till I wailed. She'd saved my life, but the band had branded me. Mom said my lesion looked like an angry scarlet snake at first. That seemed dramatic. In any case, I suspect the nurse was a little shaky when she finally handed me over. The whole fiasco wasn't exactly a job well done. Plus,

Rosemary's Baby had hit theaters a couple years before, and everyone in that room must have been wondering what had propelled me out of the womb with such force.

"It would have been bad luck to keep a baby whose own mother tried to strangle it twice," Aunt Jin finished, chucking me under my chin. I decided on the spot that it was an okay joke because Mom was her sister, and they both loved me.

Here's another nutty saying Aunt Jin liked to toss my way: "Earth. If you know what you're doing, you're in the wrong place." She'd waggle her thick eyebrows and tip an imaginary cigar as she spoke. I didn't know where that gesture was from, but she'd giggle so hard, her laugh like marbles thrown up into the sunshine, that I'd laugh along with her.

That's how every Aunt Jin visit began. The joke about drowning me, some meaty life quotes, and then we'd dance and sing along to her Survivor and Johnny Cougar tapes. She'd spill all about her travels and let me sip the honey-colored liqueur she'd smuggled from Amsterdam or offer me a packet of the biscuits she loved so much and that I'd pretend didn't taste like old saltines. Sephie would want to join in, I'd see her on the sidelines, but she never quite knew how to hop on the ride that was Aunt Jin.

I did.

Aunt Jin and me were *thick as thieves*.

That made it okay that Dad liked Sephie way more than me.

I wrinkled my nose. He was really going to town on that massage. Mom had left to refill her and Dad's drinks even though he'd offered, since it was taking him so long to rub Sephie's shoulders.

"Sephie," I asked, because her eyes were closed and I wanted that to stop, "what's *your* dream for the summer?"

She spoke quietly, almost a whisper. "I want to get a job at the Dairy Queen."

Dad's hands stopped kneading. A look I couldn't name swept across his face, and I thought I'd memorized every twitch of his. He almost immediately swapped out that weird expression for a goofy smile that lifted his beard a half inch. "Great! You can save for college."

Sephie nodded, but she looked so sad all of a sudden. She'd been nothing but moods and mysteries since December. The change in temperament coincided with her getting boobs (*Santa Claus delivered!* I'd teased her), and so I didn't need to be *Remington Steele*'s Laura Holt to understand that one was connected to the other.

Mom returned to the dining room, a fresh drink in each hand, her attention hooked on my dad. "Another game of cribbage?"

I leaned back to peek at the kitchen clock. It was ten thirty. Every kid I told thought it was cool I didn't have a bedtime. I supposed they were right. Tomorrow was the first day of the last week of seventh grade for me, though. "I'm going to sleep. You guys can play three handed."

Mom nodded.

"Don't let the bedbugs bite!" Dad said.

I didn't glance at Sephie as I walked away. I felt a quease about leaving her up with them when they'd been drinking, but I wrote it off as payback for her always falling asleep first the nights we were left alone, back when we'd sometimes sleep together. She'd let me climb in bed with her, which was nice, but then she'd crash out like a light, and there I'd lay agonizing over every sound, and in an old house like ours there was lots of unexplained thumping and creaking in the night. When I'd finally drift off, everything but my mouth and nose covered by the quilt, she'd have a sleep spaz and wake me right back up.

I couldn't remember the last time we'd slept in the same bed, hard as I tried on the walk to the bathroom. I rinsed off my face, then reached for my toothbrush, planning out tomorrow's clothes. If I woke up forty-five minutes early, I could use the hot rollers, but I hadn't okayed it with Sephie, and I'd already excused myself from the table. I brushed my teeth and spit, rinsing with the same metallic well water that turned the ends of my hair orange.

I couldn't reach my upstairs bedroom without walking through a corner of the dining room. I kept my eyes trained on the ground, my shoulders high around my ears, sinking deep in my thoughts. My homework was done, my folders organized inside my garage-sale Trapper Keeper that was as good as new except for the Scotch-taped rip near the seam.

First period tomorrow was supposed to be English, but instead we were to proceed directly to the gym for an all-school presentation. The posters slapped around declared it a Summer Safety Symposium, which some clever eighth graders had shorthanded to Snake Symposium. *SSS.* I'd heard the rumors this week that Lilydale kids were disappearing and then coming back changed. Everyone had. Aliens, the older kids on the bus claimed, were snatching kids and *probing* them.

I knew all about aliens. When I waited in the grocery checkout line, the big-eyed green creatures stared at me from the front cover of the *National Enquirer* right below the shot of Elizabeth Taylor's vampire monkey baby.

Right. *Aliens.*

Probably the symposium was meant to put those rumors to rest, but I didn't think it was a good idea to hold it tomorrow. The break in our routine—combined with it being the last week of school—would make everyone extra squirrelly.

I was halfway up the stairs when I heard a knock that shivered the baby hairs on my neck. It sounded like it came from right below me, from the basement. That was a new sound.

Mom, Dad, and Sephie must have heard it, too, because they'd stopped talking.

"Old house," Dad finally said, a hot edge to his voice.

I shot up the rest of the stairs and across the landing, closed my door tightly, and slipped into my pajamas, tossing my T-shirt and terry cloth shorts into my dirty-clothes hamper before setting my alarm clock. I decided I *would* try the hot rollers. Sephie hadn't called dibs on them, and who knew? I might end up sitting next to Gabriel during the symposium. I should look my best.

I was jelly-bone tired, but my copy of *Nellie Bly's Trust It or Don't* guilted me from the top of my treasure shelves. Aunt Jin had sent it to me as an early birthday present. The book was full of the most fantastical stories and drawings, like the account of Martin J. Spalding, who was a professor of mathematics at age fourteen, or Beautiful Antonia, "the Unhappy Woman to Whom Love Always Brought Death!"

I'd been savoring the stories, reading only one a night so they'd last. I'd confided to Jin that I was going to be a writer someday. Attaining such a goal required practice and discipline. Didn't matter how tired I was. I needed to study the night's Nellie.

I flipped the book open to a random page, drawn instantly to the sketch of a proud German shepherd.

Nellie Bly's — Trust It or Don't!

The DOG THAT TRAVELED AROUND THE WORLD IN 30 DAYS!

COACH IS A GERMAN SHEPHERD WHO WAS ACCIDENTALLY LEFT BEHIND WHEN HIS FAMILY HAD TO FLEE WORLD WAR II GERMANY. IMAGINE THE FAMILY'S SURPRISE WHEN COACH APPEARED AT THEIR NEW CALIFORNIA HOME HALF A WORLD AWAY! HE IS BELIEVED TO HAVE SNEAKED ONTO A CARGO BOAT THAT BROUGHT HIM ACROSS THE OCEAN, AND THEN HE MADE HIS WAY TO HIS FAMILY. NOW THAT'S WHAT WE CALL PUPPY LOVE!

I smiled, satisfied. I could write that. My plan was to begin drafting one Nellie a week as soon as school was out. I'd already written a contract, which I'd called Cassie's Summer Writing Duties. It included a plan for getting my portfolio to Nellie Bly International Limited before Labor Day and a penalty (no television for a week) if I did not fulfill the terms of my contract. I'd had Sephie witness me signing it.

I set the huge yellow-covered book on my treasure shelf and stretched, checking my muscles. Did they want to sleep stretched out long underneath my bed or curled up short in my closet?

Long, they said.

All right, then. I grabbed a pillow and the top quilt off my bed and slid the pillow under the box springs first. I followed on my back, dragging the quilt behind. I had to squish to reach the farthest corner. The moon spilled enough light into my room that I could make out the black coils overhead.

They were the last thing I saw before drifting off to sleep.

CHAPTER 2

"Your dad's still asleep," Mom said when I stepped into the kitchen the next morning. "Don't make too much noise."

That was code for *cereal for breakfast*.

I scowled. "You think it's fair he gets to sleep in?"

Mom was rushing around the kitchen, taking out meat to thaw for dinner, making sure Dad knew what leftovers to eat for lunch, packing her own midday meal. "If life were fair, there'd be no starving children," she said, not even glancing my way.

I wasn't in the mood. "Maybe when I'm old I can sleep in all day."

Mom stiffened, and I worried for a second that I'd pushed too far. She tolerated a lot, but when she flipped, she was *gone*. "He's keeping artist's hours," she finally said, dipping back into the refrigerator. "He's got a new project."

That explained why he'd been extra weird all weekend.

Donny McDowell was an artist and a soldier, that's what he told people. One he chose and the other he didn't, he'd say. After his discharge, he and Mom tried to make a go of it in St. Cloud, but the city was too busy for him. He declared that the future was to be found in the country, where he could return to his roots and live like a pioneer, natural and free.

Mom and Dad pulled up stakes and headed to Lilydale when I was four. My only memory of living in St. Cloud was coming home early from a friend's down the block to find Dad naked in bed with Mom's best friend. Mom's friend was naked, too. I ran out looking for Mom and found her biking around the block, crying. She wouldn't talk to me. I'd never asked her about that again, not like I asked her about Grandpa turning away from her at Uncle Richard's funeral.

Other than that, I didn't remember much about that house. For me, this was home, not a place we'd moved to. I had no recollection of Dad and Mom planting the row of lilacs that now shielded the house from the road, thick like fairy-tale briars. By the time they converted the granary to Dad's studio, I was walking. When they remodeled the red barn into a billowy Arabian den, I was old enough to help paint the interior, though Sephie complained that I spilled too much.

Dad, he liked to be outside, at least during the day. At night he'd grab a bottle and head to his studio or the basement to do "private work." Or he'd plop down in front of the television, drinking, and in either case getting tense quiet or super talky and telling us all about swallowing a bellyful of lead in some jungle and never being able to smell fish again because it was the last meal he'd eaten and he had to watch it pour out with the rest of his guts. If he kept drinking—this didn't happen very often, but it happened—he'd look at me or Sephie in a way that felt like a monster had found your hiding spot, and Mom would say it was just best if we went to bed early and stayed there until the next morning.

Game nights like last night were rare, more of Dad's weekend weirdness.

A new project explained it. He was always bragging that he could sell his work for big money but that he didn't want to be a cog in the capitalist machine. His sculptures *were* impressive, even if he didn't move many. He'd cut, bend, and weld the prettiest creatures and flowers out of sharp metal. The contrast slayed me, how he could craft a

13

ten-foot-tall bleeding heart out of steel and colored tin, so real, so soft looking, that you had to touch it to make sure it wasn't a true flower, you an ant on its stem. But it was metal you'd feel, cold in the winter, burning hot in the summer.

He'd created a Willy Wonka wonderland on our thirteen-acre hobby farm, one that only he knew the scope of. He'd reclaimed much of the wildness, forging paths through the woods with our help, twisting secret routes where you could stumble across a soaring metal bumblebee flashing wrought-iron eyelashes or play hide-and-seek through a metal daisy garden. People were impressed when they visited, which my dad made sure they did at least twice a year during his legendary (his word) parties.

"How lucky you are to have a creative father!" the guests would burble. "Your whole family is so *unconventional*. I wish my childhood had been like this! Do you know how *lucky* you are?"

I get why they said it, and sometimes they were so convincing that I'd begin to absorb a little bit of their dream fluff. That would last exactly as long as it took me to look around and see what the grown-ups were doing. My stomach twisted thinking about it.

"I can cook eggs quietly."

"Not quiet enough," Mom said.

Sephie strolled in. "I like cereal," she declared.

I turned to glare at her but was too surprised by her appearance. She'd slapped on a full face of makeup. Probably she thought she'd be safe with Dad still in bed, but fat chance Mom was going to let her leave the house looking like some nympho in a ZZ Top video.

I coughed.

Mom kept scurrying.

I coughed again, louder.

Mom spared Sephie a glance. Her eyes widened, and then they grew pinched. Then her face fell slack-tired all of a sudden. "I'll pack lunches for both of you."

I puffed up. No *way* did Sephie get to leave the house looking like Mary Kay had sneezed on her when I wasn't even allowed to shave my legs. Before I could formulate my argument, though, Sephie surprised me.

"Maybe you could give us a ride in?" she asked Mom.

I lost all my wind. *Nice job,* I told Sephie with my face. The hot rollers I'd used this morning had not gone as planned. A ride to school meant I could postpone introducing today's hair to my classmates for as long as possible. That's something with small towns. Everyone knows how you're *supposed* to look, and when you show up different, you better nail it or else.

I most definitely had not nailed it.

"Uh-uh," Mom said, unwrapping a loaf of homemade bread so she could slice six pieces. "I have to get to work to sign a grade-appeal form before seven."

I thought quickly. If I ended up riding the morning bus, I could expect at the very least to be called Curly Temple. Possibly Roseanne Roseannadanna. "My science teacher said he needs empty planting containers for summer school," I said. "Doesn't Dad have some in the basement? You could drop off the appeal, drive us and those pots to Lilydale to help out another teacher, and be back to Kimball before your first class! Win win win."

Mom's eyebrows narrowed, but I could tell she was considering it. "Fine," she finally said.

Sephie and I squealed.

"Your dad said they're in the basement?" Mom asked, which was her way of telling us to go grab them before she changed her mind.

"Yep!" I said.

Dad preferred Sephie and I avoid our dirt basement and the barn, the two places he said only adults should go. I normally had no problem steering clear of the basement, which had looked like a grave just waiting for a body the one time I'd explored it. Sephie and I figured he was growing mushrooms, among other things, because of how the basement smelled and because he passed dried shrooms around like root beer barrels when his parties started. If I had Mom's permission, though, and if it meant a ride to school, I was happy to dash down there. I turned toward the basement door and almost ran smack into Dad.

All three of us females froze, I think. I know I did, my heart triphammering against my ribs.

I backed up, avoiding meeting his eyes.

"I also said never to *go* in the basement," Dad growled, low and dangerous. He was wearing his white Hanes, nothing else. Cheeks hot, I looked away from the fierceness of the hair at the top of his thighs, the same hair just above his underwear band. Sephie and I'd saved up to buy him a robe for Christmas. The only time he ever wore it, he left it open.

"Just to grab some old pots you're not using," Mom said. I didn't like how her voice sounded like she was begging. "Cassie's science teacher needs them."

Dad's silence lay like a weapon between him and Mom. No way was she going to disturb it first, she never did, and so he finally spoke.

"I don't know what *never* means to you," he said, "but it means *never* to me."

Mom flattened like they do in cartoons when a character is squeezed between two stones and they look normal from the front until they turn to walk away and you realize they've been squished like a pancake.

"I'm sorry," she said. "You're right."

Dad glared like *damn straight I'm right*, using his smirk and his eyebrows to point at her stupid. I didn't move at all. I didn't want him to notice my hair, or anything about my body.

"I was going to drive the girls to school," Mom offered, her voice bright like winter glass.

Nononono, don't give him something else to be mad at.

I risked a peek at Sephie. I could tell she was thinking the same thing. I didn't know why she wanted the ride to school, but we'd both already gotten excited about it.

"Then you better get going," Dad said, sneering at the clock. "Unless you have a time machine."

I exhaled.

Mom glanced at the sandwiches she'd been making. I could see her calculating the money it would cost to buy us lunch versus the peace she'd have to cash in to stand up to Dad. "You're right," she said, shoving the loaf back into its bag.

She wiped at her eyes as she did it.

After she twisted the bread bag closed, she walked around to kiss Dad. I could smell him from where I was standing: sour liquor, hairy morning breath, sweat. *Gross.* And what was the big whoop suddenly about going into the basement?

Sephie grabbed my hand and pulled me outside.

CHAPTER 3

Besides teaching English, Mom was the cross-country coach in the fall and the yearbook adviser starting in December, and she coached speech in the spring. You had to sign up for everything that first year or they wouldn't grant you tenure, she'd said. All I knew was that I loved being at Kimball High School with her, even if it was only for ten minutes.

She was royalty because she was *faculty*, and Sephie and me got to be part of that. It didn't matter that Mom's hair and clothes were out of date. People expected that from a teacher. All that counted was that she was smart. And good at her job. I could tell it by the way people treated her.

"Good morning, Mrs. McDowell!" the early-bird students chirped at Mom.

She smiled back. We were heading to the office, me and Sephie strutting alongside her. She'd said we could stay in the car, but *no way*. I didn't even care how ridiculous my hair looked.

When we reached the office, Betty the secretary was already at her post. She was one of those friendly, gossipy women who wore scratchy-looking pants that rode too high. Her face lit up when we walked in.

"Love your hair, Cassie!" she told me before I was even fully through the door.

I stroked my head. I'd pet a poodle once. It got off better than me. But maybe my hair had relaxed some on the drive over? That sure would make school a lot less stressful. "Thank you."

"And Sephie, that blue eye shadow looks very pretty on you!"

Sephie glowed.

This was the best place. Everything was so normal here, like a TV show.

"Looks like it'll be a hot one," Betty said, tipping her head toward the window as she handed over some paperwork.

Mom smiled. "But it's only another week until summer vacation. We can put up with anything for a week."

Betty nodded. "It was nice of you to come to school so early, Peg. You know you're the best teacher here, don't you?"

I knew it.

"You're too kind." Mom scratched her name on the form she'd been handed. When she was finished, she tapped her mouth with the pen, studying the paper for a moment longer than I would have expected. "I've got to run the girls to school, but I'll be back by seven thirty if there's follow-up on this."

"Your work ethic is something else." Betty beamed; then that smile melted away like plastic in a campfire as her eyes cut to me and Sephie. "You girls attend Lilydale, don't you?"

We nodded, still puffy with pride. My hair was nice, Sephie's face was pretty, Mom's work ethic was something else. We waited for the next nice thing Betty was going to tell us, but she looked so uncomfortable all of a sudden.

"What is it?" Mom asked, handing over the paperwork. "Are you all right?"

Betty tossed another worried look at me and Sephie, then smiled tightly and shook her head. "I'm fine. You girls have a good day at school."

Betty tried swallowing, but her spit seemed to have gone sideways.

Mom caught it. "Something's wrong."

Did Betty flinch? "It's just . . . the rumors."

Mom's eyebrows tried to meet in the middle. "What rumors?"

Betty glanced at me and Sephie again. She clearly didn't want to say anything in front of us, but Mom was having none of it.

"I don't keep secrets from my girls," Mom said.

Betty drew in a rough breath. "A boy was raped in Lilydale this past weekend." She said it all as one word:

aboywasrapedinlilydalethispastweekend

Once I was able to parse out the words, it still didn't make sense. Boys didn't get raped. Raping was for girls. Unless maybe there was something to those alien-abduction stories? I stared at Mom, confused.

She appeared to be transforming into stone from the bottom up, though, so she was no help.

"Who was the boy?" Sephie asked.

The clipped *whompwhompwhomp* sound of a helicopter flying overhead made us all jerk our attention to the window. Dad always said helicopters were bad luck. The way Betty was behaving, she seemed to agree.

Betty cleared her throat, ignoring Sephie's question. She leaned toward Mom, her voice low. "People are saying that it was a gang of men from Minneapolis who did it."

My pulse tripped. *Gang.* A morning breeze blew through the window, riffling the papers stacked on the radiator. The air smelled thick and cabbagey, like slow-cooker skunk. Mom still hadn't moved.

Betty spoke up again, even though no one had responded to her last comment. "They think the Minneapolis gang was spying on boys, hunting them, picking out the easiest one to attack."

She took a moment, fanning her face. "I'm not here to feed the rumor mill, though. It gets plenty of gas on its own. I just wanted you to know, so you could keep your own kids safe."

I didn't know if she meant me and Sephie or Mom's students. Probably both.

"It only happened in Lilydale?" Mom asked. Her voice sounded froggy.

Betty sideways-eyed me and Sephie again. "So far."

CHAPTER 4

Mrs. Janowski, our principal, strode into the middle of the gym, a smile planted on her face, chubby microphone in her hand. "Welcome to our Summer Safety Symposium, everyone!"

No one listened to her at first. I watched to see how she'd handle it. She didn't care. She could outlast any one of us; a person could see that by looking at her. When we eventually settled down, she played it like she'd planned it.

"Thank you." Her smile widened. "Today, our symposium is lucky to host a very special guest speaker, Lilydale's own Sergeant Bauer."

A buzz swept through the audience, whispers of "Brody" and "copper," as if any of us middle schoolers had a reason to fear the police. Besides, I don't know how the speaker could have been a surprise since Sergeant Bauer had been standing on the sidelines in his full blue uniform since we'd entered the gym. His youngest daughter was in Persephone's grade—ninth. I knew him from one of my dad's parties, knew him better than I wanted to.

He smiled and ambled over to hoist the mic from Mrs. Janowski. "Hello, kids," he boomed. "Who's ready for summer?"

A hooting and stamping rocked the bleachers.

Sergeant Bauer held up his free hand. The overhead lights glinted off his silver wristwatch. "That's what I thought," he said, chuckling.

He had one of those thick red smiles that looked irritated by his bristly mustache. "I was a student here myself not that long ago, so I know you've earned the upcoming break. But I need you to listen now."

He tap-tap-tapped the microphone before continuing. "Because this is important. We have a new program this summer, one designed to keep you safe, and I need to tell you about it. It starts with a curfew."

That incited a wave of grousing, and I bet most kids didn't even know what a curfew was. They just knew you were supposed to complain when an adult told you something was for your own good. I joined in because what the heck. The teachers, who'd claimed the front row of the bleachers, had to stand and turn to silence us. That's when I finally laid eyes on Gabriel, down at the lower right. Seeing him made me feel the same warm kind of good as getting a letter from Aunt Jin.

When everyone quieted again, Sergeant Bauer continued, his expression pinched. "The curfew begins at nine p.m. sharp. Every one of you must be in your homes before the sun sets." Something had shifted in his voice, icing the room.

That sent a quiver up my spine. First, what Betty had said this morning about the boy being raped, and now this. Mom'd told us on the drive over that we didn't need to worry about anything, but Betty had most definitely seemed concerned. Bauer did, too. He suddenly had our complete attention. He seemed to sense that, pivoting so the pistol at his waist was in full view. The gun looked tiny and pretend from where I was sitting, strapped to his vicious black belt, a leather clasp securing it in place.

I wondered if he'd ever shot anyone.

He swiveled his hips to face us, and I could no longer see his weapon. "You'll hear the town siren go off," he continued, "the same one we use for tornadoes. It'll last one minute, and if you're still out when it ends, you'll be in violation."

There was no silencing the outcry this time. Kids were standing and yelling. I stayed in my seat, the wood solid against my butt bones. Four miles out of town, I wouldn't be able to hear the siren, had no reason to care about a curfew. I don't think I would have minded it, though, not if it meant I could live where I could walk to stores or meet kids at the park.

Sergeant Bauer spoke above the squall. "If you are accompanied by a parent or guardian," he said, "you won't get in trouble. Make sure you know the adult you're with."

I scratched absentmindedly at my neck scar. That was a hoser thing to say. Who walks around at night with adults they *don't* know? I stared at his watch again, imagined I could see the black wrist hairs curling around it. He'd been wearing it when I accidentally walked in on him at my dad's party, that and his dog tags. I bet he hadn't even noticed me.

All the kids were out of control again, so Mr. Connelly, the band teacher, had to take charge. Everyone loved Mr. Connelly. He was *that* teacher—young, smart, and talked to us like we were humans. I didn't have an actual crush on him, though most of the girls in my class did. I just liked how he smelled like cinnamon apple potpourri and had pleats in his khakis. He was wearing them now, stepping onto the gym floor and walking toward Sergeant Bauer, who I swear stiffened as Mr. Connelly approached. I guess the sergeant didn't want to give up his stage.

He even jerked away when Mr. Connelly put his hand over the microphone and tried to speak into the sergeant's ear. Whatever Mr. Connelly said worked, though, because he was soon holding the mic.

"Can we please give the officer our full attention?" Mr. Connelly requested.

He had to repeat it four more times, but eventually everyone closed their pieholes.

"Thank you." Mr. Connelly handed the mic back to the sergeant, who appeared none too grateful.

The sergeant coughed. "As I was saying, it's important you're all in by the nine curfew. Me and my fellow officers will be patrolling from

8:30 p.m. on, extra cars out there, looking for kids in violation. Don't let us catch you."

Sergeant Bauer's words made me think of *Chitty Chitty Bang Bang*, a movie I'd watched on television at my grandma and grandpa's house when they were still alive, obviously. One of the film's villains, the Child Catcher, was a grotesque horror doll of a human being. His nose was long, too long, and his lips were wet and red, kind of like Sergeant Bauer's. The Child Catcher held out giant lollipops and bright taffy to lure the kids into his cage.

Don't let me catch you.

I wiggled the creeps off me.

"One more thing," Sergeant Bauer said, drawing to a close the shortest and crappiest symposium Lilydale Elementary and Middle School had ever witnessed. "Always travel in pairs. I don't want to see any of you kids out alone this summer."

That shushed us all up, every last one of us.

This time it wasn't the words, or even his tone.

I think it was the first moment we caught a whiff of what was coming for us.

CHAPTER 5

"Cassie!"

My name was almost swallowed by the rumble of voices streaming toward second period classes. I couldn't see who was hollering for me.

"Cassie! Over here."

I finally spotted Mr. Kinchelhoe, my English teacher. He was a short red-haired man with a Bob Hope profile. He specialized in Jane Austen jokes. I pushed sideways against a stream of kids. "Hi, Mr. Kinchelhoe. They have you on herding duty?"

"Someone's got to make sure you ding-dongs can find your way to the right rooms," he said, winking. "I wanted to tell you, great job on that paper."

The flush was instant. It wasn't exactly pride, more embarrassment, actually, all mixed together with the roller-coaster ick feeling left over from Betty's warning and then the symposium. "You read my paper already?"

I'd written my capstone on the chronograph's symbolism in "For Esmé—with Love and Squalor." The paper was five pages typed, plus my works cited page. I had spent every study hall for the past month in the library looking up my sources and had nervously turned it in last Friday.

"Twice," he said, smiling.

I ducked my head. "Thank you."

"You're a writer, Cassie. Don't fight it."

That did it. I smiled so wide I was in danger of the top of my head cracking off. The bell rang, yelling at us that we should already be in our next classes, so Mr. Kinchelhoe waved me off. I was swept toward the band room, holding close the warmth of his praise. It wasn't the first time he'd told me I should be a writer, but sometimes teachers had to say gooey stuff about their students so they didn't feel like they'd wasted their life choosing education. I hoped that wasn't the case with Mr. Kinchelhoe, but you never knew.

There was one way to test it. I'd wait until my *Nellie Bly's Trust It or Don't* articles were published and I was up for my first award. I'd invite Mr. Kinchelhoe to the city where the ceremony was, probably New York, but not tell him why. We'd drive to the auditorium together and even sit next to each other. I'd wear glasses and a serious expression but also a strapless red gown for the formal occasion. We'd be talking about the good old days, and then they'd call my name. I'd act all surprised, excuse myself, and then saunter onto the stage, smiling and waving. I'd reach the microphone and say,

I am only here today because my English teacher believed in me . . .

If he cried then, I'd know he meant it all along.

I walked into the band room, scanning the sea of kids. Most were still talking to their friends, moving slowly toward their seats. Out of habit, I searched for Lynn and Heidi, who'd been my two tight buds until last fall. Our parents hung out and everything. But then we'd stopped being friends, and I'd been bouncing from group to group ever since.

You would think with only eighty-seven kids in our whole class we'd *all* be tight. You'd be wrong. Small-town kids are pebbles in a river, pushed around by the flow, forming pockets and piles, reforming when the current picks up and we find ourselves in a whole new cluster. Maybe it's the same in big cities, I don't know.

I didn't see Lynn or Heidi.

Gabriel either.

The cacophony of instruments beginning to warm up hit me like a wall. No Mr. Connelly in the pit, which was where he should be. My mood soared. Maybe he hadn't taken attendance yet.

I hurried to grab my clarinet.

The instrument room was one of my favorite places in the entire school. It had a secret door off the back, usually hidden behind a stack of music stands. The door only came up to knee height, a leftover from before the addition was built back when my parents went to high school here. It led to a cement room that used to store the school's water heater and furnace but now was an empty space the size of a large bedroom. The storage room used to be locked, but now it was left open, and you could sneak in there to do stuff. Some kids swore they smoked in there, but I'd never smelled any evidence of it.

I liked to hide in there because it was quiet, and dark, a peaceful tomb compared to the noise of the main room, which was currently all trumpets tuning up, drumsticks tapping, boys pushing each other around, and girls telling stories. Clarinets were stored in the back left, my secondhand case at waist level. I clicked it open and dug around, popping a reed in my mouth to wet it while I assembled my instrument. I was wondering about the logistics behind a Minneapolis gang passing unnoticed through Lilydale when a voice from the storage room startled me.

"Cassie?"

I squeaked and jumped three feet off the ground. "Lynn?"

She'd been hiding in the dead space between the shelves and the hidden room's door. Seeing it was my former best friend didn't soothe me, though. She looked terrible, her face all ashy and streaked with tears. She and I had cried a bunch around each other back when we hung out, but not like this. These tears looked like the result of scared crying. My tummy twisted further. I did *not* have the hair to handle crisis.

She nodded, which confused me. Was she agreeing that she was Lynn?

"What are you doing back here?" I asked, hearing my jagged heartbeat in my voice. "Band's going to start any minute."

She leaned forward a little bit, keeping her lower body out of sight. "I can't go out there."

I glanced over my shoulder and out the door. The instrument room was level with the top tier of the band room, which meant the only people who could see in were the drummers who ringed the back of the U-shaped practice space. "Did you forget your instrument?"

She shook her head, like *no, that's not it.*

I tried to think if I had seen her yet today. My follow-up thought chilled my blood. Had Lynn *also* been raped this past weekend by the gang from Minneapolis? She'd given me my first friendship pin back in fourth grade. We'd never fought over a boy. When she liked Larry Wilcox, I took Erik Estrada. She wanted Bo Duke? I was fine with Luke. We'd sworn we'd be friends forever until last fall, when she stopped calling.

My voice came out like sandpaper. "Did someone hurt you?"

"I got my period."

I blinked. "Just now?"

She nodded. "I think so."

She stepped into the light. The front of her tan cords had a darker spot. It could almost pass as a shadow if you weren't looking straight at it, but when she turned around, I saw there was no hiding the blood.

"That all came out at once?"

She ignored my question. "What am I going to do, Cassie?"

I tore my eyes off the stain. "We have to get you to the nurse's office. She's got supplies."

I'd never had to use them. In fact, if the circumstances were different, I'd be jealous of Lynn for getting her period first. She looked too scared now to feel anything but sorry for her.

"I can't go out like this! Everyone will see."

I glanced over my shoulder again. It was still chaos in the band room. "Maybe not. Mr. Connelly hasn't shown up yet."

She started crying again, softly.

It hurt to see it. She was right. Everyone would see. And in a town like Lilydale, they don't let you forget those things. I slipped out of my pretty aqua jacket, the one I only wore once every nine days so it wouldn't stop being special. "Here."

"You love that coat."

My smile surprised me. She remembered. "It's okay. My mom can sew another one. Tie it around your waist, and no one will see from behind. I'll walk in front."

She cinched the jacket at her waist and rubbed at her cheeks. "Can you tell I've been crying?"

"Only a little bit," I lied. She looked like her face had been stung by killer bees. "But if you look away from the main room and toward the clock, like you're really concerned about the time, I bet no one will notice."

"Thank you."

She grabbed my hand, and it felt like Christmas to have someone need me.

Except we weren't safe, not anymore.

Sergeant Bauer had made that clear.

CHAPTER 6

Little John's was one of four bars in Lilydale. It was the only one with Pac-Man, but that wasn't why it was Dad's favorite. He'd been going to Little John's since before they'd put in the game. I guess there were just some places that felt more welcoming to a person than others.

With Little John's, I almost understood. It was a corner bar with a private feel to it, close and smoky, the counter featuring bottles of pigs' feet and pickled eggs floating in murky liquid, and behind that, shelves of amber, green, and clear liquors. Dartboards lined one wall, Pac-Man flashed from another, and even though the men at the bar always stared at me and Sephie, we felt like we were part of something secret when we stepped inside.

"Can we each have four quarters?" I asked Dad, blinking to adjust to the dark cave of the bar after the brightness of the May afternoon. "Tupelo Honey" played in the background.

When me and Sephie had stepped off the bus, Dad'd seemed looser than usual. Not happy, exactly, but like he wasn't so deep in his head that he couldn't hold a conversation. He needed to cruise into town to pick up some welding supplies, he'd said, and Sephie and me would have to come along to help load them into the trailer. I hadn't wanted to go. I had mountains of homework, and besides, Betty's warning and then the awful symposium had me feeling jumpy. For the first time in my life, I wasn't sure I wanted to go to town.

Dad'd said we didn't have a choice.

Once we reached Lilydale, he'd suggested stopping into Little John's almost like an afterthought. "It's a warm one," he said. "Be nice to cool off with a drink."

That was A-okay with me. More often than not, when we'd stop by Little John's, he'd buy us a soda—grape for me, strawberry for Sephie—and in any case, he rarely stayed long enough to get drunk, not when it was daylight, not in public. But when my eyes adjusted and I spotted only two people in the bar—the bartender wiping his counter and Sergeant Bauer leaning against a wall holding a can of Pepsi—I knew better.

It was no accident that we were here. Sergeant Bauer and my dad were up to something. Knowing that made my throat go oily. Dad walked up to the bar, rested his foot on the rail, and grabbed the edges of the counter. "Whiskey water," he said.

I didn't recognize the bartender. He was older than most of my teachers, with a face like a bulldog. He kept one eye on me and Sephie and the other on the drink he mixed for my dad. He went light on the whiskey, I could see that. I was sure Dad would be angry, but he only smirked, tossing a five on the counter.

"Get each of my girls a pop," he said. "And the change in quarters so they can play your video game."

Dad grabbed his drink and loped off toward Sergeant Bauer, who wasn't in uniform but held himself like he was. He should be out catching whoever was attacking boys, I thought, not in a bar with my dad, up to all sorts of no good.

"I'll take strawberry, and my sister would like grape, please," Sephie said, yanking my attention back to the bartender.

He reached into a cooler, pulled out two sweating bottles of soda, one a purple as dark as night, the other the bright red of a maraschino cherry, and he snapped their caps off using an opener he kept on the lip of the counter. I swallowed the anticipatory spit gathering in my mouth. The bartender set both bottles on the counter. I stepped forward and reached for mine, tasting the sweet grape, feeling it slide down my gullet and fill my belly.

I almost had it in hand when he spoke directly to me.

"No kids at the bar," he growled.

The words hit me like a slap, and the heat to my face was instant. I glanced over at Dad, but he was leaning into Sergeant Bauer, almost kissing his ear he was so close. I'd been waiting for someone to kick me and Sephie out of Little John's ever since the first time we'd stepped inside. That was part of the thrill of being here. But I hadn't wanted the moment to come, and I for sure wasn't prepared for how small it made me feel.

The bartender seemed to be trying not to smile, but not in a nice way. He knew he was being mean, opening those pops and then telling us we couldn't have them. I couldn't take that grape soda, not after he'd hit me with those words. It'd be a beggar thing to do. We faced off, he and I, and we might have locked eyes forever if Sephie hadn't reached forward and snatched both bottles, quick, careful not to touch any part of the bar.

"Sorry," she said to the bartender. "Sorry for my sister, too."

The bartender glowered at her, but he took Dad's five-dollar bill and slapped four quarters on the counter. I had no problem grabbing for those, but I didn't make eye contact with him. Sephie nudged me with her elbow, but she didn't need to. I was already on my way to the corner where the Pac-Man machine was, the one near Dad and Sergeant Bauer.

It was still weird to see them together. Up until a year ago, Dad had hated the police worse than lice. Said they were government shills trying to take our freedom. Then suddenly, he decided to invite Sergeant Bauer to one of his parties. That idea had alarmed Mom, but he couldn't be talked free of it. Reminded her that he and Bauer went back pretty far, all the way to high school, and so it was no big deal that they'd recently decided to look out for each other. Bauer'd only attended that one party last fall, but him and Dad had seemed to find all sorts of reasons to run into each other since.

"I'll go first," Sephie said, pulling my focus back as she slid a quarter into the Pac-Man machine. The booping music got my blood moving. I was really good at Pac-Man. Sephie was crap at it, but she kept trying.

Out of the corner of my eye, I saw Dad stride back to the bar. The bartender had another whiskey water waiting, plus a bottle of beer for Bauer. Dad banged down some money and grabbed both. I wondered how much of Mom's paycheck he was spending.

Sephie kept chomping dots with her Pac-Man. Dad walked back to Bauer. They were louder with these drinks.

". . . fuck her until—" Sergeant Bauer said, quiet enough that you wouldn't have heard it unless you were my dad, or playing a video game nearby.

My dad chuckled.

I leaned into the Pac-Man game, wishing I were wearing armor.

". . . there are mushrooms," my dad said, still laughing.

I perked up at that. Once he'd bought us pizza at Little John's. It was one of those perfectly round frozen ones that the bartender slid into a toaster oven. I could have rolled in it, it was so delicious. I tried to hear more, but the two of them were quieter now.

I think they were conversing about the boy who'd been hurt the weekend before. The words "raped" and "every few years like a plague" floated toward me.

Part of me wanted to ask Bauer if a Lilydale boy had really been attacked, like Betty said. If it really had happened, I'd bet I knew him. Kids had been hot-whispering about nothing else after the symposium, but I didn't have a close friend at the moment I could ask about the attack.

Then it was my turn at Pac-Man. I almost earned a free play on my first round.

CHAPTER 7

There was no pizza, only more drinking and bad words.

Sephie and I ran out of quarters and huddled near the safety of the Pac-Man game, taking the tiniest sips from our pops to make them last.

Not all men are like my dad and Sergeant Bauer and that raping gang from Minneapolis, I thought. *There are good ones out there.*

I knew that because of Gabriel.

Gabriel Wellstone.

I'd begun planning a future with him last December.

I'd already known who Gabriel was, of course. He was a year older than me and cover-of-*TV-Guide* handsome. *Ricky Schroder* handsome. His dad was a dentist and his mom a receptionist at his dad's clinic. He rode my bus and was the only town kid who never mocked my hand-sewn blue jeans with no brand, no brand at all, not even Lee. (Mom had embroidered a smiling golden sun on the butt pocket, so no pretending.) I would have crushed on him simply for that human decency, but then came the December day when I was riding the school bus without Sephie because she was home with the vomit flu. That left an empty spot, which Gabriel slid right into.

Sitting next to me for the first time *ever*.

My heartbeat had picked up. I'd been studying the lacy frost pattern on the inside of the bus window, thinking Rorschach could have saved a buttload on ink if only he'd moved to Minnesota. Those thoughts crashed to the ground, splat on their backs, as soon as Gabriel's thigh touched mine, though. There were plenty other seats he could have taken. *This was a Life Event.* He was so close that I could smell the chemical-sweet dryer sheets his mom used. It smashed my heart to be this near to him. Were people staring at us? Was he going to ask me out? Did he have a true-love confession to share?

Nope.

"Hey, here's some mittens." He stared straight ahead as he thrust them toward me. His voice was glossy and too fast.

A forest fire of shame torched my cheeks. My hands fell from my armpits, where they'd been tucked for the entire bus ride, and every bus ride since the temperature had dropped below Eskimo. Pretty sure I'd seen penguins in parkas huddled around a burning barrel on the way out of town. The air was so cold you could *see* it, a bluish-gray fog, and if you breathed in too fast, your nostrils would freeze closed. I owned mittens, of course I did, but I preferred Popsicle fingers to wearing the homemade argyle atrocities that Mom had repurposed from hand-me-down sweaters. (Really, where would the madness end?)

Gabriel was sporting his own pair of gloves, leather, a curve of the warm-looking fleece interior peeking out at his wrists. The ones he was offering me were the same style, but worn. They looked so toasty, like heated hand pillows, and the bus was so glacial that I was sure someone had left a door in hell open. But I couldn't take them, obviously. I yanked my scrubby used-sweater mittens out of my pocket. "I have gloves."

His brow buckled. "That's what I told my mom."

My blush grew so nuclear that it was a wonder the whole orange pill of a bus didn't explode in flames before rocketing us to the moon, powered entirely by my mortification. Gabriel and *his mom* had talked about me. I'm sure they'd discussed how poor we were, how my winter jacket had a glued-up rip in the back that shot out white feathers like a popcorn fart if I sat down too quickly, how me and Sephie had displayed identical hairdos—long with bangs—since I was three and she was five because it's the only way Mom knew how to cut hair. Crap on a cracker, I bet he had a pair of gloves in his pocket for Sephie, too. Jeezus. Could people die of embarrassment? Because if so, sign me up.

Gabriel continued talking, staring straight ahead, and that's when I noticed he was no Ricky Schroder. He was cuter. Dang it, he was Rick *Springfield* handsome up close. "But Mom said you'd be doing me a huge favor by taking these. That if you didn't accept them, I'd have to lug them to the Salvation Army because we don't have room for them in our house and that I'd have to bike there myself. In the cold."

I could tell he was lying to help me save face. God. He was just thirteen. How could he be so sophisticated? Clearly, my only option was to pull this Band-Aid off quick. "Thanks." I snatched the gloves and jammed them into my jacket pocket. It was tough with my hands swollen from the cold, but I couldn't slide into the mitten comfort, not then. I needed to wait at least a day for my blushroom cloud to recede.

Once the gloves were out of sight and I wanted to dissolve into the Naugahyde seat (because what's the small-talk protocol after your life has ended?), Gabriel slam-dunked the impossible. He slid me a secret "parents are the worst but we're cool" smile. I don't know how he pulled it off, but that smile made me feel good for letting him do *me* a favor.

Messed up.

That's when he tugged at his coat collar, Rodney Dangerfield–style, and I first spotted the necklace that would change my life.

I pointed at it. "Is that new?"

He smiled, looping his thumb under the chain so he could hold out the charm. It was a tiny golden paper airplane. "Yeah. My mom got it for me for Christmas. I'm going to be a pilot."

"It's so pretty," I sighed. My hand went to my neck. I massaged the familiar ropy warmth of my scar. I was wondering if the necklace would cover my disfigurement, but I swear it was just a fleeting notion. I never would have given it a second thought if not for what happened next.

"It would look nice on you," Gabriel said.

And that's when I first legitimately imagined him as my boyfriend.

Believe me, I get it. Hand-me-down Pete (guess how I earned that nickname) me, dating the most popular boy in Lilydale? It was a long shot, such a ridiculous, impossibly fat chance that I'd walk naked across the tundra before I'd confess it to anyone, even Aunt Jin. But there was something in his kindness that zapped straight into my heart, and wasn't that love? It would be a Cinderella story, except instead of my prince bringing me a shoe, Gabriel would offer me a necklace that would perfectly cover my scar. When he went off to school to be a pilot, I'd go with him. We'd be old enough. We'd make a whole new life together, a normal one.

Ever since that bus ride, I'd been carrying my love for him around in my pocket. I should have handed it to him then and there in exchange for the gloves, but the briars and brickles of shame had been too sharp. By the time they receded, it felt stupid to bring it up. Then that faded, and all I could do was wait for an opening, some situation where he and I were hanging out and shooting love darts at each other.

When it arrived, I'd say, all joshing, *Hey, you remember when you thought I needed gloves?*

Yeah, he'd laugh. *I've wanted to give you my paper airplane necklace ever since.*

And our relationship would bloom from there.

Every day, I looked for this opening.

It could be tomorrow.

"Time to go," Dad said, finally. His face was glistening. Me and Sephie's pops and quarters were long gone and our stomachs were growling. We'd been sitting near the door, wishing Dad would take the hint and leave, but he'd kept up at that hot conversation with Bauer. We followed him outside.

"Keep your friends close and your enemies closer," Dad said when we finally slid inside the van, his voice full of bravado.

Except I could tell he was scared.

Mom wasn't going to be happy that we were out so late on a school night and that Dad was driving drunk, but that wasn't it. No, he looked jumping-ghost scared, and that made me uneasy.

It did even worse to Sephie. It must have. That's the only explanation for why she broke the rule about inviting conversation with Dad when he'd been drinking. "Are you okay, Daddy?"

She hardly ever called him that anymore. I didn't think he was going to respond, but he finally did, his voice all bluster.

"As okay as a man can be in a country where nothing's sacred."

I wondered what he meant. He and Bauer had talked about so many things. Well, I wasn't going to ask, not with Dad in this mood. I glanced out the window, my hand to the glass. I imagined the sparkle of town lights were connected to my fingertips, that I could direct them like a conductor leads an orchestra. We never had picked up welding supplies.

When neither Sephie nor I asked a follow-up question, Dad grunted. "Bauer said they're developing the lake property by our house and putting in new power lines to feed it. Will be all sorts of digging and construction in the area. Our property taxes are going to rocket through the roof."

I nodded. That made sense. Dad was scared we wouldn't have enough money. That's why he'd been so unsettled.

But that didn't explain why I felt so hunted all of a sudden.

CHAPTER 8

"Tomato soup. Grody."

I shook my head. Heather Cawl would complain about winning the Publishers Clearing House Sweepstakes. Tomato soup was fine by me, especially since it was served with grilled cheese and a side of apple pie. I'd saved up my last punch for this. A lunch card cost $8.50, eighty-five cents per meal, and I'd bought it with my babysitting money. I only ate hot lunch for my favorite meals. The rest of the time I brought a brown bag that smelled like old apple no matter what was packed inside of it.

"I'll eat your tomato soup if you don't want it."

Heather turned to glare. I didn't take it personally. I'd known her since half-day kindergarten. It was just her face. "I didn't say I didn't *want* it."

I glanced around the cafeteria to find a seat. The air was noisy with the clinking of metal forks on plastic trays, barks of laughter, and hummering conversations. Because school was almost out for the summer, the teachers were not riding our nuts and shooing us out after our twenty minutes of designated eating time.

That meant there wasn't a guaranteed spot for me to sit.

The only empty seat was next to Evie, who had also been in my grade since half-day kindergarten. Her left eye was brown, poop brown. If you saw a rock that color, you wouldn't slow down to kick it. The other was as green as sea glass. My neck scar and her eyes should have brought us together, but they didn't. If we hung out, we lost any edge our oddness gave us. One weirdo = quirky; two weirdos = weird.

Evie caught my eye. She didn't smile, just glanced at the open spot to indicate I could have it if I needed it. I liked her for that. We both knew the score. No pretending we were going to be friends.

"Hey," I said, sliding into the seat.

"Hey," she said, a marker in one hand and a cheese sandwich in the other.

She was fox-faced up close. You forgot about that with her off-color eyes overshadowing everything. She had a pointy nose and little sharp teeth, though, and that's something I should have remembered. "What're you working on?"

She sliced off an end of that sandwich with her razor teeth, set the rest down, and held up the sheet of paper she'd been drawing on. We were at the misfit table, kids who smelled like farm, fat kids, circus freaks like me and Evie, some new kid, none of us interacting. For sure no one here I could confess my crush on Gabriel to.

I focused on Evie's hand-drawn flyer, reading it out loud. "Playtime, every Saturday from eleven to two, Van der Queen Park." She'd colored in the bubble letters and sketched two girls swinging. I winced. It was so childish. "You're setting up playground get-togethers?"

She rolled her eyes and laid the flyer back on the table, drawing blue ribbons in the girls' hair. "You haven't heard?"

If there's a question designed to make a person more defensive, I haven't experienced it. Besides, people were no longer whispering about the boy getting attacked over the weekend. They were all but yelling it. I'd heard every rumor you could think of this morning, and not just gangs and aliens anymore. Now there were vampires, too. In some versions of the story, the boy had been tortured, made to drink the blood of his captors, and forced to walk home naked. Except no one seemed to have a name to go with their stories. Who had been attacked?

I'd about decided that no one had, that it was nothing more than a rumor dog running through Lilydale, biting people on the way, before disappearing.

I tore off a corner of my grilled cheese and dipped it into the soup. Popping it into my mouth, I relished the creamy cheese blending with the salty soup. I searched for Gabriel and found him across the room, sitting at the head table. Of course. He could be the *king* of this lunchroom. He was the cutest, nicest, oldest. He had friends who were mean or snooty, but not him. I couldn't see the paper airplane necklace from here, but I was certain he was wearing it.

He unexpectedly glanced my way, a smile igniting his dimples. My heart thudded, my eyes plummeting to my plate, cheeks burning. Had he been looking for me at the same time I was looking for him? Had I been chewing with my mouth open?

"Kids are being taken."

I looked over at Evie. I'd forgotten she was talking. "What?"

She tapped the flyer. Even her fingernails were pointy. "Someone is attacking kids. There's a Peeping Tom in town, too. I think they're probably the same person. I'm not going to let them steal my childhood, though, so I'm creating a playtime, someplace safe and in the open, where all us kids can get together."

I'm not going to let them steal my childhood, though. For the love of Betsy, who talks like that? No wonder we were at the loser table.

I tipped my head toward Evie's flyer. "Good luck with that."

She shrugged and went back to her drawing. Something about her manner put me on edge. She was just so . . . confident. Everyone else was swapping rumors, but Evie seemed to know something. I didn't like the prickly chill that sent across my skin.

"What are *you* looking at?" I asked the new kid, who I'd caught staring at my neck scar. He didn't look older than ten, maybe a small-size eleven-year-old.

"Not much," he said, his eyes shooting back to his lunch tray.

I scowled.

"He just moved here," Evie said, not glancing up from her drawing. She talked like she was his tour guide. "His name's Frank, and he'll be in sixth grade next year, but they didn't know what to do with him today. His parents wanted him to come to the last few days of school so he could meet kids before summer."

I squinted at him. He was studying his food like it contained all the answers. Well, there was no point in getting to know him with only three days of school left. I had more pressing concerns. For example, Evie hadn't touched her apple pie. I thought of asking her if she was going to eat it—she'd scored one of the corner pieces, and those chunks were dripping with extra powdered sugar frosting—but I didn't want to start up a new conversation. A pat on my shoulder made me forget the pie altogether.

"Here's your jacket." Lynn stood there, Heidi at her shoulder.

I took it, relieved to see that it appeared clean.

"I'm having a birthday party." Lynn held out a pink envelope. "Here's your invitation."

My heart did a cautious happy-jump as she slid the envelope into my hand. It smelled like Jean Nate After Bath Splash Mist and was decorated with bubble gum stickers. I was afraid to look at it, worried that "Cassie Lassie Dog" or one of my other less savory nicknames would be scrawled across the front. But it had no name on it, none at all. She hadn't planned to invite me, not before what had happened in the band room yesterday.

I swallowed the ball of food I'd been chewing, but my words still came out gooey. "When is it?"

Obviously I knew when Lynn's birthday was. It was one week before mine, and we'd celebrated with each other every year since kindergarten. One summer our parents had even held a joint party.

"This Sunday. It says on the invitation." She smiled, but it was small and tight.

"Thanks."

She nodded and twirled away. Her jeans were Guess. I sighed.

"I thought you guys weren't friends anymore."

I looked over at Evie. She was still sketching. Small towns, everyone knows everything. Except was that sadness in her voice? I suddenly felt ugly for holding an invitation to a party she hadn't been asked to. I shoved it in my back pocket. "Probably I won't go."

Evie slid her tray closer to me. "You can have my apple pie."

I reached for it, my mouth watering.

"Be careful if you go to the party, though," Evie said. "You don't want to be out alone. When the kids get taken, it's not forever. They come back. And when they do, they're changed."

My stomach full-on lurched at this. "What do you mean?"

She pointed across the lunchroom toward Mark Clamchik. Everyone called him Clam because of his last name, plus he was quiet. His dad drove the "Wide Load" pickup truck that followed houses being driven to a new location, so he was on the road a lot, leaving Clam and his brothers to mostly be raised by their mom. Their house was literally on the wrong side of the tracks, and I'm not one of those people who says "literally" when what she means is "really." The Clamchiks lived on the side of the train tracks where folks' lawns were more dirt than grass and where loud dogs paced behind peeled-paint fences.

Locals called that area the Hollow.

All the Hollow kids rode my bus, so I knew them well.

Clam had taken his unruly environment to heart, which meant you could find him sitting out front of the principal's office more days than not. "Clam was the one who was attacked last weekend?"

She nodded. "My mom was working an overnight at the hospital and was there when Clam was brought in. It happened Sunday. That's why they have the curfew now."

The tomato soup curdled in my throat. This wasn't gossip-from-Betty anymore, wasn't a rumor dog at all. This was something Evie's mom had *seen*. Across the crowded room, Clam held Ricky Tink in a headlock as Wayne Johnson looked on. Because the three of them were friends, it might have looked like boy fun to an adult's eyes. If you grew up with Clam, you knew that sort of behavior was a warning that he was in a foul mood. "But he came back to school?"

Evie nibbled on her bottom lip, her sharp teeth a startling white against her deep-pink flesh. "Yup. The very next day. Yesterday."

The lunchroom was doused in shadow as a cloud rolled over the sun. Today's high was forecasted at seventy-five degrees, but it hadn't been spring long enough to chase the chill from the dark corners. "Is it gangs from the Cities that did it to Clam?"

Evie rolled her eyes. "I told you, it's probably the Peeping Tom who took him. Chester the Molester is what everyone is calling him. My mom said Clam had to spend the night in the hospital. Said he had to wear diapers."

A thousand needle-footed ants crawled across my ankles and began marching toward my scalp. "I don't want to talk about this anymore," I whispered, my lunch bucking in my belly. "I just want to get that airplane necklace."

"What?"

I shook my head, grabbing my tray and walking toward the kitchen.

I fought the urge to turn around to see if Evie cast a fox-shaped shadow.

There was a girls' bathroom at the end of the school where the woodworking shop was. It was never used. After I dropped off my tray, I headed to it, needing some alone time. There were three empty stalls inside. I chose the farthest from the door. I perched on the toilet, gripping my knees so my feet were off the ground. If I didn't get out of here soon, I was going to be late for algebra, but I had to catch my breath.

Maybe it wasn't money Dad had been afraid about last night.

Maybe he knew something about Clam being attacked.

I heard someone entering the bathroom.

"—better for the school," a woman was saying. It sounded like Mrs. Puglisi, the home economics teacher. My heart sank. Being in the bathroom with teachers was the *worst*. It was unsettling to hear them make those human noises.

The water faucet turned on. Maybe they were just freshening up. I peeked under the stall and saw two sets of feet. That's when I realized that if they'd done the same, they'd think they were alone in here because I was still holding my knees, even though my legs were beginning to shake from the effort.

"Mr. Connelly is good at his job, and that's what's best for the school," the other woman responded. I was sure it was Mrs. Janowski, the principal, and now that they were talking shop, no way could I let on that I was in here.

"Even if he's the Peeping Tom?"

My mouth grew dry. Mr. Connelly?

"He's *not* the Peeping Tom, Carol," Mrs. Janowski said. "I'd bet my career on it."

"That's exactly what you're doing," Mrs. Puglisi responded. "You know he's a queer."

"Carol!"

I could almost hear her shrug through the thin metal partitions. "I'm not telling you anything you don't know. A grown man, still living with his parents besides. His mother had a heart attack last week. Did you hear about that? It would explain why he wasn't able to control his urges anymore. That sort of stress drives a man crazy."

Heels clicked over to the stall next to mine, followed by the whirring of toilet paper being unwound and then the honk of a nose blow. Mrs. Janowski wasn't responding to Mrs. Puglisi's bait, but that didn't slow down Mrs. Puglisi at all. "The boy who was attacked could turn queer now, too. Did you ever think of that?"

That sent a thrill of terror through me. Was that sort of thing contagious?

"What do you want me to do?" Mrs. Janowski asked from near the sinks. "Kick a child out of school for being attacked?"

Mrs. Puglisi stepped out of the stall next to me, a light *phiff* telling me she'd tossed her used tissue. "Now you're being ridiculous," she said. "I'm only telling you to be prepared. You're going to hear the same from parents."

Mrs. Janowski sighed. I didn't hear her response because they click-clacked out of the bathroom before she got a chance to respond.

Mrs. Puglisi had not washed her hands after she'd blown her nose.

I dropped my legs and shook the cramps out of my fingers. I scrubbed my mitts and checked both ways before leaving the bathroom.

All clear.

Except I didn't think it would be all clear in Lilydale ever again.

CHAPTER 9

The air pouring in through the school bus windows smelled like fresh-squeezed limes, and despite the wackadoodle day, I was full of wandering hope. *Summer was coming.* I was telling Sephie about what I'd overheard in the bathroom, but not with much investment.

"You shouldn't have spied on them."

She had our regular seat saved, the *new* regular seat across the aisle from Gabriel, the one I'd convinced her to move to after the glove incident, but he hadn't yet boarded. The Lilydale school buses picked up high schoolers first, which was backward in my mind, but I suppose they figured the older kids could handle extra motoring time better than the little kids.

After picking up the high schoolers, the buses arrived at the combination elementary and middle school to load up on us K–8 kids before the route officially began. Town kids were dropped off first, followed by the Hollow kids who lived on Lilydale's perimeter, with deep-country kids getting off very last. That route was reversed in the morning. That meant that Seph and me were first on—the sun barely peach fuzz on the horizon—and last off.

An itty-bitty bonus of this crap deal was that on the days he rode the bus, I got to watch Gabriel walk to and from it. Some afternoons, his mom was waiting for him on the front porch of their clean-looking, roomy rambler, a row of hostas bordering each side of the sidewalk, turning it into a green carpet. She always appeared happy to see him. I wondered what she'd think of me.

The thought gave me a shivery thrill and brought me back into the moment.

"Yeah, big duh I shouldn't have spied on them," I said to Sephie. "It wasn't like I tried to."

Clam swaggered down the aisle, his elbow connecting with my shoulder, maybe accidentally. I studied his back, looking for evidence of him being attacked. He still seemed like he was behaving rougher than usual, but that was it. I rubbed the sore spot he'd made, wondering if Sephie knew he was the one that Betty had been referring to. Clam'd been on our bus route forever. Sephie knew him as well as me, maybe better. Plus, Clam's best friend, Wayne Johnson, had a crush on Sephie, and she seemed to be returning the favor. He was a year younger than her and even poorer than we were, but Sephie liked the attention. Maybe Wayne had mentioned something.

I dropped my voice. "You hear what happened to Clam?"

Sephie shrugged, her face a full-on pout. I realized she'd been crotchety since I'd boarded, only giving me half her attention.

"Jeez Louise, Seph, what's your problem?"

The bus lurched away from the curb. No Gabriel.

Karl, our ham-faced bus driver, seemed to be checking over all the boys, maybe watching for Gabriel, just like I was doing. Sephie took so long to answer that I thought she didn't hear me. Finally, she looked me square in the face. "I'm failing chemistry."

That jolted me like a snake bite. "Dad's not gonna like that." He hated any attention drawn to us or our house.

She stared glumly at her hands. "I know."

My gut sank lower and lower. Dad was an equal-opportunity rager. If he was mad at her, *everyone's* life was going to be miserable. "How could you?"

She shrugged and kicked at the worn book bag at her feet. "It's a stupid class, anyhow."

Her chin quaked. This was going from bad to worse. Sephie'd made herself invisible by being a shy, mostly C student who was good at volleyball and never stepped out of line. If she wept right now, though, she was done for. Tears guaranteed her a terrible nickname, as soon as the doofuses around us could figure out anything that rhymed with "crybaby."

The bus pulled away from the school. I continued to massage the spot Clam had bumped as something occurred to me. "Hey, you said you're failing. That means you haven't failed *yet*, right? Want me to help you study?"

Sephie leaned forward to tug an envelope out of her book bag. "You could try, but it won't make any difference. I still need Mom and Dad to sign this letter saying I have two days to get my grade up to a D, or it's summer school for me."

"Silly Sephie, it makes *all* the difference. If we work hard tonight and tomorrow and you get a good-enough grade on your final, you pass. Ergo, no summer school, which means no angry Dad. You know he always likes it better when we come up with a plan rather than just bringing him bad news."

I could see her wheels spinning. "You think I could learn all of chemistry in two nights?"

I moaned. "You don't know *any* of it?"

"It's a hard class! And Mrs. Tatar is the worst. You'll see when you get to high school."

I doubted it. Besides, Mom always said a bad teacher was a window, not a wall. I opened my mouth to argue, but before I could squeak out a word, the whole mood of the bus exploded.

"Green Goblin!"

I don't know who shouted it, but our response was automatic. Everyone on my side of the bus sucked in their breath and glued their faces to the windows to search for the green Chevy Impala. Those across the aisle yelled at us to confirm the Goblin sighting. He'd had that nickname forever, maybe gotten it when he was in high school. He'd gone to Lilydale, graduated about the same time as Dad.

Goblin had a harsh face, all angles and stubble, lips so thin they weren't more than a cut, black porcelain-doll eyes. He looked like he smelled sour, though he couldn't be older than forty. He mostly kept to himself, but he exuded that creepy frequency that kids' radars picked up on. It was a hard-and-fast rule that we all yelled out "Green Goblin" and held our breath on the occasions his car passed our lumbering bus, which was more often than you'd expect because he lived at the end of the bus route, just down the road from me and Sephie. We were supposed to hold our breath when we ran into him in public, too, but since he was our neighbor, Sephie and me let that rule slide sometimes. This time of year in particular, we'd spot him when we'd bike over to check out his patch of wild strawberries. They grew just off the road, on his side of the ditch, but we were both always too chicken to run over and grab them, even though they fruited early and shone like rubies in the sun.

"False alarm. It's not Goblin!" I yelled, and air whooshed out of our mouths so loud it sounded like an accident at a balloon factory. The excitement of a potential Goblin sighting on the last week of school revved us all up, though, and Karl gave up trying to silence us, though his droopy eyes were still scanning the boys. Sephie forgot about her grade, and all us kids laughed and talked about summer, and I felt just fine right up until Karl pulled up to our driveway, Sephie and me the last two kids on the bus.

We stepped off into the road-dust cloud, blinking the dirt from our eyes. We were laughing and elbowing each other, but those good vibes fell away like a bad coat when we saw what was waiting for us. I don't know about Sephie, but my pulse was fluttering because there stood Dad, a storm brewing in his face. His top lip was pulled back in the sneer that told you he was feeling bad and that you were welcome to join him, thank you very much.

CHAPTER 10

He stood, arms crossed, as the bus pulled away, and I forgot all about what Evie had told me, what I'd overheard in the bathroom, Clam, a Goblin sighting, Lynn getting her period before me, even Gabriel's necklace because Dad's face was pointed at us like a missile. The school must have called him in case Sephie "lost" the letter on her way home. Some kids would do that. Not us. We were taught never to lie to our parents.

A strip of sweat rolled down my back and was absorbed by my training bra. The cicadas were whirring, and the air smelled dusty purple from the lilacs tossing up their pollen like Mardi Gras floozies. I licked my lips and tasted salt.

Dad and Sephie stared each other down like gunslingers, except she was already wilting. When Dad was this mad, his green eyes whirred in their sockets, flashing dragon anger. I wanted to hide behind Sephie, but that would be cowardly.

"Hi, Dad," I said, slicing through the tension. "What's our chore list?"

He ignored me, which pushed Sephie over the edge. She had already gone floppy, but his stony silence forced her tears. "I'm sorry, Dad, but I'm failing chemistry," she sniffled. "I might have to go to summer school."

I grabbed her hand. "*Might.* Not for sure. I already told her I'd help her study. If she does well on the final, I bet she'll pass the class, and no one will come out here to check up on her."

I was talking too fast. Dad still hadn't looked at me. He hadn't spoken yet, either, which was worse than yelling times ten.

After another full minute of staring at Sephie like she was something grody on the bottom of his shoe, Dad abruptly turned on his heel and stormed up the driveway toward the house.

"Dad?" I yelled.

Sephie's cries escalated to wails.

"It's not that bad," I soothed her. "Wait until he's out of sight and let's see if Mom is home."

Mom could almost always coax Dad out of his spells. Sometimes I thought it was her main job on this planet, other than paying the bills. Dad veered off the driveway, paced through the orchard, and stomped into the house, slamming the door behind him. My shoulders drooped in relief. The house was the best possible location for him in this mood. He'd be out of the sun, and if he got a drink, he would calm right down.

I wasn't worried about him spanking Sephie or anything. He'd never hit either of us, and he took great pride in that. His mom's third husband had been violent. He'd beaten Dad for any infraction and sometimes just for shits and giggles, Dad said. That had lasted until Dad was big enough to fight back. Dad would pause, slyly, at this point in the story.

I'm not someone to mess with, his curled lip would say.

But there are worse things than hitting.

We crested the small hill between the main road and the house. The VW van was parked in front of the summer kitchen, which meant Mom was already home. I let out a huge breath. "Come on, Sephie! Mom'll mix him a drink, and we can figure all this out."

We jogged toward the house, scaring up dandelion fuzz. Meander, my calico kitty, dashed up and wanted me to pet her, but there wasn't time. We rushed through the sunporch, dropped our backpacks on the living room table, and found Mom and Dad in the kitchen, where, sure enough, Dad held a tall drink, no ice.

Mom's eyes were cramped when we entered, but she tossed us a smile. I was struck by how good-looking they were, even with Mom wearing her worried face and Dad his mad one.

"How was school?" she asked.

I made myself as tall as I could. "Sephie is failing chemistry, but I'm going to help her study and she's going to pass, and it'll be fine."

Mom kept eye contact with Sephie even though her words were clearly directed at Dad. "I agree."

Dad glugged his whole glass of clear liquid and held it out to Mom, who refilled it wordlessly with half vodka, half water.

When he had a good grip on that second glass, he finally spoke. "Sephie, you know how important school is."

I'm positive I'm not the only one in that room whose butt cheeks immediately relaxed. Sephie stopped crying, and the squeezed look left Mom's eyes, rushing out like bathwater after you've pulled the plug. You could tell how Dad was going to play it, always, by his first words after a silent time. Sometimes he'd go dark, or creepy. But he was saying normal things this time. Me, Mom, and Sephie were quick to encourage that.

"Yes," Mom said. "It's the most important thing at your age."

"I know," Sephie said, wiping her face, eager to agree. "I made a mistake. Mrs. Tatar is impossible, but I should have gotten tutoring."

"You think I should help her, don't you, Dad?" My liver felt yellow at this, joining in coddling Dad like he was a babyman, but it's what worked.

He took a swig of his drink, finishing half in a swallow. "You're lucky I'm a rational man, Persephone, and I want you to listen to this, too, Cass. My own stepfather was an asshole. He'd beat me bloody if I failed. I want better for you girls."

Mom put her arm around Dad's waist. Sephie and I donned our sympathetic faces, except I think she really meant hers. We'd heard this story a hundred fifty zillion times.

"You know how reasonable I am?" he continued. "I stopped my outside work to help our new neighbors move a couch. Isn't that right, Peg?"

Mom smiled. "Lovely people, we think. Their last name is Gomez."

"Salt of the earth," Dad said, his words gone woolly around the edges, "but not too educated."

He and Mom nodded at each other. They were proud of the master's degree they each held, Dad's in art history and Mom's in education.

"The old Swenson place?" I asked. We passed it on our bus route, right before turning at Goblin's and then a straight shot to our place. Mrs. Swenson used to have a beauty parlor off her kitchen where she'd make extra money. She'd pierced my ears for five dollars an ear, though one of them had grown so infected that I'd had to remove the stud and let the hole seal up.

Mom nodded. "That's the one."

"The 'For Sale' sign is still out front," Sephie said.

"They'll take that down soon," Dad said. He was relaxing, his tone growing high-minded. "They have three kids and said they'll need babysitters from time to time."

Sephie lit up. She was saving for a Make Me Pretty Barbie head. For sure this wasn't the time to tell Mom and Dad that she'd decided to forgo college to pursue her dream of being a hairdresser.

"I can do it!" she said.

Dad snorted. "Not if you don't pass chemistry. Cassie can babysit."

"All right," I said, too quickly.

He finally acknowledged me, his eyes beady with vodka. "How's school going for you, Cassie?"

I knew what he was after. He liked to end his lessons with a glob of shame, no matter how they started. I didn't want to answer him, didn't want to take part in humiliating Sephie. "Fine."

"You still have that best friend? Lynn? Haven't seen her for a while."

My cheeks burned. Now wasn't the time to mention the birthday invitation. "Naw, not anymore."

"Her parents finally came to one of our parties last fall, isn't that right, Peg? Didn't seem too good for us then."

Mom patted his arm. "Can I get you some more water?"

He finished his drink and handed it to her. Seph and I watched tensely to see if she'd add vodka. She didn't, thank god, holding the glass under the ceramic water dispenser. We filled ten five-gallon jugs at the public spout in St. Cloud. They filtered the water straight from the Mississippi, and it tasted clean as clouds. Way better than our metallic well water.

"Girls," Mom said, "why don't you both go study until suppertime? Your dad and I have some planning to do for the next party."

"What?" I asked, clutching my hands together. The previous one had been in September, the first and only one Lynn's parents had attended and Sergeant Bauer's first. I could have guessed another party was coming, but I always hoped the last was the *last*.

"Yep, Saturday," Dad said. "We'll celebrate the beginning of summer. This party is going to be big. Bigger than any before. Maybe our last, before the state puts in those power lines and we lose all our privacy."

Sephie and I didn't look at each other, but I didn't need to see her face to know that she—like me—would be just fine if this were the last party. We trudged off to her room and dug right into chemistry. A couple hours of me quizzing her and she had the basics down. She'd been dumb about it because she hadn't tried, but she was smart underneath that. If we worked together again tomorrow night, I knew she could pass.

"Hey, Sephie," I asked, once she had the periodic table as memorized as she could in a single sitting. "I tried to tell you on the bus. Clam was the boy who was attacked, the one Betty talked about yesterday morning. We had a symposium about it at school, even though they didn't tell us exactly why we were there. There's going to be a curfew in town."

"I know," she said.

I could tell she didn't. "Evie said he was hurt pretty bad. She doesn't think it was a gang. She figures it was the Peeping Tom. You've heard about him?"

"Everyone has."

I sighed. Sephie really needed to feel smart. "Sure. But here's what I think. I think that it doesn't matter if it's one man or a whole gang of 'em. If someone hurt Clam and got away with it, they're going to try again."

I watched Sephie roll that around in her head. "The police will catch whoever did it."

I pictured Sergeant Bauer. I wasn't so sure. "I'm going to try to get to the bottom of it," I said without even thinking. But once the words were out, they felt right. I was going to be a writer for *Nellie Bly's Trust It or Don't*, and wasn't that just like investigative reporting? Besides, how many people would want to be my friend if I figured out who'd hurt Clam?

Lots, that's how many.

Once the idea took root, it grew. By the time Mom called us down to supper, I'd even started planning what sort of clothes I'd wear when investigating.

My excitement all but disappeared when I saw how boisterous she and Dad were with party planning. Her chicken tasted like ash to me, thinking about what was coming on Saturday. Sephie didn't really dig in, either. We ate quickly, did the dishes, and headed to our rooms.

By the time I finished my homework, it was nearly eleven o'clock. My bedroom window was open, inviting the dirt-scented cool of a late-May evening to drift in, making my room the perfect temperature for sleeping. I was beat, but I had a duty.

I opened *Nellie Bly's*, jamming my face in the pages to smell the paper, running it along my cheeks. I pulled the book back and pretended the words were written in braille, closing my eyes and tracing my fingers over them. When there was nothing left to read it with but my eyes, I dove in.

Nellie Bly's — **Trust It or Don't!**

TREE MAN WHO CARRIED 13 POUNDS OF WARTS!

SUKARNO BAMBANG, A FORMER ENGINEER IN INDONESIA, IS COVERED IN BARK-LIKE WARTS THAT HAVE EARNED HIM THE NAME OF TREE MAN! HIS HANDS AND FEET ARE COVERED IN THE GROWTHS, WHICH ALSO APPEAR ON HIS ARMS, TORSO, AND FACE. HE HAS HAD THE WARTS FOR SO LONG THAT HE NOW CONSIDERS THEM A PART OF HIM.

I closed the book and sighed. Sukarno and I would have had a lot to talk about. Sometimes I didn't know where I stopped and my problems began, either. Life would be fine if we didn't have to live with Dad. I'd told Mom that, a bunch. She'd say I was being dramatic.

Bedtime. My body wanted to sleep short.

Inside the embrace of my closet, I nestled into the cloudy purple quilt my grandma had sewn me that was so puffy Sephie and I could perform standing somersaults on it without hurting our shoulders. If

I stretched overhead, my fingertips could play the hangers like wind chimes. Their sweet Tinker Bell song settled my bones, usually.

Everything was arranged perfectly for sleep, but it was a no go. And I knew exactly why. It was the thirst. It had started two hours ago, but I couldn't leave my room. Dad was lumbering around in the kitchen below, his sounds magnified by the grate in my floor.

The grate had been installed to allow warmth to rise to the second story back when this was a drafty old farmhouse with wood heat. We had a furnace now, so Sephie and I had repurposed the floor hole into a spyhole. We'd spent hours with our ears pressed to the wrought iron, listening to Mom and Dad fight, or party, or do gross stuff. Once we'd even rigged up an empty oatmeal tube by punching holes in its sides and lacing twine through them. We'd remove the grate and drop the oatmeal dumbwaiter through the hole. Mom'd insert food into it, and we'd jerk the canister back up and eat whatever was inside, giggling until our stomachs hurt. That lasted until we forgot to clean out the apple cores we'd tossed back in and she got slimed.

Distracting myself with memories wasn't working.

My thirst was driving me bonkers.

I shifted, burrowing into my quilt nest. I swallowed, but my spit only rolled halfway down my throat before it was absorbed. It didn't help that if I opened the closet door and peeked down through that grate, I'd be able to see the water dispenser. One flick of the knob and I'd have enough liquid to fill me up to my eyeballs. I supposed that's how the lions successfully hunted the antelope, just lurked around the watering hole until the weaker, fleshy animals couldn't stand it anymore and came for a drink.

I wouldn't be so stupid.

Mom had gone to bed around nine. If she were still up, I might have hollered down for her to hand me up a glass of water and hoped Dad didn't intervene.

What was he doing? This time of night, he usually parked himself in his chair on the opposite side of the house. Tonight, he seemed to be moving between the garage and the pantry, with its door to the basement. His breathing sounded heavier than usual.

I was so thirsty, but I couldn't leave.

That was one of my handful of life rules, those lucky charms that I rattled to stay safe.

Sleep where you're protected.

No leaving to go to the bathroom after Mom was in bed. I stored a bucket under my bed just in case.

And definitely no getting a drink of water after dark.

CHAPTER 11

"Next!"

Our middle school band room has a peculiar locker room tang, a product of all the horn section spit that pooled in the brass instruments, then dripped onto the floor. I plowed through that odor, yanking the reed I'd been sucking on out of my mouth and securing it to the tip of my clarinet while I hurried toward the small practice room Mr. Connelly was summoning me into, one of its walls a bank of windows looking out onto the band room floor.

I'd managed to scrape out a few hours of shut-eye last night, which meant I looked like a *Dark Crystal* Muppet this morning. I was almost grateful Gabriel hadn't ridden the bus. Normally, a bright spot would be that I had my band lesson first thing on Wednesdays, which meant I got to hang out with Mr. Connelly. After overhearing Mrs. Puglisi and Mrs. Janowski talk about him in the bathroom, though, I was feeling apprehensive, not excited, for my lesson. If Connelly was a potential suspect in the attack on Clam, I needed to investigate him.

"Hi, Mr. Connelly," I said as I closed the door behind me and took my seat. Heather Cawl and I hadn't acknowledged one another as her lesson ended and mine began. She was first chair, me third with no chance of promotion. I was in band to round out my résumé, let's say.

He smiled that movie-star grin, and it made all my worry about what I'd overheard in the bathroom melt away. No way was Connelly someone who could hurt a kid. We all loved him. Lots of my classmates called him Connelly, all informal, or Mr. C. I wanted to be cool like that and had rehearsed it at home. *Hey, Connelly! Did you party hearty last weekend?*

That's as far as I'd gotten.

He pointed at my garage-sale clarinet. "How's the goose whistle?"

"Sweet like ice cream." I held it up. I'd wanted to play the flute, but Mom and I hadn't found one despite scouring every rummage sale in the county. The only other option was this clarinet or drums—sticks were cheap enough we could buy them new. Unfortunately, I couldn't keep a beat to save my soul.

Connelly, which I at least called him in my head, laughed. "It's a beautiful instrument, you know."

I dropped into the practice chair. It was a familiar conversation. "A real work of art."

"You know what Artie Shaw and Benny Goodman had in common?"

"Not smart enough to play the saxophone?"

He chuckled. "You're not going to make first chair with that attitude."

"Or these fingers." I waggled them at him. "Yet the world continues to turn."

This one got a roar of laughter, loud enough to turn the head of Charlie Kloss, who was waiting on the other side of the glass for his piccolo lesson. Poor kid hadn't got the memo about what instruments were cool for boys to play.

"Let's start with 'Apache.'" Connelly opened my music book and started the metronome before blowing on the round pitch pipe tuner that might as well have spurted glitter for all the use it was to me. I readied my hands for the first note and dove in, making up in volume what I lacked in talent.

We ran through the song five complete times before he was satisfied. "You're coming along nicely, Cassandra."

He used my full name. I liked that, too. "Thank you."

He folded up my practice book and handed it to me, standing as I stood. Our fingers brushed. It was an accident, but he jerked his hand back like I'd burned him.

"Sorry," I said, fiddling with my clarinet's keys.

He slid his hands into his pants pockets. It felt like an invisible wall had dropped down between us, and I couldn't figure out why.

"You in for selling some popcorn?" Connelly asked, ignoring that wall.

I tried to swallow but made a clicking sound instead. "Is that this year's promotion?"

It was tradition for the fourth to eighth graders to sell food, usually chocolate bars, over the summer to raise money for the fall band trip the high school kids took every year. I rarely sold much because of how far out of town I lived. Most farms were at least half a mile apart, and they could buy their own chocolate bars at the store, *thankyouverymuch*.

"Yep." He opened the cardboard box near his feet and yanked out a glossy brochure, its front cover featuring nine varieties of popcorn. He held it out to me, careful to keep his hands far from touching mine. "Instructions inside."

I grabbed the brochure and walked out as Charlie went in, my eyes pinned to the bright images. It was the best way to hold back the tears. I didn't know why it had grossed out Connelly to touch me, but there you go. Better to think about the popcorn. I bet the cornfetti flavor was the best, cheerful reds and purples and blues in fruit flavors. I was still studying it as I made my way to the instrument storage room but had to set it down to dismantle my clarinet. Hand-lettered masking tape marked my case, not that anyone would want to steal a secondhand clarinet.

Once my clarinet was tucked away, I peeked toward the band room, my throat tightening. No one was coming, which meant it was all clear. I could look through people's stuff. I'd been doing it since I could remember, rifling through my classmates' backpacks and purses and instrument cases. I'd find Lip Lickers, Twinkies that I'd smell, notes. I never took anything. I just liked to hold it. I wasn't proud of the behavior, so I tried not to think about it too much.

My pulse was hammering nicely as I knelt to pull out Heather's clarinet case. I knew for a fact she'd stored her new Avon lip gloss in there. It was shaped like a chocolate chip cookie. A couple weeks ago, she'd screwed off the top and shown her friends the two separate flavors—caramel and chocolate—inside. After, she'd tucked it in the compartment in her case where she kept the extra reeds. I wasn't going to use any of it, I was pretty sure. I just wanted to hold it.

"What's a good girl like you doing digging in people's stuff?"

I spun guiltily, shoving the chocolate chip cookie compact into my pocket to get it out of sight. I was surprised to see Clam standing in the doorway. He wore high-water jeans, an oversize belt buckle, and a dated '70s collared shirt.

"You're not in band." It was a stupid thing for me to say, but my chest was fear-knocking too loud to think. My decision to solve the case of who'd hurt him suddenly seemed distant and ridiculous.

Clam twitched and looked over his shoulder. Was someone behind him? His face was shadowed when he turned back. He was small for his age, but he had ropy muscles. He could rip through you like the Tasmanian Devil if he wanted, every kid knew that. I wasn't afraid of him, though, at least I'd never been before. Clam only beat up boys.

Except this didn't seem like the Clam I'd grown up with.

I thought of Evie's story, that he'd spent the night in the hospital, that he'd been put in a diaper. My mouth grew dry. I'd been a baby to think this was some Nancy Drew mystery.

"You here alone?" He moved a step closer.

I could smell him now, the scent of fried food on his clothes. His eyes held a wildness that I'd never seen before, something between terror and danger.

I couldn't run past him. Trapped, I made myself larger, hoping he couldn't see my knees shaking. "You come one step closer and I'll slap you."

Now I was in *Dynasty*? But I still couldn't make sense of what was happening. I was in Lilydale Elementary and Middle School, standing in a lit room. Mr. Connelly wasn't more than fifty feet away. I could even hear Charlie Kloss's ragged notes splitting the air. But my stomach held a bag of ice suddenly, and I grew light-headed. I was afraid, really and truly, and I'd known Clam my whole life.

Just not this Clam.

He sneered, hooking his thumbs into his belt loops. His flood pants were thick denim, the grommets and zipper an ugly copper. "I could hurt you," he whispered, "but I won't if you do what I say."

His words sounded weird, like an echo, or a new language he could recite from memory without understanding it. My brain pinged off reassuring markers, like the light switch that I'd flicked on a hundred times or the rainbow Trapper Keeper stored under my clarinet case. None of it helped. Something was wrong with Clam.

"I know someone attacked you," I said.

He grew still and clear, like his colors became brighter. "You don't know shit."

"Who did it?" I asked. It came out as a rush. My jaw felt locked, and I couldn't seem to draw a full breath.

Clam opened his mouth like he was going to say something, and then he slammed it shut. The movement worked like a bellows, lighting the crazy fire in his eyes. Somebody had hurt Clam, and he was going to do the same to me.

Charlie continued to squeak through his piccolo lesson a million miles away, and I found I couldn't even yell, because I'd feel stupid if I was making a big deal out of nothing. Clam must have seen the surrender in my eyes, because he lunged closer. I stepped back, tripping over a cornet case that hadn't been pushed fully in. My fall brought a stack of cymbals crashing to the ground.

A door opened in the main band room. Footsteps rushed toward us. Mr. Connelly appeared in the doorway, his eyes wide. I could have cried with relief at seeing him there.

"Heavens, Cassandra, are you okay?"

I nodded, jumping to my feet to stack the cymbals. My right wrist smarted from where I'd landed on it, and my scar pulsed with my racing heart. I hated how ashamed I suddenly felt.

"Good. Glad to hear it." Mr. Connelly's face tightened as his focus shifted to Clam. "Mr. Clamchik, I can only assume you've decided to take the yard-work job I offered you?"

Clam's shoulders slumped, and his thumbs dropped out of his loops. Mr. Connelly deflated him just like that, letting all the bad air out of his balloon. "Naw," Clam said, pushing past Mr. Connelly.

Mr. Connelly watched him go before turning back to me. "You sure you're okay, Cassandra?"

I blinked back tears. I didn't want Connelly to see me crying because it was stupid, this was all so stupid. I didn't even know what had just happened. "Yep, just putting my clarinet away. Is Charlie's lesson done?"

"We might as well finish early." He was looking at me funny. "Want me to walk you to class?"

"No, thank you."

Connelly stepped to the side to let me pass. My legs were still trembly, but I grabbed my popcorn brochure and Trapper Keeper, putting one foot in front of the other toward the exit.

I shrugged off the crummy panic of having Clam go all animal on me. No one had seen it.

I made it all the way to fourth period civics before a worried-looking secretary called me to the principal's office.

CHAPTER 12

My fingers and toes itched on the walk to Mrs. Janowski's. I'd never been called in before. Did she know I'd spied on her and Mrs. Puglisi in the bathroom? My heart sank. Maybe it was even worse. Maybe Connelly had told them about Clam being weird in the instrument room this morning. Were they asking me in as a witness, to tell on him? This theory gathered strength when I spotted Clam sulking out of Mrs. Janowski's office at the end of the hall. I shuddered at the sight. He didn't glance my way.

The secretary led me straight back to the principal's office, where she was on the phone.

"She just walked in," Mrs. Janowski said into the mouthpiece.

My ears burned. Who was she talking *on the phone to* about me?

She hung up and indicated the chair in front of her desk. I collapsed into it, I think, but my body had gone cold and I couldn't really feel anymore.

"Do you know why I called you here, Cassandra?"

My full name didn't sound as good in her mouth as it did in Mr. Connelly's. "No, ma'am."

Her lips tightened. "Can you empty your pockets for me?"

I was falling, plummeting deep down inside myself, looking up toward the holes that were my eyes. Heather's chocolate chip cookie compact was still in my front right pocket, where I'd shoved it when Clam surprised me. I glanced down at its outline in my jeans, then back up at Mrs. Janowski. She looked so disappointed. I yanked out the cool plastic and held it out to her.

"Is that yours?"

I shook my head, my hair falling in my eyes. It sure wasn't.

"Who does it belong to?"

"Heather," I whispered.

"Cawl?"

"Yes, ma'am." The shame was complete. Tears threatened, but I crammed them down.

Mrs. Janowski dropped her face into her hands for a moment. For a brief flash, I thought she was going to let me go.

"I've called Sergeant Bauer," she said.

My breath intake was loud enough to startle her.

"He won't take you to jail," she said, misreading my shock. "He's just going to talk to you about what will happen if you do this again. I must say I'm surprised you stole at all, Cassandra. You're one of my best students. Is there something going on at home?"

The word shot out like a cannonball. "No."

Mrs. Janowski's eyes glittered. For a moment, I thought I'd blown it. *People won't understand how creative we are,* Dad always said. *If you tell them how we live, they'll split us up, make you kids live with strangers. It's your choice if you want that, but I sure don't.*

But she didn't ask a follow-up question, not about my home life. "You'll have to apologize to Heather for stealing from her. She's on her way right now."

God himself couldn't have stopped my tears then. Why had Clam told on me? I wasn't going to keep the lip gloss, but Mrs. Janowski wouldn't believe that. Neither would Bauer. *I just wanted to smell it, to pretend I owned it.* Yeah right.

"Finally, you'll have detention after school today." Mrs. Janowski's voice grew kinder. "But I won't note this on your permanent record, Cassandra. Stop crying now. We all make mistakes. If you don't repeat it, you'll be fine."

I nodded, miserable. Never in my life had I gotten detention. Same with Sephie. Detention meant parents getting involved, and Dad had been clear: stay below the radar. This was for sure worse than Sephie failing chemistry. The sun shone outside Mrs. Janowski's window, its brightness surreal. I didn't feel like I deserved to even look at it. Sergeant Bauer's black-and-white pulled up. He must have been patrolling nearby when the call came in.

"There he is," Mrs. Janowski said. Her voice was businesslike again.

Heather beat him to the office. She appeared scared, as I had, when she was ushered in. A jealousy burned in me, fast and hot, and then dissolved. She was going to get to walk out of here.

"Mrs. Janowski?" she said.

The principal pointed at me. "Cassandra has something to tell you."

I couldn't make eye contact with Heather. I snatched the plastic chocolate chip cookie container off the edge of Mrs. Janowski's desk and held it out. "I took your lip gloss. I'm sorry."

Heather plucked it out of my hand but didn't immediately say anything.

I peeked at her. She was staring at the lip gloss, a line between her eyebrows.

"I said I'm sorry," I said.

"I forgot I had this." She looked at Mrs. Janowski. "Can I go?"

"Yes, Heather. Thank you. And there's no reason to share with your classmates what has transpired here."

Probably Mrs. Janowski meant well, but she sure didn't understand how middle school worked. I wondered what my new nickname was going to be.

Heather left as Sergeant Bauer entered. He turned to watch her go before studying me, his head cocked. I saw him putting the pieces together. Mrs. Janowski must not have told him my name when she'd called him.

One of our students is a thief. Can you come by and put the fear of Jesus in her?

My pleasure.

"You're Donny's girl?"

"Yessir," I said. I kept my stare locked on his. I'd been ashamed in front of Mrs. Janowski and Heather, but I wouldn't be for him. I remembered what I saw him doing to Kristi at Dad's party, all hunched over, their eyes slammed shut, their skin sweaty and soupy smelling, him wearing only that silver wristwatch and dog tags that made a metallic *tink tink* sound as he thrust.

"I'll take this from here," Bauer said to Mrs. Janowski, like he could dismiss her from her own office.

"I'll stay if you don't mind," she said.

I wanted to hug her. *Fucking*, he and Dad had talked about at Little John's. *Fucking and mushrooms and every few years like the plague.* I'd only heard those crude bits, the words grating like out-of-tune piano blonks.

"All the same to me," Bauer said, perching on the edge of her desk, his hat in his hand. He drew a pen from his shirt pocket, but he didn't reach for paper. He just pressed the button on the pen. *Click click. Click click.* "You know stealing is wrong, don't you?"

"Yeah." *Do you know that what you did at my dad's party was wrong, too?*

"What's that?" *Click click. Click click.*

"Yessir."

"Your dad would be very disappointed to hear his daughter is a thief," he said. "Don't you think?"

"Yessir." *But only because it might get him in trouble.*

"You do this again, you'll end up in juvie." *Click click. Click click.* "Do you want that?"

"No, sir."

The way he stared at me, I could tell he didn't like that I wasn't more ashamed. And I was, but like I said, I wasn't going to let *him* see it.

"All righty," he finally said.

CHAPTER 13

We'd read *The Scarlet Letter* in Honors English last year. After walking out of Mrs. Janowski's office, boy, did I understand it on a whole new level. The worst part wasn't the way kids stared at me the rest of the day. It was how a couple teachers, like Mr. Kinchelhoe, treated me extra nice. Pity feeds humiliation like spinach tools up Popeye. I survived the day, though, and walked the long mile to detention at the end of classes. Once there, I focused on my homework like my life depended on it.

I didn't know who was going to pick me up, Mom or Dad.

Obviously, I wanted it to be Mom, except I didn't want to see how bummed out she'd be. I couldn't tell her the truth of what I had been doing, either, because it would make her so sad that I'd felt compelled to smell someone else's stuff. The more I thought about it, the more I hoped it was Dad. He'd be mad, raging, but it'd keep some of the heat off Sephie.

By the time he strolled through the detention door, I was almost happy to see him.

"Come on," he grunted, not bothering to acknowledge the room monitor.

I scrambled to gather my books and Trapper Keeper. "Thank you, Mrs. Cunniff," I said to the teacher on my way out. She nodded without looking up from the book she was reading.

Dad marched stiffly toward the front door. The halls were mostly empty except for kids finishing up with track and making their way to the locker rooms and a couple eighth graders staying late to work on projects. I was so happy that Gabriel wasn't around to witness me leave detention.

I tried to read Dad's mood, but he was walking so fast and saying nothing. I prepared for the worst. I would take my knocks, no complaining. I would be grounded and given extra chores. I could handle that. Probably Sephie would get the babysitting jobs now that I was in the hot seat, and she needed the money more than me.

The sun outside the school was blinding. It took me a second to notice that Sephie was sitting in the front seat of the van. Her face looked grim. *Dang.* Okay. This was worse than I thought. I opened the side door and slid in. Sephie didn't turn around. Dad crawled into his seat.

We sat in a suspended second before he swiveled, his face split into a wide grin. "Broke you out of there, didn't I?"

He held up his right hand, and Sephie high-fived it. He turned the hand to me, palm out, and I did the same, confused.

"My daughter the criminal," he said, chuckling. "Guess you really needed yourself some lip gloss."

Sephie turned to face me, nodding, her eyes wide. "Did you have to give it back?"

"Yeah," I said. My brain was spinning. "You're not mad, Dad?"

He started up the van and chugged it into reverse, peering at me in the rearview mirror. "I will be if you do it again, but everyone gets to make a mistake. Plus, it's bullshit they brought in Bauer. I don't truck with bullshit."

The ice that had been around my heart since I'd been called into Mrs. Janowski's office melted. "Thanks, Dad."

"Yep. Now let's get some shopping done. We need to stock up for the party."

My breath hitched. That explained his good mood. Well, I'd take it.

"What do we need to get?" Sephie piped up.

Dad held up his list, reading while he drove. "Whiskey, beer, mix, potato chips, cheese, and cold cuts."

My stomach grumbled. We got to eat well during the parties, that was something at least. I started to get into the spirit of the trip. "Is Sephie going to drive on the way home?"

"That's a great idea! What do you say, Pers?"

She shot me the stink eye over her shoulder. Sephie was a pretty good driver in an automatic. In this big metal suppository with a ball-topped stick to shift with? Not so much. I felt small about bringing it up but told myself I'd done it to help her.

Dad caught her glare. "Practice makes perfect, Persephone."

"Fine," Sephie said, her mood buoyed as we pulled into the liquor store that gave out Tootsie Pops. She might be fifteen, but her tooth was sweeter than mine. That's when I spotted the Lilydale police cruiser in the lot. I twisted the skin at my wrist. What were the odds it was Sergeant Bauer?

There were two open spots in the nearly full parking lot. One was next to a white sedan, the other next to the police car. I thought for sure Dad'd park next to the sedan, but he pulled in alongside the cruiser. He turned off the ignition, stepped out of the van, closed the door, and tapped on the police car's passenger-side window. The officer stretched over to unroll it.

Yup. It was Sergeant Bauer.

"Hello, Donny," he said to Dad. "What can I do you for?"

Dad leaned in through the window. They exchanged words, followed by a shared dark laugh. Both Sephie and I had stepped out of the van and were waiting behind Dad. She grabbed my hand when Dad stepped aside so Sergeant Bauer could address us.

"Twice in one day, girl," he said to me. "Your dad and I agree I won't ever be seeing you again in an official capacity. Is that right?"

"Yessir," I said, the word glucky in my mouth. They were both pretending, playing the role of Concerned Adults. I was sure they'd mostly been talking about the party.

I thought of the symposium, the rumors of torture and alien abduction, how evil Clam had turned, of Evie coloring her playtime posters. *I'm not going to let them steal my childhood.* I didn't want his eyes on me, but I needed to know the truth. "Sergeant Bauer, why is there a curfew?"

Dad glared at me.

Sephie huddled closer, but I wasn't going to back down. I studied my own reflection in Sergeant Bauer's mirrored sunglasses. I was gnat-size and upside down, me and Sephie two lollipop heads blocking the sunlight from reflecting a perfect circle in each.

Bauer finally spoke. "Nothing too serious. No need for kids to be running around getting in trouble is all." He turned his face toward Dad. "Keep an eye on your girls, hear?"

Dad saluted him, two stiff fingers tapping his forehead.

If you were across the parking lot, you would have missed the look Dad and Sergeant Bauer passed each other right then, a quick smirk from one man to the other. They shared a secret, the two of them, something coiled and wet. Seeing it made me want to tug on a sweater even though the sun was shining down like a lava ball.

"I best be off," Sergeant Bauer said, rumbling his car to life. "Looks like I'll be seeing you girls Saturday!"

Sephie, ever polite, said, "Sounds good."

I glowered.

Dad slapped the top of the cruiser and stepped back so Sergeant Bauer could drive away. When he pulled out of the parking lot, Dad threw his arm around Sephie. "That's how you do it, honey. If the police are at the party, they won't bust it, right?"

Sephie beamed up at him. "Makes sense."

I was simultaneously disgusted and jealous. I hated it when she played up to Dad like that, but I had to admit, there were perks to being his favorite. I followed them into the liquor store, Dad's arm still around Seph. I was running through ways I could butter him up while weighing if it was worth it, so lost in thought that I didn't see the man tramping around the whiskey aisle until I collided with him.

"Sorry!" The word shot out my mouth at the same time my skin shivered like I had to pee.

I was standing face-to-face with Goblin.

Every rumor I'd ever heard about him rushed at me like a wave as I sucked in and held my breath out of habit. *He tortures animals. He worships Satan. He eats fingers. When he tastes blood, he goes berserk and turns into a demon. He used to be a football star until he got in a terrible car accident that took off the top of his head, which is why he always wears a hat. He sits alone at home and rocks in a chair, only leaving his trailer to buy food and beer.*

Goblin's feed cap was pulled tight to his ears, his hollow eyes shaded under its brim. He had a wormy tattoo, like the "Don't Tread on Me" snake. Its head licked out of his collar, then showed up again coiling around his arm. I wondered what it looked like under his shirt, where it ended. He was bulky and barrel-chested but not overweight.

I'd never stood this close to him before.

I realized that he didn't smell like sour old man but rather like my dad first thing in the morning, before he had a chance to shower. It embarrassed me to know that about Goblin. I found myself laughing, but I swallowed it quick. It didn't stay down, rising as a burp, full of black oil and stink.

That's when I realized I was still holding my breath. I let it out in a whoosh.

"Excuse me," I said, caught in Goblin's stare. He was glaring at me.

"Cassie, stand behind me." Dad squeezed my shoulder, and for the first time in my life, I welcomed his touch. It flushed me with a gratitude so strong I momentarily mistook it for anger.

"Of course, Father." My words were formal, weird, but we were on a large stage, acting out a play that none of us had rehearsed. My father felt it. So did Goblin.

They stared at each other, neither backing down, their hackles raised. We were country neighbors, with Goblin's house one of the nearest, but Mom and Dad never talked about him or any of the other people who lived around us, except that Gomez family who had moved into the old Swenson place. It was best to keep to yourself, Dad said, but he clearly knew Goblin, the way they were punching each other with their eyes.

Goblin kept switching his weight from one leg to the other, making a soft, repetitive sound in the back of his throat, a nervous tic, like *cuk-cuk-cuk*. Something about my dad made him terribly uncomfortable.

Goblin broke first. "You seen my dog?" he sputtered.

Dad waited a beat before answering. He wanted Goblin to know he was in charge. "You should keep that thing tied up. It chases cars."

"I asked you seen it?"

"No."

Goblin seemed to chew on this, separating seed from shell before spitting the whole works out. He pushed past Dad, jostling him, but Dad kept solid on his feet, watching Goblin march out empty-handed.

"Both of you, never go to his house. His dog is a mangy thing," Dad said, talking to us though his eyes stayed on Goblin. "I'd as soon shoot the bastard as bring him back."

He squeezed my shoulder once more, but this time was different. He was testing me, seeing if I intended to finally join his team, and the possessiveness in his eyes when he looked my way confirmed it.

"I'm talking about the man, not the dog," he said.

CHAPTER 14

Supper was almost festive. Dad had recovered from the strangeness with Goblin, and he was *on*. He told Mom about rescuing me from school, and the way he spun it, we were almost Butch Cassidy and the Sundance Kid. Besides springing his youngest, he'd gotten everything on Mom's list for the party, he said, and he'd saved her money by using coupons.

He didn't tell her about Goblin, but maybe he didn't get a chance because when he mentioned the new curfew, Mom's face closed up like she'd pulled a zipper over it.

"Lilydale's under curfew?"

Dad had scooped a big spoonful of mashed potatoes and stopped with it almost to his mouth. "Yeah. Two boys claimed they were abducted." He spit out the word "claimed" like it'd been soaked in vinegar. "Supposedly only one of them went to the police."

My mouth dropped open. *Two* boys. That wasn't right.

A year of Mom's life seemed to fall away. She turned to me and Sephie. "Do either of you know anything about this?"

Sephie shrugged.

"I heard it was only Clam. Mark Clamchik," I corrected, when Mom looked confused. "He's an eighth grader."

"That poor boy," Mom murmured.

"If it's even true," Dad said. "Kids lie."

"I heard after he was abducted, he ended up in the hospital," I offered, not sure exactly what I was saying. I hadn't wanted to use the word "raped," but neither was I 100 percent clear on what it meant to be abducted.

"A friend of mine's mom is a nurse," I continued. "She said Clam was in bad shape."

"Who's the other boy?" Mom asked.

We all stared at Dad. He was digging into his grub, this time going for the cow liver. He loved the stuff, said the iron in it gave him superpowers. The texture made me want to gag. It was like chewing on a wet book.

"Another Hollow boy," Dad said.

Sephie twitched, looking as startled as I felt. If what Dad was saying was true, it meant the second boy also rode our bus.

"What's his name?" I asked.

Dad kept chewing.

"What's his name?" I repeated.

"That's other people's business," Dad said, his eyes sliding. He was hiding something, I could tell. I wondered if it was connected to the secret he and Sergeant Bauer shared.

"That's enough," Mom said. "We're not going to speculate about other people's troubles." She reached into the radish bowl, coming out with one as bright and plump as a cherry. She'd grown it herself. Along with the spinach, it was the first crop of the year. She bit in.

The crunch made Sephie and me jump.

Mom and Dad moved to the living room while Sephie and I cleaned up supper. Mom brought out a stack of papers to grade, and Dad settled in front of the television like he did most every night. He watched a lot of TV. I guess many people did. Maybe like him, they preferred their lives delivered to them in a box.

"Do you know who the other boy is?" I asked Sephie.

She'd offered to wash dishes, me to dry and put away. She stoppered the sink and squirted out some green Palmolive before twisting on the hot water. "There's a lot of talk, but it's just rumors. Clam seemed fine on the bus."

I scraped the leftover potatoes into a plastic container, licking the spatula when I was done. "He looks okay, but he's not the same. He cornered me in the band room today."

"Clam?"

"Yeah," I said. "Except different."

She seemed to chew on this for a while, riling up the water to make bubbles. "Why'd you steal the lip gloss?"

"I didn't." I fitted tinfoil over the top of the plastic bowl. "I just wanted to see it. That's when Clam found me. I shoved the gloss in my pocket without even thinking."

"What? Why didn't you tell Mrs. Janowski?"

"Because that sounds even stupider than saying I stole it."

Sephie began dipping dishes into the hot, soapy water in the order Mom had taught us. Glasses first, so they didn't streak. Then silverware. Plates and bowls came after that, pots and pans last because they greased up the works.

"I'm sorry," Sephie said finally.

I looped my hands around her waist and squeezed. "Thanks."

"Get offa me!" she said, laughing. "Hey, you're going to help me study again tonight, aren't you?"

"Do bears poop in the woods?"

I'd crammed all the chemistry that'd fit into Sephie's head before padding back to my bedroom.

The night was humid, the color of ink. A storm was coming, I could smell it in the air, all hot and electric. It was definitely a stretch-out-under-the-bed night, but if I did that, I wouldn't be able to flip my pillow to harvest the coolness underneath. That's why I chose the closet, and I stuck with my decision even though a mosquito found me, buzzing and burrowing into my sticky skin when I'd drift off.

To take my mind off the heat and the bug, I imagined my summer. Tomorrow was the last day of seventh grade for me. Soon I'd be running through the corn rows with my hands out to catch the pollen, the air exploding with the smell of green juice and earth. Summer meant everything detonating in fruit and flowers. Clouds the color of rose quartz would fluff overhead, and Sephie and I would pedal so fast that we'd make our own breeze, racing through the air, rich and spicy with the smell of secret forest and water bug swamps.

Maybe Gabriel would want to join us. Shame threatened to creep back into my heart when I thought of him, but I wouldn't let it. Gabriel might not know about the lip gloss, and even if he did, he would forgive me once I explained myself. Sephie had. We'd bond over that mistake, maybe, and fall in love.

He'd give me his paper airplane necklace.

But how to stay in contact with him once school was out? No way would I accidentally stumble across him. We ran in different circles, you know? The only way I was guaranteed to run into him this summer was if I joined his church, which seemed unlikely. We were an atheist family, at least that's what Dad said. When I asked why, he said, "Over in 'Nam I realized the only god is the sun coming up one more day. I swore if I survived, I'd never take another sunrise for granted."

That started out okay, he said, but then there were only so many kinds of sunrises after a while, and they all started to look the same.

So no worshipping anything at our house.

No, I had one day—tomorrow—to connect with Gabriel before school was out, and the only way I could think of to do that was to have him sign my yearbook. That idea came to me whole. Once I had my plan, I was able to fall right asleep, mosquito or no.

◈

I woke with a start, my blood pumping a warning. I held my breath even though I didn't know what had woken me. My clock was outside the closet door. I'd have to open it to see the time, but something under my skin was telling me to be still.

The crack of thunder made me squeal, but then I relaxed.

A storm.

That's what had woken me. The weather had finally broken. I sniffed, inhaling the close sweetness of a spring rain. The temperature had dropped a couple degrees. I snuggled into my quilt nest, a smile on my face.

But then I heard the *clip*.

And another.

Clip.

Two more.

Clip. Clip.

It sounded so near. Dad must be right below my floor grate, clipping his nails.

How many nails had he trimmed before I woke? How many left before he came to the bottom of the stairs? The silence crackled. My arm hairs were electric. I smoothed them over, trying to quiet the blood-thump of my heart.

The slap of the clipper hitting the kitchen counter chilled me.

Dad sauntered to the bottom of the stairs.

He'd done this on and off since December. Mom had started as yearbook adviser the same month. It meant she worked late, and she'd be so tired when she finally got home that she'd stumble to bed.

Some of those nights she was gone, not every but some, Dad would clip his nails and then creep to the steps, every floorboard groan like a map of where he stood.

He'd walk to the base of those stairs and stand there for minutes at a time, never putting his foot on the first tread. My bedroom was the first one off the stairs, Sephie's at the end of the hall. There was a room between us, mostly storage. I didn't know what Dad wanted out of the storage room, but it made me feel trapped-in-a-haunted-house that he could never seem to remember to grab it during the day.

The first time he'd stood at the bottom of the stairs was the last night I'd slept on top of my bed, like a normal girl. Dad'd never gone beyond that first step, not any of those nights, but he could.

Tonight he could.

I knew that I should have hollered down one of those nights that it was okay to grab whatever it was he needed to grab already, that . . . that if he was worried about waking up me and Sephie, lurking at the bottom of those stairs was just about the worst way to go. But I couldn't open my mouth. That haunted-house feeling wouldn't let me. Then morning would come, and there would be the sun all bright and safe, and I couldn't find a single good reason to bring up the stairs thing.

But I'd land right back here, quivering under my bed or in my closet, wondering why the heck I *hadn't* brought it up because Dad was standing there, at the bottom of the stairs, I could almost see him through the wood and the walls. I couldn't quite make out his face, but I knew how it would look, half-erased from drinking, his body swaying.

hurry up, morning

I tried to slow my heartbeat to keep the fear poison from spreading. I bet this was how Clam had felt when he was abducted. The other boy, too, if there was one. I wanted to help them so bad right then, find out who'd hurt them and make it stop even if Clam had gone weird on me. Another rip of thunder tore through the sky, and I bit my tongue to keep from yelping. The wind stretched the branches as close to the house as they could reach, whipping leaves and twigs at the siding, warning Dad not to walk up those stairs.

He didn't listen.

He stepped on that first tread slowly, I could tell by the tone of the creak, like he was tasting it with his foot. Then came the second stair, its cry as familiar to me as my own name. My intestines gurgled, and I suddenly had to poop so bad I thought I'd die. I shifted, scaring up the wind chime noise of the hangers. I tried to squeeze my eyes shut and breathe regularly.

Mom, I said, but my throat was too bleached to make noise.

Dad paused on the third step.

He'd never gotten this close.

Fear gobbled me.

My senses fell away, leaving only a two-word drumbeat in my skull. *Run. Hide. Run. Hide.*

Except there was nowhere to go.

The wind screamed at Dad, the lightning sliced through the night, turning the crack under the closet door as bright as day.

Dad listened to that last warning, finally, backing down those three steps. He shuffled off to his and Mom's bedroom, banging the door closed behind him.

I unclenched my hands, feeling the ridges my fingernails had tattooed into the soft meat of my palms.

I'd die if he ever came all the way up those stairs.

It was a true thought, truer than any I'd ever had, and suddenly I wanted to write about it, not in a way that people would know what I was saying but like a message in a bottle, a secret code that Dad couldn't crack. I reached for the pencil and spiral-bound notebook that I stored inside my closet. I couldn't risk turning on a light, but the lightning came often enough that I managed to write the words burning up the space between my brain and hand.

Cassie's — Believe It or Don't!

THE EMPRESS WHO DIED EVERY DAY!

THIRTEENTH-CENTURY CHINESE EMPRESS LIU ZHENG WAS ATTACKED BY A LION AS A CHILD. SHE SAVED HERSELF BY PLAYING DEAD. SINCE THAT DAY, SHE COULD MIRACULOUSLY AND SPONTANEOUSLY FALL INTO A COMA THAT LASTED FROM SUNRISE TO SUNSET. DOCTORS WERE BROUGHT IN FROM ALL OVER THE WORLD TO VERIFY THIS MIRACULOUS CONDITION. EMPRESS ZHENG'S MEDITATIVE STATE INDEED MIMICKED DEATH. SHE COULD ONLY BE AWOKEN FROM HER "DEATH SLEEP" WITH THE REPEATED CLANGING OF A BRONZE GONG THAT WEIGHED OVER A TON!

Writing it took longer than it should have, but when I was done, I felt like I could sleep. I closed the notebook and tucked it back into the shelf along with the pencil before falling into a heavy slumber.

CHAPTER 15

Bad news still finds you on sunny days.

If that saying of Aunt Jin's was true, then the converse must hold as well: good news could arrive during a monsoon, and man, was this a tree-bender. Usually storms finished off before morning, but this one was holding on. I wondered what Mr. Patterson, my biology teacher, would have to say about the downpour. An early summer with a lot of rain seemed like it'd be a good thing for farmers.

But of more immediate concern: today was the day.

Not the last day of seventh grade, though it was that.

Today I was going to ask Gabriel to sign my yearbook and cement our relationship.

Eeeeeee.

The way I envisioned it, as Gabriel was leaning in to sign my *Lilydale Ledger*, I'd make a joke about how hard Mr. Kinchelhoe's finals were. Then Gabriel would say that he was looking forward to seeing *Cujo* at the Lilydale Cinema come August, and I'd say *no way me too*, and before you knew it, he'd offer his phone number and our summer would be a bliss of dates with his dad driving, Seven Minutes in Heaven for that first melty love-and-rockets kiss, and him pushing me on a swing with my toes pointed toward the moon. He'd tell me my scar was beautiful but offer me his necklace just the same. He'd remove the link that would make it just the right length, drape it around my neck, and clasp it.

The air would flood with the pink-honey smell of roses.

Like that, my disfigurement would disappear.

I'd rehearsed the interaction until I knew it by heart.

Unfortunately, I couldn't locate Gabriel.

He hadn't ridden the morning bus. As if that weren't bad enough, Wayne, Ricky, and Clam were more aggressive than usual. Made sense with it being the last day of school, but I wondered if it was something more, if Wayne or Ricky were the other Hollow boy who had also been abducted. Sephie and I talked about it and decided we couldn't tell for sure.

Gabriel missed band, the only class we shared. Also, no passing him in the hallway during morning classes, though I kept my yearbook clutched to my chest just in case. I made it all the way to lunch without spotting him, which I hoped didn't portend anything.

I started to plan and organize a million miles a minute, which is what I did when I felt nervous. If I didn't see Gabriel for the rest of the day and he didn't ride the bus, I'd walk to his house after school. I would. I'd do it. I needed that necklace.

If you want it, go for it. Aunt Jin.

"Free lunch!" someone yelled as I cruised into the cafeteria. I stood up straighter. Mom had woken early to pack our noon meals, which was something she hardly ever did now that she was full-time, but I suppose she wanted to send us off to our last day feeling good. Unfortunately, I could guess without looking that the brown bag held too-thick home-made bread slathered with co-op peanut butter, the kind you had to stir with a cement mixer to get the oil to blend back into the nuts, an apple (of course), and maybe some almonds.

Heather's friend Bonnie was standing next to me wearing the prettiest rainbow shirt. For sure she knew about me and the cookie lip gloss, but I didn't care, not in that moment. "What's this about a free lunch?"

She stood on her tippy-toes to peek at the menu. She had to raise her voice to be heard over the rain pelting at the cafeteria's roof and window bank. "I think they're cleaning out the kitchens. Doesn't matter if you have a lunch card or not," she said, managing not to glance at my brown bag. "We get to eat until it's gone."

"Thank you!" I said too loudly, even considering the storm happening outside.

I wove through the crowd to dump my brown bag in the trash and then jogged all the way to the rear of the line. When I finally reached the front, there wasn't much depth, but there was so much breadth! Green beans and fish sticks and cinnamon rolls and applesauce and white-bread-and-butter sandwiches and instant mashed potatoes. I tucked my yearbook under my arm so I could hold the tray with two hands; then I stacked the food up as high as I could before searching for a spot to sit.

The only feasible opening was across from Evie and Frank, same as before.

Oh well. Nothing was going to break my stride, not when I was holding a tray of free lunch.

"Hey, guys!"

Evie smiled at me with her sharp little teeth. "Hey, Cassie."

"Hi, Frank," I even said. Free cinnamon rolls made me magnanimous, a word I did not know how to pronounce but appreciated when I read it.

"Hi." He sounded mad.

"What's wrong with you?" I asked.

He scowled. "Your face."

"Gawd," I said, digging into the lump-free mashed potatoes. "What's your prob?"

When he didn't answer, I studied him. He was trying to make an angry face by clenching his jaw, but his lower lip was quivering. I shifted uncomfortably. The kid was a mess.

"It's hard being new," Evie said. I wasn't sure if she was telling him or me.

"Yeah," I said, as if I had any idea. Really what I was thinking was that he'd moved to town about the same time as Clam—and maybe another Hollow boy—had been abducted. Probably it was terrifying for him. "You shouldn't be so defensive, though. There's better ways to make friends."

He rolled his eyes and ignored me. Fine by me. I wolfed down my lunch while Evie picked at hers. Eventually, a deep sigh and long stare signaled someone special had crossed her line of vision. I glanced over my shoulder and saw Gabriel striding into the cafeteria. My pulse tripped over itself. That wasn't who Evie was looking at, though. Mr. Connelly stood on the perimeter of the cafeteria crowd, joking with some students. Evie was flashing Mr. C. the lovey eyes.

Well, she was one of many.

I grabbed my nearly empty tray with one hand and my yearbook with the other. "I gotta skedaddle. I need Mr. Connelly to sign this bad boy."

I hadn't planned on having the band teacher sign it, but now that he was in the lunchroom, it gave me an excuse to get away from Frank and Evie and then make my way back to Gabriel.

Evie couldn't have cared less. She'd gone back to tapping and toying with her food. Frank didn't even look up. As I walked away from them and the loser table, a cloud ditched the sun. The brilliance lit up the bank of windows opposite the gym, refracted a thousand times by the raindrops still falling.

I wove through the jostling crowd to dump my two milk cartons and that second cinnamon roll. I'd eaten everything else, including the soupy green beans and applesauce. I dropped my fork into the soaking bucket, slid my tray into the stack for the wide-hipped kitchen ladies to clean, and speed-walked toward the closed doors of the gym into which Gabriel and then Mr. Connelly had disappeared.

"Where's the fire?" Wayne Johnson said, dropping a hand onto my shoulder when I tried to squeeze between him and Ricky Tink. Wayne wasn't a great-looking kid, and he came from the Hollow, same as Clam, but three years ago he'd said this funny thing that had instantaneously launched him to the top of Popularity Mountain.

The fourth- and fifth-grade class had been outside for recess, playing Troll Under the Bridge. We had a German foreign exchange student that year, a quiet kid with eyes like lakes. He also smelled like sausage. The kid's name was Deter. Deter, Wayne, and all the rest of us were waiting our turn to dash over the troll-bridge jungle gym when the ice cream truck drove by, dingle-inging its bell in the hopes of tempting the day-care kids.

Without a second of self-consciousness, sausage-scented Deter shouted, "Ice cream!"—only his *r* was long and his *ea* was short, and it sounded like "ice crrrim!"

"No," Wayne yelled louder, proudly. "That bell means they're *out* of ice cream."

We'd gone silent, all of us within earshot, wondering for a split second if we'd been lied to our entire lives. Then someone laughed, and just like that, Wayne was promoted from troubled kid to Official Class Clown.

The thing was, it'd been an accident. I could tell *no questions asked* that Wayne had believed what he'd said, that ice cream trucks only made noise when they were out of ice cream. He'd been gloating that he knew something Deter hadn't, not telling a joke. He'd wiped that confusion off his face lickety-split, though, and jumped into the laughter because while Wayne was not the sharpest knife in the drawer, he was smart enough to recognize when he'd hit a bull's-eye.

That's the thing about small-town boys. All they had to do was come up with that one shtick, a crack at just the right time, or a Hail Mary touchdown, or nail the part of Romeo in the class play, and they were set. They never had to try again. Here's the thing about small-town girls: we let them get away with it. But not now. I didn't have time for it.

"It's a gas fire, and it's in your smelly pants," I responded, twisting free of Wayne's grip. Ricky sniggered. He was a year younger than me, two years younger than Wayne, best known for the Band-Aids covering his finger warts. He was the only one of the Hollow boys who was in band. He played one of the school-issued trombones, and no one else would touch it because of the warts. I thought he was a nice kid. He never bothered me on the bus, anyhow.

Wayne didn't follow up, so I slipped into the gymnasium, breathing in the quiet, the raucous noise of the lunchroom mellowed into a background hum. Two high windows let in squares of murky, stormy sunlight, dust motes floating lazily inside them. The bleachers were rolled back and pinned to the wall, revealing a glossy sea of golden oak flooring. Overhead, the basketball hoops were tucked in tight, ready for the long summer slumber.

Gabriel and Connelly were nowhere in sight. I was alone in the gym for the first time in my life, and all that space was whispering at me to run across that big floor. Students weren't supposed to be in here unsupervised, but it was the last day of school, and I wasn't the only one bucking the rules. I glanced at all the doors. I really *was* alone in here. I charged off toward the opposite side, toward the locker room doors, my China flats as quiet as butterfly wings.

I was racing, flying, free, speeding with such power that my hands made an echoing slap when they hit the cool cinder block of the far wall.

"Cassandra!"

I squeaked as Mr. Connelly appeared from the shadows at the top of the locker room stairs. My only consolation was that he appeared more startled than me, his face white, his hair mussed. He flicked on the stairwell lights. They were harsh against the amber glow of the floor.

I glanced around. Connelly was alone. My heartbeat, which had been pleasantly pumping from the jog, skipped a lurch before it got back on track. I held out my yearbook. "Will you sign it for me?"

Connelly ran his ring finger across his forehead, moving a stray hair back into place. His eyes were hidden for a moment, and then there they were, his warm smile in place. That grin could light up a room. "You caught me meditating. My apologies."

I smiled. It felt like I had less lip to work with than usual. This was the first time I'd been alone with Connelly. Where no one could see us, I mean. He gave private lessons to everyone in band, but the lessons were stacked, which meant someone else was always waiting for their lesson after you, so you were never technically *alone* with him, especially since the lesson room had windows for walls. Still, it'd always felt good to sit in that small practice room with Connelly, who smelled like an Italian actor and dressed like a fresh envelope.

But here we were truly alone, and something felt off.

Mrs. Puglisi's words played across the television screen of my brain. *A grown man, still living with his parents besides. His mother had a heart attack last week. Did you hear about that? It would explain why he wasn't able to control his urges anymore. That sort of stress drives a man crazy.*

My hand was shaking. Connelly wasn't taking the yearbook. I pulled it toward my body.

The soft wheeze of one of the locker room doors closing below wafted up the stairs. We both tensed at the noise, swathed in the oily smell of the antique locker room heaters that were needed to heat the wet and frigid basement no matter the season.

Soft footsteps padded toward us.

Gabriel appeared, a confused smile on his face.

Gabriel! My heart thumped. He reminded me of a feather-haired Greek god. He was so close, so unexpected. The air grew syrupy like it does when life tumbles out of your hands.

Connelly seemed to blend into the darkness of the bleachers before changing his mind and stepping toward Gabriel, who wore a turquoise T-shirt that matched his eyes. Gabriel's top lip was dusted with the lightest of incoming mustaches. My glance shot to his paper airplane necklace. The world shifted as I imagined the cool metal licking the tender skin at my throat.

"You have one, too," Gabriel said, pointing toward my neck.

My knees buckled. *Could Gabriel see my imagination?*

Connelly reached out and held me up. "Whoa there!"

I steadied myself and blinked, which was all the time I needed to realize that Gabriel had been referring to the green padded yearbook I was clutching to my chest, identical to the one he was holding. Of course he couldn't see into my brain. I swear, sometimes I felt like a monkey wearing clothes, hoping nobody noticed. "I'm having Mr. Connelly sign it."

"He asked me for mine, too," Gabriel said, smiling that honey smile. Being on the receiving end of it felt like returning to the sunshine after a life underground.

"Can't let my best students leave for the year without a proper message to carry them through the summer!" Connelly produced a pen out of his back pocket with a flourish. His words and jovial tone made me smile, even though I knew I was far from his top pupil. I decided to write off the momentary weird vibe he'd given me. Who had the energy to be freaked out when all their dreams were coming true?

"Is Connelly giving you summer lessons, too, Cassie?"

Connelly had announced to all band students last week that he'd be providing private music lessons to interested students this summer. He said he'd only charge $20 an hour, which might as well have been $2,000 an hour for my family. The good news was, who wanted to learn how to play the clarinet better?

"Naw, I'm just here to get my yearbook signed." I held it out to him, proud of how cool I sounded. His hair appeared so soft. I imagined running my fingers through it, and goose bumps erupted on my forearms. "You might as well sign it, too."

"Hey now." Mr. Connelly laughed, snatching it from my hand. "Me first. And if I won't see you for lessons, I can at least count on you to sell those popcorn kits."

"Sure!"

"Great. Stop by my house this summer. Maybe you and Gabriel can sell together?"

"Will do!"

And we stood there, in that safe pocket of smiles and laughter, summer dreams and yearbook autographs, and it was the last time we'd all three be together again.

Alive, I mean.

CHAPTER 16

Sephie swiveled her knees toward the middle of the bus so I could squish in next to the window. She took in my grinning face, my hair gone pancake in the humidity, my backpack stuffed to capacity with the end-of-school locker clean out.

"What's wrong with you?" she asked.

I ignored her. Instead, I stood and rested my elbows on the pane of the open window, chin in hands, and studied the front of the school, hoping to spot Gabriel walking out.

I'd waited until final period to read his inscription in my yearbook.

Cass, sweet lass, hope your summer doesn't go too fast! I will see you around, promise.

Sweet lass.

I will see you around.

promise

The first time I read "swoon" was in one of Lynn's mom's romance novels that I borrowed (secretly) back when Lynn and I were tight. I'd been immediately disgusted by the word. As if a girl couldn't even hold up her own head for the sheer manliness of some guy. But here I was, swooning over a cursive-scribbled yearbook note.

Sephie tugged on the back of my jeans. "I can see your plumber's crack."

Impossible. My shirt was tucked in. Still, I fell back into the bus seat, eyes closed and smile intact, letting the sweet smell of rain-washed lilacs and the last-day bus fumes wash over me. "Gabriel signed my annual."

"Should I book the church now?"

Her tone chiseled through my joy. I opened one eye. "What's riding you?"

Her head drooped, the ear nearest me poking through her brown hair. She clutched a letter, the Lilydale High School, ISD 734, rubber stamp marking its corner. It was crumpled, as if she'd been twisting it.

Both eyes were open now. "Sephie! You didn't?"

"I failed the final. I have to go to summer school." She was too despondent to even weep.

"Dang." I scrambled for a way to make it better. "But hey, Dad already knew it could be coming, and besides, this weekend is a party, so he'll be in a good mood. This is perfect timing!"

"Easy for you to say."

"Guess what?" I asked, hoping to distract her. I leaned over, unzipped my backpack, and rummaged around until I located the pink invitation. "Did I ever tell you uptight Lynn invited me to her birthday party?"

Something like jealousy darkened Sephie's face, but her inner sun won out. "No way! I thought you guys weren't friends anymore."

Another bus driver stepped onto the bus. He looked over us kids like an auctioneer at a cattle sale, then leaned to whisper into Karl's ear. Karl glanced up at all of us in the mirror, his jowls waggling, eyes seeming to settle on me and Sephie, only that didn't make any sense. He nodded at the other bus driver, who got off.

The bus lurched away from the curb. No Gabriel. *Oh well.* We'd already decided we were getting together this summer. The plan was in motion.

I tapped Sephie's knee with the envelope. "I didn't think we were friends anymore, either! Probably they're going to sacrifice me."

I didn't know Wayne had been listening, but he snickered, leaning over me to snatch the envelope. "It'd be a virgin sacrifice."

Sephie had Wayne's ear in one hand and my pink party invitation in the other before I spun all the way around.

I grabbed the envelope, feeling big with Sephie on my side. "I heard what happened to Clam," I said. I was safe saying it, mostly because Clam wasn't riding the bus. He'd gotten detention on the very last day of school.

Wayne's face slammed closed like shutters in the wind. "You didn't hear shit."

Sephie and I exchanged a look. It felt like I was on the edge of something big. "Did too. I know somebody whose mom works in the hospital."

He pinched and twisted a soft bit of flesh at his throat, quick and violent. His eyes appeared extra shiny. "Yeah, well, it was his own fault."

"How do you mean?"

Wayne shrugged, only it was disjointed, like someone had yanked his shoulder strings.

"Wayne?" Sephie asked.

He wasn't going to respond, so I asked the question I was sure both Sephie and I were thinking. "Did you get attacked, too?"

He stood abruptly and made his way toward the back of the bus. Middle schoolers never sat there. It wasn't a written rule, just the way things were. Sephie and I stayed quiet until all the townies, including the Hollow kids, stepped off the bus. Without Wayne and his weird, angry sadness, we could finally relax. It was the last day of school, after all.

Karl even agreed to crank up the radio when "The Stroke" came on. I'd already gotten burned by thinking Olivia Newton-John's "Let's Get Physical" was about exercise, so I was going to assume this one referred to sex. One by one, the country kids streamed off the bus until it was only me and Sephie choking on the gravel dust pluming in the open windows as Karl swung past the old Swenson house, the one that a new family had moved into last week. I was hardly paying attention. *Summer.* I felt wild and large, bigger than the bus, huge as the sky.

Straight ahead was Goblin's house. Looking at it, I was gripped by the best idea.

"Sephie! Let's go pick those wild strawberries from Goblin's ditch."

She shook her head so hard that her hair fell across her eyes. "You're crazy."

"Am not!" I stood, grabbed my backpack, and hollered to Karl, "Let us off here, please!"

Karl never said much, and he looked like a grumpy hound dog, but he handed out jelly beans on Halloween and Easter, wouldn't yell at a kid who got sick on the bus, and broke up a fight a couple years ago without turning anyone in. He'd been staring at some of us longer than comfortable this past week, but I imagined it was the same on all the buses since Clam had been attacked.

Karl grunted a response. I wondered what bus drivers did in the summer. Construction work? In any case, he pulled over, tapping his blinker lights and pulling out the stop sign.

"Come on, Sephie!" I squealed. I didn't look, but I knew she was following me even before I heard her feet hit the gravel. We watched the bus pull away, lumbering down the road and finally past our house.

"Dad's gonna be mad that we got off early."

"He won't even notice," I said, grabbing her hand. "And if he does, we'll tell him we had to pick strawberries. He'll get a kick out of that."

Sephie didn't respond. There wasn't much to say because here we were. I crunched across the gravel until I was standing on the lip of the ditch separating the public road from Goblin's private land. Summer bugs were whirring and clicking. I smelled clover and the rich, gritty scent of rain-soaked gravel. The ditch looped down, sandy by the road, turning green as it neared Goblin's, and between, the patch of early wild strawberries, ruby jewels like I remembered.

I swallowed. I bet they tasted like pink lemonade, sweet-tart and happy.

Goblin's farmhouse was one hundred yards beyond the wild strawberry patch. Sephie pointed at the No Trespassing sign driven into the ground.

I pursed my lips. "The berries are on *our* side of the sign. Technically, we wouldn't be trespassing. Come on, Sephie. You only live once."

I thought I'd have to do a lot more convincing. I was wrong.

To this day, I'm not sure what made Sephie bolt across the ditch and grab at those berries like a starving animal. I'd always been the one to lead, always pushing the line, but without warning, it was like she needed to get at those berries more than she needed to breathe.

I was laughing when I took my first step into the ditch, following her. She looked so silly stuffing those strawberries into her mouth, like Cookie Monster on a binge. I swear she was even making the gobbling noises. I kept giggling as I neared her, would have laughed all the way to the berries if Goblin's dog hadn't caught wind of us and started barking to beat the band from inside the house.

We both froze.

Goblin charged out of his farmhouse moments later, ferocious dog at his ankles, shotgun in his hand. Only his mouth was visible below the brim of his hat, an angry slice of red across his face. He racked his gun, the crack echoing in the countryside.

Sephie screamed. So did I.

We sprinted toward our house, not looking back.

It was almost a mile, but we ate that road up in record time, running so hard that our sneakers slapped our butts. Once we were safely on the other side of our mailbox, we fell into a giggling heap. I felt so alive. My side was all stitched up from running fast, and it hurt to laugh, but I couldn't stop hooting.

I look back at that day and wonder where we'd be now if I'd eaten those strawberries, too.

It wasn't fair that only Sephie had to bear that.

CHAPTER 17

Birds sang, crickets rubbed their rear legs together, the green-juice tang of crushed fiddlehead ferns drifted up from the bottom of our sneakers, the chickens in our coop clucked and warbled, and a far-off car zoomed.

But there was no nearby sound of nailing, or mowing, or sawing or welding.

"I don't hear Dad working," I finally said, still on my rump, the giggle stitch fading.

"Me neither." Sephie stood and brushed herself clean, offering me a hand. A ratty-looking black cat ran up to her, twining between her legs.

"Hey, Bimbo," she said, petting him. I'd named him that because he'd let *anyone* pet him, but he especially liked Sephie.

"Race you to the house!" I called, dashing ahead.

She didn't even try to catch up. Probably that letter was weighing her down, now that the exhilaration of being chased by Goblin had passed.

"Down here!"

Mom was kneeling in the one-acre garden at the bottom of the hill that tilted away from the driveway and barn. She waved her spade. My stomach dropped. No way was she going to have us slave in the garden on the last day of school. What was she even doing home so early?

"I know you see me!" she yelled, laughing, when I hesitated.

"Mom!" I whined. "Can't we have a day off?"

"Yes, Peg," Dad hollered from behind me. I jumped. I hadn't heard him come up. "Can't the girls have a day off?"

His green eyes were dancing. He held a sketch pad with a tiger lily drawing on its open page. It would make a gorgeous sculpture. I tilted my head, gauging his mood, his alcohol level. He seemed both sober and happy, which made no sense. I tossed a nervous gaze at Sephie. Her expression said she was as confused as me.

Mom stood, wiping dirt off the front of her cutoffs before grabbing a basket and strolling toward us. "I still have planting to do," she said when she reached us. "And I have to drive in early tomorrow to get my grades in, so it has to be today."

"We could plant, or we could go to town," Dad said. "Who wants to join me?"

"Me!" Sephie raised her hand.

Mom had probably an hour's worth of seed packets in her basket.

"Me too!" I said. I was worried Dad was meeting up with Bad Bauer for more of their Bad Business, but it would be better than working.

Dad gave Mom his full attention. "What do you think, love?"

Mom smiled. It was tired. "I'll keep Cassie. We'll plant the rest of these seeds and have supper waiting for you two when you get back."

Dad leaned over to kiss her, in full preparty mode, a regular Richard Dawson striding onto the *Family Feud* set, ready to charm the ladies and wink knowingly at the men.

I stink-eyed him and Sephie's back as they walked away, toward the van that would take them to freedom and town. "That's not fair," I said.

Mom wiped a bug off her arm. "Life isn't fair. If it was, I'd make a million bucks for teaching."

"But why does Sephie get off and I have to do chores?"

Mom started walking toward the garden. "The school called. We know Seph has to go to summer school. Your dad wanted to talk to her. If that sounds like a good time to you, we could arrange it."

I slammed my mouth closed. That was *not* my idea of fun. I wondered if Mom had received the call about Sephie while she was at work. "How did you get home before us today?"

She handed me a pack of seeds. Garden Sweet Burpless Cucumber. "I left the same time as my students," she said. "I have a pile of grading to do, and I can work faster here."

I nodded, mulling things over. "Are you guys mad at Sephie?"

"Disappointed." She reached for a hoe and handed it to me.

I sank it into the mucky dirt, building a hill before slicing a divot across the top. "Have you heard anything more about Lilydale kids getting taken?"

She'd been ripping a sprig of apple grass out of her spinach bed. She stopped weeding but didn't turn. "Not much more. The boy who went to the police, Mark Clamchik? He says he was taken by a man wearing a mask."

My chest grew hot. The agony of it, of being grabbed by a faceless man, the white terror of feeling so powerless. I felt it every time Dad clipped his nails. "A mask?"

"Yes," Mom said. "Poor boy. You said you know him?"

I nodded mutely. She couldn't have seen it, but she went on talking. "We're safe out here, in the country. The police are focusing on the Hollow area on the edge of town."

I heard the distaste in her voice, the disdain for people who lived in trailers. She wouldn't say it out loud, but there it was. I wanted to ask her what she thought of people who lived in houses with scary drunks, but I didn't. Those sorts of questions only made her angry.

She rubbed her hands on her pants, leaving streaks of mud, and turned, her mouth in an O like she'd just remembered something neat. "How'd you enjoy your lunch surprise?"

For a second I thought she knew about free lunch, but that seemed unlikely. "What?"

"The Girl Scout Thin Mints I stashed in there. I know they're your favorite. I bought a box last February and was saving it for today."

My chest stuffed with emotion. *I'd thrown away Girl Scout Cookies.* Mom would be devastated if she discovered that I'd wasted her thoughtfulness. "Thanks."

She smiled but didn't hug me. She'd never hugged Sephie or me, not that I could remember. But the thought of her saving cookies for me was as good as any embrace.

CHAPTER 18

The late afternoon smelled like purple clover and then, as I ducked my head to enter the chicken coop, like smut, feathers, and the acrid paste smell of bird poop. The chicken house used to be a storage shed, three rooms long, and briefly a glorious playhouse for me and Sephie. Now the three rooms were divided into laying hens in the far west room, with off-the-ground nesting boxes to choose from so the skunks didn't eat their brains at night; a middle room for eating hens; and in the east room, a storage space that housed chopped corn the color of lemons and oranges, oyster shells for grit, and spare waterers and food troughs.

We would butcher most of the eating chickens tomorrow morning. For now, I placed the halved plastic milk jug over the heads of the nesting chickens to calm them before slipping my hand under them to remove their warm, smooth eggs. The chickens warbled suspiciously, a *heyyyybroody*, *heyyyybroody*, but with their heads covered, they let me slide out their cackleberries. We used to own Araucanas. Their eggs were pastel greens, blues, and pinks, ready-made for Easter. Now we had plain old rust-colored hens, with boring brown eggs.

The egg-gathering rhythm soothed me. I thought about Clam, how frightened he must have been when the masked man took him, and Wayne's face—angry and broken—when I'd asked him about it on the bus. What had Wayne meant by it was Clam's own fault he'd gotten attacked? If Dad really knew the details, he wasn't telling. Him and Sephie had been extra quiet since they'd returned from town, Sephie's face red and puffy as if she'd been crying. Mom put her straight to work while she made supper. Me, I hadn't stopped working since Sephie and I'd run home from Goblin's place.

A swarm of gnats buzzed near my face, trying to drink the water off my eyes. I swatted at them as I returned the egg-picking jug to its nail and unlatched the wire door before stepping outside. My skin lapped up the fresh air. It was cool now—late May chilly—but the stillness told me tomorrow was going to be a scorcher.

Dad appeared from behind the chicken coop, rolling the butchering stump in front of him. Apparently we were returning to chopping off heads. That's how we killed them the first year. Sephie would hold them by the beak, pinching it between chubby girl fingers, and Dad would hold the legs with his left hand and swing the hatchet with his right.

Chop.

You'd think after war that Dad wouldn't want all that blood and violence. He seemed to crave it, though, always grimly happy on butchering day.

Once the chickens were headless, I was sent to retrieve the animated corpses. They jiggled when held upside down. I'd bring them to the feather pot boiling over the camp stove, an enormous metal vat in which we'd dunk the newly killed hens. The dirty smell of wet feathers would be in my hair for days, no matter how much I scrubbed, but I preferred this job to holding the beaks so near Dad's swinging hatchet. We'd watched *Roots* in school, and that scene when Kunta Kinte loses his foot stuck with me.

Thunk.

I couldn't hold that beak, not for love or money.

Dad, he didn't mind the gore. He made sure to mention that any chance he got.

"How many?" he asked, still pushing the butchering log, pulling me back into the here and now.

"What?"

He stared at the bucket I was holding, then back at me. "How many eggs?"

I hadn't even counted them. "Nine," I guessed.

He stopped rolling the stump directly in front of the coop. The chicken blood that had pooled in the hatchet divots had grown black. I squinted. The sun radiated directly behind him. He was wearing raggedy work clothes, but he possessed the outline of the statue of David. Tall, strong, muscled. When I thought of stepping forward and hugging him, I shuddered. He could just as well be crawling with maggots for how close I wanted to get to him. I realized that with curiosity. It had been that way for as long as I could remember. Maybe that's how it was for all girls and their dads.

He spun on his heel toward the chicken coop.

"Dad?"

He stopped but didn't turn. "Yeah?"

"Since we have to butcher tomorrow, can Sephie and I have the rest of tonight off?"

He stepped into the coop without answering me. He appeared a minute later with an egg in his hand. "You missed one."

I stood in place as he brought the egg over and placed it in my bucket. It was covered in poop. It'd be a pain to clean. A roar on the gravel road drew my attention. I turned. A huge truck was rolling past on our quiet road. It had a bucket on its back, STEARNS COUNTY ELECTRICAL on its side.

Dad tensed. "Goddamned invasion is happening already," he said.

I could hear the hate in his voice. He'd moved us out here to escape the real world, to find a place where he could hold his parties and build his sculptures and create his magical forest pathways without anyone telling him different.

"They can't take our land," I said, heated.

He was quiet for a while. "Yeah, you can play," he finally said. "But no complaining when it comes to butchering time tomorrow."

"Okay," I said. I started to walk away and then stopped. "Dad?"

He hadn't moved, his eyes pinned on me. "Yeah?"

I almost lost my nerve, but I couldn't shake the image of Wayne on the bus, scared and mad at the same time when I asked him about Clam. "Did Sergeant Bauer tell you any more about Hollow boys getting attacked?"

A clot of blackbirds took to the air in Mom's garden, probably scared off by Meander.

Dad laughed, an ugly cut of a sound. "They're not getting attacked."

I took a step back. "What do you mean?"

"I mean they're lying if they say they are."

But he couldn't know that. He hadn't looked into the eyes of the animal that'd taken up house in Clam's body, or the terror in Wayne's face. Dad was hiding something. Something different than he usually hid, I could feel it, something to do with Bauer.

I'd have to poke through his drawers.

I'd done it before. It hadn't felt good, digging through those dirty magazines, those red-and-black pictures he sketched that were so different from his sculptures, that book he claimed to always be writing but that read like a diary except everyone owned laser guns. I hadn't discovered anything surprising, nothing except some letters that Aunt Jin wrote him when she was a little girl. She called him her best big brother. That caught me off guard, but I suppose they'd all had a life before I was born.

I'd never snooped in his studio, though. Or the basement. That's probably where I should start, as soon as Mom and Dad were both out of the house. Maybe I could talk Sephie into helping me.

I found her on her knees in the bathroom, cleaning the bathtub grout with an old toothbrush. "Dad said we can have the rest of tonight off!"

She sat back on her heels. "Doubt it."

"For real! Cuz we have to butcher chickens tomorrow. He said we only get it off if we play willowacks, though." I grinned. It didn't matter if she knew that last part was a lie. It was funny either way.

We'd been playing willowacks since we were five and seven. It involved covering ourselves in sheets with a headband over our eyes holding them in place, tying ourselves to one another, removing our shoes so we were sock-footed, and blundering through the woods circling our property. Where we ended up was anyone's guess. We lost hours playing willowacks, laughing, collecting cockleburs. It was the best fun, but Sephie had refused to play since last summer. She'd said it was because she was starting high school. I'd told her it was probably her little boobies throwing her off balance.

Seph rolled her eyes, but they had a spark in them. "I'm too old for that."

"You're never too old to be sheet-seeking. Please? We only have a little bit before it's suppertime."

She looked at the toothbrush, and at the line of grout she'd cleaned. It was white to the remaining grout's gray. I could tell she was wondering what more she could squeeze out of this deal, but her better nature won out. "Fine."

"Yee-haw!" I wasn't going to allow her time to change her mind. I sped off to locate the materials, then led her outside. The giggling started after we were covered in the sheets like Halloween ghosts but before we'd donned the headbands that would hold them in place.

"We should tie ourselves together at our ankles," Sephie offered.

That's when I knew she was full in. The ankle tie was the most challenging. It required us to orchestrate every step or fall over like a sack of potatoes. I let Sephie tie the knots. She was always better at it than me.

"Hey," I said while she wound the twine around my ankle, "I really do think Wayne has a crush on you. He asked about you in school yesterday. I forgot to tell you."

I couldn't see her face, but I knew she was grinning. "What'd he ask?"

"What your favorite color is."

A yank on the twine told me she'd wound her end of the rope around her own ankle. Bimbo peeked under my sheet, and I pushed him away.

"Do you think he was attacked by Chester the Molester, like Clam?" Sephie asked.

The humiliation and fear I'd felt when Clam cornered me in the instrument room returned, wrapping itself around my ribs like a too-tight rope. "I think Dad might know. I think him and Sergeant Bauer have talked about it. Want to help me look through his stuff later?"

"What would we be looking for?"

I shrugged under the sheet. "I dunno." I thought of what Mom had said, that the man who'd attacked Clam wore a mask. "Clues, I suppose. Like maybe Bauer gave Dad a copy of a police report, and it lists the names of the boys who were hurt and what happened to them?"

We were quiet for a while.

"Do you really think Wayne likes me?" she asked softly.

"What's not to like?" I shook off the uneasiness and stepped forward, testing the rope. Sephie glided with me without needing to be told. "Except that you snore. Oh, and you smell like donkey. But other than that . . ."

"I don't snore."

We were cruising now, nearly running, hands held in front, the anticipation of a collision tingling along my skin. The mowed lawn gave way to the thick grass and crunchy sticks at the forest perimeter. We headed into the woods, the smell of secrets and rotting leaves growing stronger, the air cooler.

"And besides, you smell like a donkey's *sister*," Sephie finished.

I laughed, and she did, too. "Tree!" I called, my hand meeting the solid wood. We both shifted to the right, bonking against each other.

"Another tree!" Sephie giggled and stumbled.

I caught her hand before she fell. "Hey, Sephie. I bet Mom and Dad will be okay with you wanting to be a hairstylist." They wouldn't be. I was feeling good, though, and I wanted to share that.

"You think so?"

"For sure." We crunched along silently for several minutes. When a narrow valley appeared beneath us, we both pitched into it. My elbow grazed something sharp as I crashed to the ground. "Ow!"

"Where are we?" Sephie asked from beside me. The rule was that we couldn't look, couldn't remove the sheets until we were hopelessly lost. Her voice was too thin, though.

"I don't know. Are you okay?"

A flurry of fabric told me she was removing her sheet, which was expressly against the rules. "Sephie!"

"I'm bleeding."

I gasped, pushing the headband off and then the sheet. We were so deep in the woods that the trees cast underwater shadows. Sephie and I lay hip to hip in a grove of wet-looking oaks, a place we'd never seen before. It smelled like loam and rot and copper. Sephie's knee was bleeding a thin red streak. Tears streamed down her cheeks.

"What happened?" I asked her.

She pointed past our sheets, which were a shocking white against the moldy forest floor, to bones nearly the same color jutting from the ground.

I screamed.

CHAPTER 19

My dad killed someone.

It came to me all clean and laid out, just like that, landing in my belly rather than my brain, like most thoughts did. When I tried to grab on to it, though, to examine it up close, it slithered away. Of course my dad wasn't a murderer. By the time he'd heard Sephie's sobbing and my yelling and found us in that moldy oak grove, I'd marked the thought as outrageous.

Once Dad pointed out that the skeleton belonged to a vulture—*look, you can even see some of the wing feathers here*—and not a small child, I almost couldn't even remember that I'd had it.

Almost.

Dad carried Sephie to the house, where Mom cleaned and bandaged her punctured knee. The phone rang in the middle of the process. Surprisingly, Dad went to answer it. He must have been expecting a call, because normally he hated talking on the phone. He said the government was always listening and that anything you had to say you should say in person. When he returned moments later, he was working his jaw. "The new neighbors need a babysitter for tonight," he said.

"Yay!" Sephie squealed.

"No," he said, sounding irritated. "They're not going to want a limping sitter. Cassie, I told them you'd do it. They're on their way, so clean yourself up."

I'd only babysat for one family before.

Over the winter, I'd taken on one of Persephone's cast-off babysitting jobs, this one for the Millers. Their four blond boys were indistinguishable except for height: John, Kyle, Kevin, and Junior. The oldest was five, and having them so close together meant their mom couldn't laugh too hard anymore or she'd accidentally pee. (She'd told me on the uncomfortable ride home.) Because I couldn't tell them apart, I said the boys' names all at once when they were naughty, which was regular. *JohnKyleKevinJunior, do not light that match. JohnKyleKevinJunior, do not hold your dad's golf club over your brother's head. JohnKyleKevinJunior, get your hand out of your pants.*

At the end of an exhausting evening, I discovered that the only way the monsters would sleep was if I let them crowd the nappy rust-colored couch and watch TV with me. Not much was on that late and that far out in the country but *The Twilight Zone* (which seemed like a mean trick). The boys fell asleep before the episode got too spooky, and I wished they hadn't because it terrified me. I'd have changed the channel except JohnKyleKevinJunior had crashed out on my lap and looked like boogery angels. The best I could do was close my eyes and plug my ears.

I hoped things would go better with the Gomezes.

"Your parents keep their property very neat." Mr. Gomez's accent was faint, his vowels longer than if he'd been a native Minnesotan. That and his black hair told me he was from Mexico, but a while ago.

I smiled and nodded, crammed into the farthest corner of the pickup cab. Mr. Gomez hadn't done anything wrong. It was just my standard response to being in a car with a stranger. "Thank you," I said.

I was grateful that the ride was so short, a little over a mile from our house as the crow flew. Making conversation with adults was the worst. Plus, Mr. Gomez drove with his window down, and one of the area farmers had recently spread manure. The air was tangy with the odor of composting hay and ammonia.

I wondered if Mr. Gomez knew about Clam being attacked and the curfew in town. If he did, I bet he was regretting moving his family here. "Do you like your new place?" I asked.

Mr. Gomez nodded. He had deep creases around his eyes that reminded me of a cozy leather chair. "Having a larger house is nice."

Dad said they'd moved from Rochester, that Hector was a farmer and his wife a redheaded Minnesotan who'd fallen in love with him on sight when they'd met at a bar. It was clear how Dad said it that he didn't approve. I don't think it bothered him that Mr. Gomez was Mexican. Both our parents were clear to me and Sephie that immigrants were good people. The problem was that they were uneducated. To Peg and Donny, being not-book-smart was a crime.

It made me feel tall when I thought about my parents' master's degrees, and my grades. It was good to be a brainiac. Dad said his mind moved too fast for most people. Because it raced so hard, he needed to work extra hard to entertain it. Books worked, he said. So did all those magazines, some thick with science fiction stories, others with popular mechanics (which, if that's what you name your magazine, you're trying too hard), and the others, the ones I hated, bursting with pictures of naked women with their hands between their legs and soft smiles on their faces.

Dad had tossed a warning my way when Mr. Gomez pulled up. "Don't let your guard down when you're there, Cass, and don't talk about what happens over here. You can't trust anyone but family." A thought popped into his head, I could see it skitter across his face, and he turned to Mom. "Hey, love," he said, face bright with the pleasure of his good idea, "maybe we should invite the Gomezes to our next party? We could welcome them to the fold."

Mom had been facing away from us, stirring green pepper slices with a wooden spoon. Her shoulders tightened. "Maybe. Cassie, why don't you wait outside to get picked up."

I was more than happy to. Mom was cooking up tofu stir-fry with brown rice for supper. I didn't know if the Gomez family expected me to cook for their children. I didn't even know how many kids they had, but I knew whatever I'd find in their fridge would be tastier than what Mom was cooking.

My stomach had been audibly growling when I pulled myself into Mr. Gomez's dusty Ford pickup. It'd had the good graces to shut up on the drive over. I think me and Mr. Gomez would have stayed silent after the initial small talk, if not for the fist of squawking black birds he plowed through taking the corner by Goblin's house.

My arms shot up reflexively.

"The hell!" Mr. Gomez said, braking and swerving. The birds had been hiding in the unmowed grass on each side of the road until we were nearly on top of them. It was a wonder we hadn't hit any.

The back end of the truck skidded before Mr. Gomez brought it to a full stop at the lip of the ditch, near where Sephie had gathered those wild strawberries. I dropped my hands and smoothed the cloth of my sundress, tasting the road dust pouring through Mr. Gomez's open window.

"I didn't know crows gathered this late in the day," I said, my voice small.

Mr. Gomez looked at me straight on, for what seemed like the first time. It was too shadowed to read his eyes. "Feed truck must have dropped some corn," he said.

"Yeah," I responded. What else was there to say?

He put the truck into gear, and we didn't say another word for the last half mile of the drive. Mr. Gomez didn't step out with me when we pulled up to their house, either.

"You can go right in. Tell Sally I'll wait for her out here," he said.

I nodded and wiggled out of the truck, still shaken from driving through a cloud of crows.

"Hello?" I asked tentatively when I stepped into the strange house. The living room was stacked high with boxes, the largest sectional couch I'd ever seen crowding the middle. The kitchen was probably off to the left, just like in my house. I smelled something rich and cheesy, maybe lasagna, plus garlic toast. My stomach approved.

"In here!" Mrs. Gomez stuck her head out of the kitchen, a big grin on her face. Her curly red hair was spilling out of her upsweep. "You must be Persephone. Sorry for such short notice on the babysitting!"

"Cassandra," I apologized. "Persephone is my sister. She had to stay home tonight."

"Well, we're happy to have you. You hungry?"

She disappeared into the kitchen. I followed the good smells.

Her kitchen had the same charmless cupboards and yellow-and-brown linoleum ours did before Mom and Dad ripped it out and Dad built the maple cabinetry from scratch. In our house the linoleum had looked horribly dated, but in this kitchen it felt like sunshine. Three kids sat at the table, two little girls facing me and a boy with his back to me.

When he turned, I gasped.

It was Frank, the new boy who had sat by Evie at lunch and was all smart mouth and sass.

Sally laughed big. "Frank, you see Cassandra's face? She's also wondering why a boy your age needs a sitter."

There was that, but more pressing was the fact that we didn't like each other. Plus, I was freaked out that I hadn't known he lived so near.

He hadn't ridden the bus, even though he'd be on our route. His parents must have driven him to school.

Frank rolled his eyes before turning back to dig into a glorious melty pile of cheese, noodles, and red sauce. A tinfoil sleeve of store-bought garlic bread was within arm's reach. The bowl of green lettuce was untouched. Near it stood a bottle of Wish-Bone Western Dressing. I had to swallow so the drool didn't escape my mouth.

Sally looped an arm around me. It was so natural. "Frank's dad thinks boys can't babysit. Other than that character flaw, he's a good man. So now you've met my son. The girl who has more sauce than face right now? That's Julia, my youngest. She's three. Her older sister, the one unfortunate enough to get my coloring, her name is Marie. Frank will show you the ropes. We have the phone hooked up in case there's an emergency. We'll be back before midnight. Any questions?"

Can I live here? "Does anyone have a medical condition?"

Sally laughed, but it felt like a hug. "I see you've taken the Girl Scout babysitting class. No, my kids are wash-and-wear. Hope you like lasagna. I made a double batch." She kissed all her kids before she left, and then she planted a smooch on my head, right in my part. "Have fun!"

"Milk!" the youngest screamed, reaching for it.

I ran over to help her, listening to the front door slam and the pickup truck pull away. I looked at my hands before shyly grabbing my own paper plate. "You guys haven't unpacked your dishes yet?"

Frank shrugged. "My dad has been here for a couple weeks. He didn't unpack anything. We came last Sunday, and Mom hasn't had time to go through all the boxes."

"And they made you go to school anyway?"

"Yeah."

I could tell he was as nervous as me. That made me more comfortable, that and the fact that I was in charge. "Well, let's finish supper and then clean up. We can probably get this kitchen squared away before your parents get home."

I ate lasagna until my eyeballs were cheese colored, and then all four of us cleaned up. Little Julia held the garbage bag while we dumped in the disposable plates and forks, Marie wiped, and Frank and I packed up the leftovers and hand-washed the plastic cups.

Once the table was cleaned off, Frank helped me scrounge up crayons and paper for the girls, and they colored while me and Frank scrubbed out the cupboards and unpacked all the dishes and silverware. I didn't think Sally would care where we put stuff, that's just the kind of person she seemed to be. The more Frank talked about his mom and dad, the more I knew I was right.

"What was Rochester like?" I asked.

He shrugged. "We lived out in the country, like here."

"I wish I lived in town," I confessed. "There's so much more to do."

He leaned toward me, shaking his head. "No you don't. Town is where bad things happen. Someone was taking boys in Rochester, just like here."

I blinked. "Only town boys?"

He nodded.

I thought back to the vulture bones, and Dad, and Bauer. "Is that why you moved? To get away from boys being attacked?" Because if so, they must have felt awful that it was happening here now.

"Naw," Frank said. "We needed a bigger house."

"This isn't very big," I said, then felt like a heel when I saw his face drop. I tried to take back my words. "It's built like our house, is all."

"Does yours have a creepy dirt basement, too?"

I nodded vigorously. "It's dirt, all right. Mom keeps most of her canning down there, and Dad stores stuff in it, I think. My dad doesn't let us go down there."

Frank shuddered. "Dirt basements are haunted. Always."

CHAPTER 20

Here's the thing. If you'd told me when I woke up that I'd have a best friend by the end of the day, and that he'd be a *boy*? I'd call you crazy cakes. But Frank and me found ourselves practically finishing each other's sentences after that first hour together. We had mountains in common, once we got through the fact that he'd been mean to me at school because he didn't know anyone and thought I was snotty. First, we both liked to watch *The A-Team*, and when I told him I had a copy of the latest *Nellie Bly's Trust It or Don't*, he made me promise to bring it over next time. I didn't tell him that I only allowed myself to read one entry a night, because I knew it was weird. I told him all about Aunt Jin and how great she was, that she was an artist who said I could come live with her if I ever wanted to.

Frank had been duly impressed. When the girls started fussing, we uncovered the TV, plugged it in, and twisted the antennae until a grainy single channel came in. It featured a riveting (not really) show on the *Alaus oculatus*, commonly known as the eastern eyed click beetle. It made the same back-of-the-throat noise as Goblin had made when I literally ran into him at the liquor store, which I told Frank all about. Frank loved the world of bugs, it turned out.

The beetle show was interrupted by a commercial featuring a hard-working lady who couldn't catch a break until she finished her workday, fed her family, and tucked in her kids. Then she got her big treat: alone time. Our view was whisked to a bottle of bubble bath poised on the edge of the tub. The bottle was blue, the label white. It read **My Time**.

A deep male voice rumbled the only words in the entire commercial: "Take charge. Make this your time."

Frank punched my arm. "Hear that? You should make this your time."

I bopped his arm back. "Shut up, young pup."

He giggled and hooked my neck, pulling me down into a wrestling move. I laughed, pushing him away and then thinking better of it and twisting his arm behind his back, just enough to hold him in place. Or so I thought. He squirmed out and yanked me onto the floor, where we began wrestling for real. We were about evenly matched, but my long hair messed me up. We kept at it for nearly ten minutes, laughing and hurling insults—*Bag your face! Eat my shorts!*—neither of us able to keep the upper hand for long.

Finally, exhausted, we declared a truce. That's when we noticed the girls had fallen asleep on a bare mattress in the corner.

"Hey, you wanna see something?" Frank asked, still trying to catch his breath.

"Sure. Hold on." I stood, opened the bag marked "blankets," and pulled out a musty orange afghan to cover Julia and Marie. "Where?"

"My parents' bedroom."

"Okay." I wiped the back of my hand across my forehead. I was sweaty from wrestling.

We wove through the maze of boxes, by the steep staircase that I hadn't yet used, past the bathroom that I had, and toward the rear of the house.

The Gomezes' bedroom was the same size as my parents' but seemed larger because it wasn't dominated by the gurgly waterbed Mom and Dad had in theirs. Liquid moonlight poured in through a bare window, lighting up the double mattress and dousing everything else in shadowy relief.

"Where's the light switch?"

"I dunno," Frank said, heading straight toward the dresser. "Maybe we should call the A-Team?"

I lowered my voice and started to recite the TV show opening from memory. "'In 1972, a crack—'"

"Yeah," he said, distracted. He tugged open the top drawer, and then the second.

"Let me help." I felt along the wall shadows until I bumped the light switch. I flicked it on. A bare bulb illuminated the room. "Your parents unpacked here already?"

"Mom told Dad that if he was going to make her move to Bumtruck, Egypt, that he better plan on having her bed ready and take her dancing the first week."

"Smart." I ran my hands along the buttery brown wood of their bed frame. "What are you looking for?"

He turned, a lopsided expression in his sea-colored eyes. He held up a round plastic disk that he'd fished out of the drawer. "This."

I leaned in. "What is it?"

His voice was church-serious. "Drugs."

I showed him the whites of my eyes. "What kind?"

"My mom calls them her Happy Pills. Dad says they're the best thing since sliced bread."

My scar cord tightened around my neck. I'd thought Hector and Sally were different from my parents. "Did a doctor prescribe them?"

"I don't know." He snapped open the disk and pointed at his mom's name typed inside the clamshell lid. The bottom half was a miniature Stonehenge of white pills.

I started giggling. Once the laugh tickled my belly, it rolled to my mouth and squeezed water out my eyes. It was hard to wedge my words past all that laughter. "Do you think we should try those *drugs*?"

Frank pooched out his bottom lip. "What are you laughing at?"

"Those are birth control pills!"

He held them close to his face, as if he'd be able to spot a picture of a baby with a red line through it, like a no smoking sign. "You sure?"

"Hundred percent. Mrs. Smith passed some around in health class this past winter. They were in a different packet, but there were twenty-one white and seven green, just like those."

"Aw dang."

I thought about telling him I could get him real drugs, if he wanted them. The temptation to impress him was strong, but then he looked at me with those ocean eyes and I decided I'd rather be kind. "What do you want to be when you grow up?"

It was a nobber question and he knew it, but we both wanted to change the subject. "A pilot," he said.

I gasped. "Just like my boyfriend!"

He squinted and returned his mother's birth control pills to her drawer. "Who's your boyfriend?"

"We're not technically dating. Yet." I followed Frank back to the living room. Julia and Marie were still asleep, Julia audibly snoring. "You know how you sometimes get a sense about something before it happens?"

Frank wasn't buying it. He was still sore from being wrong about the pills. "Naw. And you shouldn't say you have a boyfriend if you don't."

Headlights played across the ceiling. His parents were home. I didn't want to end the night like this. I wanted to ask him if he'd come to my place next. I hadn't had a slumber party in forever, but you can't ask boys to spend the night. "Want to go biking with me?"

"When?"

"This week. We could investigate the abduction of those boys. We'd be heroes if we cracked that mystery." It felt right when I said it. He could be my sidekick, and then I wouldn't be so scared.

His shoulder twitched. "We'll see."

"I pity the fool who doesn't bike with me." I poked his armpit. He pushed me away, but he was smiling.

"I have to use the bathroom real quick before I go," I said. "Will you tuck the girls in tighter so it looks like we took really good care of them?"

Frank was leaning over his sisters when I darted back toward the master bedroom. My plan wasn't fully formed, just a foggy vision of Gabriel and me kissing, and another of Mrs. Smith passing around those birth control pills, lecturing past the point of hearing. Sally wouldn't miss one out of her packet, and I'd need it if Gabriel and I decided to make love. I yanked open the drawer, popped the top of the clamshell, and dispensed a tiny white pill into my hand before closing the container and stuffing it back into the drawer. I ignored the icky feeling of stealing from Mrs. Gomez. It would be better to be a thief than to be pregnant, and I knew she'd agree with that.

Frank was sitting on the couch holding a book when I came out. "You might as well meet my dad outside," he said, tossing his thumb toward the front door. "He doesn't like to get in and out of the truck more times than he needs to."

I grabbed my jacket. "Bye." My heart was still bumping.

"Bye."

CHAPTER 21

May 26, 1983

Dear Jin:

Thank you for the <u>Nellie Bly's Trust It or Don't</u>! You probably know my birthday isn't until June— finally, I'll be a teenager!

I don't know if you've heard that a boy was attacked in Lilydale, maybe two? People are really jumpy around here, you wouldn't believe it! I'm going to find out if it's true about the second boy so I can let you know in my next letter.

School is officially out, and 7th grade wasn't so bad. I ended up second in my class. I have a plan to catch and pass Erica next year. It involves a tinfoil hat, electrodes, and a summer storm. Just joshing! I do have some great plans for this summer, though, and I'll tell you all about them next time you come by. I'll just start by saying that I am going to begin shaving my legs (I know!!!) as soon as I can convince Mom.

I babysat tonight and met my new best friend. His name is Frank, and he lives up the road. I know—a boy for a friend! Maybe one of these days I'll have an actual boyfriend. JJ 2!

Toronto looks beautiful from the pictures you sent (and thanks for the PO box #!). I looked at a map and you're not that far from Minnesota. Maybe you could stop by? Dad has been extra-weird lately, and Mom and Dad are having one of their parties Saturday.

Maybe I'll sneak out on my own. Send help if I go missing (haha!). Just kidding. But I know you'll always save me if I need it.

XOXOXO,
Cassie

CHAPTER 22

Morning was a muddy-brown promise against the flat line of the horizon, and Dad, Sephie, and me were already outside, working. Mom had to take a phone call with the school. Dad said when she was done, we'd start butchering, but he'd said that over half an hour ago.

The air chilled my meat. My heart and arms, anyhow, which is why I wore my hooded jacket zipped to my chin. My legs were bare. I hadn't bothered brushing my hair, because it would only get messy. I'd been too tired to even wash the crust out of my eyes, though the nip of spring-coated summer air was bracing, waking me up against my will.

"You can carry more." Sephie had been growly since we'd started.

She dropped her armful of mossy sticks into the wheelbarrow. Dad was working ahead of us, removing the trip wires he put out so he could tell if anyone trespassed. It was our job to clean off the trails behind him. Sephie and I still hadn't talked about the upcoming party. We were too scared. The older we'd grown, the harder the gatherings were to tolerate.

I dropped my own admittedly lighter bundle of sticks, scraping off the nubby worms that had spilled from the woodbelly. "You're being a crab since I got to babysit and you didn't."

"Am not."

"Are too. And I know you were lying about the wound on your knee making you fall asleep before I got home." We had a rule that we stayed up for each other. I'd done it a million times for her because she did most of the babysitting. Last night was only the second night she would have had to do it for me.

Sephie turned away so I couldn't see her face. "Was not either lying. Dad says it takes extra energy to heal our bodies. The hole in my knee wore me out, and I couldn't stay awake. But look, it's good I slept so well. My leg hardly hurts at all this morning."

"Yeah, well, you're lucky Dad was asleep when I got home."

Or I'd wanted to imagine he had been. I shuddered. I'd run so fast from the front door to my room that my feet had only touched the floor twice. The dark of the house left too much room for hiding. "When does summer school start?"

"Monday." She was sullen.

"How long does it last?"

"Two weeks."

"Aw dang, Sephie, that's not so bad! And summer school is super easy."

She slowed down, letting me catch up. "Mom and Dad said I'm grounded from *everything* until I get a passing grade. I can't even have people over."

I sensed this wasn't the time to point out that she'd *never* had people over. Me neither, not since Lynn had dumped me. It would take too much explaining to break in somebody new. But maybe Frank would be different. "You and me can still hang out. I have a kitty clinic coming up!"

Every summer since I was seven I'd held kitty clinic. When I was younger, I trained them to jump from high spots, mostly. As I got older and realized they didn't need me for that, I'd switched to more medical pursuits, including cleaning out their infected eyes, gently opening the crusted-shut lids with a washcloth soaked in warm water, wiping away the pus, and dropping in eyebright tea that Mom bought at the co-op.

Sephie made a noise of disgust, but her shoulders were loose. I'd won her over. "Just while I'm grounded. And I don't want to touch their gross eyes. I'll brush 'em, though, and help you dry the catnip bundles."

I clapped my hands.

"Hey," Sephie said, loading up my arms. We had two more stacks of wood to transport to the burn pile. The sun was finally up, its yellow kiss promising to warm my bones. "You never did tell me. How was it at the new family?"

And just like that, all the distance melted away and we were sisters again.

"Good!" I spilled all about the night, everything except the birth control pill that I'd hidden in my jewelry box next to four baby teeth and a glittering earring stud that I'd found on the floor of Ben Franklin and hoped was a diamond.

"Wait," Sephie said, tapping her chin as she interrupted me. "Frank said that boys were taken where he lived before?"

"Yeah, so what?" I asked.

Sephie flicked my head. "And then they move here, and Clam gets attacked? Seems like a big coincidence."

I rubbed the spot she'd flicked. "Mr. Gomez is a nice guy."

Sephie rolled her eyes so hard they creaked. "That's what everyone says, dummy. 'I had no idea he was a serial killer! He seemed so nice!' You better keep an eye on him."

She was right, and I didn't like that one bit. "I need to use the bathroom," I said.

"You better hurry back."

Dad was up ahead of us, still removing trip wires. I couldn't see him, but I heard him. I hoped mom was still on the phone, fully immersed in a conversation. I tore past Dad's studio, toward the house.

I didn't have to pee.

I was going to follow through on my plan to go through Dad's stuff, the plan I'd made on chicken-butchering day. Sephie was wrong thinking Mr. Gomez was the one taking the kids. No one married to someone like Mrs. Gomez would ever do that. My dad and Sergeant Bauer, though? That was a different story.

Mom met me on her way out of the house, her face cramped.

"Is something wrong?" I asked her.

She rubbed her temples. "No. It's time to butcher."

"Meet you by the chicken coop," I said. "I gotta pee real quick."

I had the house to myself, but not for long. I left my shoes at the front door so as not to track in mud and raced toward Mom and Dad's bedroom. Their waterbed had no drawers below, only a big box to hold the bladder, so I started in Dad's nightstand. It held dirty magazines, some half-smoked joints, and sketches I didn't want to look at too closely. I found the same in Dad's dresser, plus his clothes.

I didn't like how much it smelled like him, but I held my nose and kept digging. I didn't know what I was after. A signed note saying he and Sergeant Bauer had attacked Clam? The mask they'd worn when they'd hurt him? Something to prove that Mr. and Mrs. Gomez were nice people, just as they'd appeared?

I didn't find any of that. In fact, there was nothing new since I'd last scoured his drawers, right around when Sephie had gotten boobs and Dad had grown extra weird.

There wasn't much time. Sephie was surely already complaining about how long I was taking and how much more work she had to do. Maybe Dad was even stomping toward the house, ready to catch me in the act. I made sure all his drawers were closed, peed really quickly because it would be a while before I got another chance, and was almost to the front door when I thought of our basement.

Dirt basements are haunted, Frank had said. *Always.*

When was the last time I'd been in ours? Surely it used to be a place Sephie and I could go, but I didn't really remember being down there other than that one time years ago. The thought chilled me. Dad had been up late this past week. I'd thought he was skulking around the kitchen, but had he been going in and out of the basement?

My feet motored toward the pantry.

I flicked on the light.

I watched my own hand reach toward the basement door. The knob was cool. I twisted it. The smell of damp dirt crowded in my nose. The absolute black below gobbled up the weak pantry light, panting for more. I put my foot on the top stair. The steps were a glorified ladder, really, not much wider or deeper, built into the wall.

The top step creaked under my weight.

My heartbeat was thundering.

"It's just a damn basement," I said out loud, swearing to give myself courage.

It didn't work. I couldn't force myself any farther, and once I made the decision to close the door, I couldn't escape that house fast enough. I pulled my shoes back on in the bright sunlight, shaking like a dog.

CHAPTER 23

If Sephie thought she was going to get out of chicken butchering because she had a fresh wound, she was dead wrong. We got to work like usual, Dad chopping off the chicken heads and me, Mom, and Sephie running the processing line.

"Hey, Mom," I said, once Dad had finished his chicken murdering and gone into the house. I had to lean over the butcher table to talk across Sephie, who was sitting between us, her bandaged knee propped up. "Did you and Dad go to school with Sergeant—Mr. Bauer?"

"Sure did," she said. *Slick slice*, her chicken was open, into the chest cage went her hand, out came the first wash of guts, good stuff like heart and gizzard in the stainless-steel bowl, entrails to the cats.

"How about Karl the bus driver? Or Mr. Connelly?" I was listing everyone who'd behaved peculiarly lately.

"I'm afraid I don't know either, unless you mean your music teacher?"

"That's him," I said.

"I only know him from parent-teacher conferences. He seems like a nice man."

I nodded. "What do you know about Goblin?"

Sephie twitched at the mention.

"Who?" Mom asked.

I realized I didn't know his actual name. "The guy who lives at the end of the road, right where you turn left to go to the old Swenson place."

"You kids call him Goblin?" Mom fake shuddered. "Yes, he graduated high school with me and your dad. He's strange, that one. Has been forever, though I think he and your dad were friends for a time back in the day. Your dad can't stand him now. The man's a draft dodger. Mr. Bauer's not so bad, though, not once you get to know him."

Mom leaned toward Sephie, talking girlfriend to girlfriend. "I used to date him in high school, did you know?"

"Sergeant Bauer?" I asked. Hearing that hollowed me out.

Mom giggled. It was a little-girl sound. "Don't sound so disgusted! I wasn't always married."

Sephie burped.

Mom nudged her. "What do you say?"

"Excuse me," Sephie said.

"My favorite ladies still hard at work!" Dad appeared behind Mom and wrapped his arms around her. His mood had changed yet again. He must have downed a drink.

I tugged out feathers, my eyes on Sephie. She shifted her wounded leg.

Dad kissed Mom's neck, and she leaned back and laughed. "Not now! I'll get us both dirty."

Dad growled something in her ear, and she laughed again. "Fine. Ten minutes. You're on your own, girls. I have to help your dad with a project."

"There's a dozen chickens to go!" I wailed.

"You're always so dramatic," Mom said, hosing off her hands.

A fly buzzed down and landed on the chicken I was plucking. The insect was fat and black, glossy, its back legs rubbing together as it rested on the hen's pimpled flesh.

"I'll finish the plucking," Sephie murmured. "You gut them."

Mom turned off the hose. "Don't get that leg wet, Sephie. It'll get infected."

Sephie nodded.

"I don't want to gut them," I said, a poor sport to the end.

"Okay, then let's pluck together," she said. "When we're done, you slice them open, and I'll pull everything out."

"All right."

I kept at the stinky chicken corpse I'd been working on, feeling her eyes on me.

"Why'd you ask Mom about Goblin and Sergeant Bauer and those other guys?" she asked.

I poured a cup of water over the bumpy flesh, clearing the plucked feathers. The water ran pink. "I dunno. Don't you ever wonder what Mom and Dad were like when they were younger?"

"Not really."

"Sometimes I do. They went to Lilydale. Bauer too. And the way Dad treated Goblin at the liquor store the other day, I figured he knew him from a while back." I paused. "And Dad's been acting bananas lately. Even more than usual. Don't you think it's funny he started meeting up with Bauer around the same time Clam and maybe another Hollow boy were attacked? And that seeing Goblin made him so upset?"

Sephie rolled her eyes. "Like Mom just said, Dad doesn't like Goblin because he's a draft dodger. Stop being so weird."

"You're the one who's gonna stick her hand up a chicken."

"What're we making?" I asked Sephie, hopping from foot to foot.

"Spaghetti, I think, and a spinach salad. Shouldn't be too hard."

"Sephie!" I grabbed her hand and tugged her up the stairs behind me. "If we're making spaghetti, we've got plenty of time to try on those dresses. Pleeeeaaassseeee."

A box from Aunt Jin had been delivered today while we were breaking for lunch, after Sephie and I had finished cleaning the chickens and in the middle of more trail cleaning. Inside was white tissue paper, with a handwritten note on top: *To my favorite princesses, who are going to grow up whether their parents like it or not.* I'd peeled back the lacy paper, revealing two flowing taffeta dresses, one the color of pomegranate seeds, the other a rich eggplant shade.

They were so beautiful it hurt to look at them.

Dad wouldn't let us try them on then with so much work left to do, so I ran them to my room. The four of us kept toiling until it was time for Mom to head off to work and hand in her final grades, leaving me and Sephie in charge of dinner. We'd cleaned ourselves up and had a whole hour before it was time to start supper. I was desperate to try on those beautiful gowns.

Sephie pretended to pull back, but she was smiling her dimpled smile. "I get the red one!"

We dashed upstairs. She vibrated with joy when I opened my closet and showed her where the dresses hung. She snatched the scarlet one off the hanger, not even giving a second glance to my nest underneath. She'd caught me sleeping there enough times.

"I want the purple!" It was held up by my only skirt hanger because it was strapless. I turned away from Sephie, yanked off my T-shirt, and slipped into the dress. "Zip me!"

She stopped in the middle of tugging on her own dress to close mine.

It was a little big on me. I rustled over to my full-length mirror and stared. I had to hold the dress up with one hand, but I could see how in a couple years I would fill it out. I piled my hair on top of my head with my free hand and smooched at my reflection. Sephie appeared behind me, the red dress fitting her perfectly. She was never going to make the *Solid Gold* dancer cut, but that dress made her graceful and curvy in ways I'd never noticed before.

"Sephie," I breathed. "You're so pretty."

Her eyes were wide and trembly. "No way."

I turned her so we were both staring in the mirror, side by side. "You bet. Let's go show Dad!" I felt a pinch of doubt when I said this, but we were too pretty to waste it on each other. I tugged her downstairs just as I'd dragged her upstairs. We giggled in a corner of the dining room until Dad finally hollered at us from his chair, asking what all the noise was about.

"Introducing Miss Minnesota, Persephone McDowell!" I pushed her into the living room, directly between Dad's view and the TV. "And her companion, Miss Preteen Minnesota, Cassandra McDowell!"

I waltzed in, still holding up the bust with one hand, the other swishing the grape-colored taffeta skirt. I stood shoulder to shoulder with Sephie but was staring toward the ceiling as I imagined a model would. "We both pledge to create world peace and cure dolphins of cancer." I nudged Sephie and tittered.

"And for your pleasure, we will dance the dance of the Fairy Queens," she said, moving loftily, her mouth quivering with the force it took to keep from laughing.

Dad set down his drink and began clapping, a goofy grin on his face. "Dance for me, my princesses!"

And we did, twirling and preening like little girls until it was time to cook dinner, when we slipped out of our beautiful gowns and into regular clothes so we wouldn't mess them up.

We had full bellies and the dishes done by the time *The Dukes of Hazzard* came on. I was hoping Dad could hold it together until *Matt Houston*, for Sephie's sake. I'd never seen her carry a torch like she did for Lee Horsley.

Me, I didn't have time for mooning over actors. That's why I liked *Remington Steele*. Laura Holt did all the work. She was the real deal. She didn't waste time being romantic.

Plus, Mom was always home Tuesday nights when *Remington Steele* was on.

I could tell by the way Sephie kept glancing from a *Dallas* rerun on the screen to Dad in his chair that she was measuring his mood, just like me. When Dad started to get too loose, it was time for bed, no matter how great the show.

At the next commercial break, he leaped out of his chair to give Sephie a foot massage. She tried to pull her leg back.

"Hey, we can probably get you those braces you want pretty soon," Dad said.

Sephie lit up like a torch, letting him at her foot. "Really?"

I scowled. *No, not really.* He was in his "generous" phase. Mom and Sephie fell for it every time.

"You bet," he said, reaching for one of my feet. I tucked them both underneath me, and he returned his full attention to Sephie. "We just need your mom to sell that ol' sewing machine, eh?"

He smiled conspiratorially, but Sephie kept her face closed on that one. She knew Mom's sewing machine had been a gift from Grandma.

"Who wants a drink?" Dad said after he'd given both of Sephie's feet a good rubdown. He stood slowly.

"I'll take some water," Sephie said.

"Cassie?"

"I'm good." I was thirsty, but I could tell right now that this was going to be an early-to-bed night, and I didn't want to need to pee in a couple hours. "But thank you."

He swayed in front of us, not quite ready to go. "Have I ever told you two that you're beautiful and that I love you?"

Sephie snuggled closer to me. "Yes."

He squinted like he was auditioning for the role of Thoughtful Dad. "So beautiful that boys are going to want to ask you out soon. Or maybe they already are."

My hand flew to my neck scar. It was pressing tight, almost choking me.

Dad leaned closer, but it threw him off balance, so he straightened. "We should talk sometime about what those boys are gonna want to do to you. Some of it is going to feel good. Real good." He smiled and nodded slowly, mostly looking at Sephie. "Some of it won't. Your mom talk to you about any of that?"

Sephie was pushing fully into me now.

"That's gross, Dad," I said, a burning setting up in my head. Mom should be home soon. Where was she?

"Should have thought of that before you paraded your bodies in front of me in those dresses. But yeah, I suppose it is gross," he said, chuckling. He tried for a little leprechaun heel click and almost made it.

"Gross gross, the man who loves you the most," he sang-mumbled as he shuffled to the kitchen.

The commercial break was almost over. A preview of the upcoming *Matt Houston* episode played, humor and action blended over its jumpy horn-based theme song. But there was more! Sonny Bono and Zsa Zsa Gabor were guest-starring.

"No way!" Sephie wailed.

"It doesn't matter," I hissed, leaning forward to peer toward the kitchen. "We have to go to bed. Now. You know that."

Sephie nodded morosely. Her face was swollen with sadness. Everybody in the world had seen that episode but us, and now we were going to miss the rerun. She pointed at today's *Lilydale Gazette* lying near Dad's chair. "I heard there's some good garage sales this weekend. Maybe we could talk Mom and Dad into taking us?"

"Do you think Dad already read the paper?"

"He's not reading anymore tonight," she said, tossing one last miserable glance at the TV.

"I suppose you're right." I grabbed the *Gazette* and followed Sephie toward the bathroom.

"We're going to bed!" I yelled in Dad's general direction, hoping it would deter him from following us. We locked the door and Sephie used the toilet while I brushed my teeth, and then we switched. The TV was still blaring when we opened the bathroom door. We swapped a worried look with each other before bolting up the stairs. I checked Sephie's room with her, and then she did the same for me.

"Night."

"Night," she said.

I was in my closet ready to sleep before I remembered that I hadn't read today's *Nellie Bly's Trust It or Don't* yet. I figured I might as well skim the garage sales while I was at it. I stepped out of the closet, grabbed my flashlight, and opened the paper.

The headline screamed at me.

Another Lilydale Boy Is Attacked.

CHAPTER 24

The article said neither of the boys could be named because they were minors, but I knew the first was Clam, and the writer included a photo of the second boy's run-down house. Anyone who rode my bus could tell you that's where Teddy Milchman lived. Teddy was small, and he was quiet, and he had soft-looking black hair like puppy fur, and he was only a fourth grader.

He lived in the Hollow, just like Clam.

Had the police noticed both kids who were on the record as being attacked were from the same neighborhood? I reread the article but didn't find anything making that connection. I stared at my door, desperate to dash through it like the cartoon Road Runner. I wanted to hurry downstairs and convince Dad to call the police and let them know that the Hollow connected the boys. Maybe if the police knew, they could watch that area. They could save any more boys from being attacked and hurt so severely they had to wear diapers, from feeling powerless in their own bodies.

The breath rushed out of me as I heard it.

Dad was clipping his nails.

I blinked back tears. I felt like I was holding my breath past the point of drowning, it hurt so bad. I swiped at my face and quietly burrowed back into my closet, yanking out my journal and pencil. I would write fast, and I would write good, so good it would keep Dad from coming up the stairs.

Cassie's — Believe It or Don't!

REAL-LIFE MERMAID GIRL!

12-YEAR-OLD ARINA IONNIDES OF THE GREEK ISLAND OF KALYMNOS CAN HOLD HER BREATH UNDERWATER FOR OVER NINE MINUTES! TRY SLOWLY COUNTING TO 540, AND YOU'LL GET A SENSE OF HOW LONG THAT IS!

BORN INTO A SPONGE-DIVING FAMILY, ARINA LEARNED TO LOVE THE SEA FROM AN EARLY AGE, WHICH IS WHY EVERYONE WHO KNOWS HER CALLS HER MERMAID GIRL.

I finished writing it.
Then I waited.

CHAPTER 25

Dad had risen as far as the fourth step before turning back. Even though I'd heard him finally shuffle off to his bedroom, and then Mom came home shortly after, I hadn't been able to fall asleep until the sun pinked the horizon. Sephie discovered me in my closet and roused me without comment. When I told her that my story had kept Dad from making it all the way to the landing and that she should thank me, she looked at me like I was cuckoo.

Whatever. It was light out. That meant I could tell Dad that Teddy Milchman lived in the Hollow, same as Clam, so the police could catch whoever was hurting those boys.

Dad was as scruffy looking as a hobo when I found him in the kitchen. He looked as if he'd slept as poorly as me. I pointed at the scrunched-up newspaper I held like I could make him see their houses and the monster hunting those Hollow boys.

"Dad, you know this article?"

He rubbed his raspy face and poured himself a cup of coffee, black.

"Both these boys live in the Hollow, Dad. Both boys who were taken. You said there was another boy attacked, too, and that he was also from the Hollow. You need to tell the police. They're practically neighbors, Clam and Teddy."

"The police know," Dad said. His voice sounded terrible, like a rusty engine screeching to life.

I set the article down and planted my hands on my hips. "You sure?"

He turned on me, bleary-eyed. "They're too stupid to listen if they don't already know that bit."

Tears pushed hot against my eyelids, and the thought that I was going to cry made me so angry. Dad laughed at girls who cried. Didn't matter if it was me, Sephie, or Mom. He got a real kick out of it. So I swallowed those tears. "Promise me you'll tell the police those boys are practically neighbors. That they both ride my bus."

Something in my voice gave Dad pause. "Fine."

"Promise me."

He did a crisscross over his heart. "Hope to die."

I had no choice but to believe him. Then do my outside chores. And think about how I should have told Frank that I liked to sneak around and hide in dark places and snoop and that that would come in handy when we became detectives, his Remington Steele to my Laura Holt. I peered at the cornfield across the road, at the spears of corn no taller than my ankles, and thought of the Indonesian tree man who didn't know where his skin ended and his warts began, and how I wished Jin were here.

By the time the first party guests started arriving, Sephie and I had set up all the potluck tables and decked them out with paper plates, plastic silverware, and matchbooks. Dad had placed out bottles of his homemade strawberry wine. I'd tried it once. It tasted like a fruit burp smells. Most of the ladies went for the wine, though, and were sure to praise Dad on how good it tasted. The men wanted beer or mixed drinks, which is where Sephie and I came in.

When we'd first been asked to bartend, both of us had been so proud. The job wasn't too hard. Two fingers of whiskey, the rest pop or water. We received quite a few compliments, but as the day wore on, the praise felt more like probing fingers. It was nice of Sephie to take the bullet on that one and offer to bartend today.

She always looked out for me.

"Holy cats have you grown!"

I smiled up at Mr. Frais, who'd just arrived at the party. He and his wife, Mary Lou, were friends of Mom and Dad's from way back. I'd always liked them. They were both professors. They hadn't attended one of Dad's parties since I was little.

I glanced hopefully toward their car. "Peter and Lisa aren't with you, are they?"

Of course they weren't. People used to bring their kids to Dad's parties, and *man*, was that sweet like cherries. We'd explore all over our property with those kids. It really was a magic garden back then, even though Dad didn't have half as many sculptures up as he did now. We'd play capture the flag, kick the can, TV tag. The parties were always potluck, and Dad would roast a whole pig, the smell so good it made your teeth ache. There'd be Tupperware containers crammed with every salad you could dream of, from the healthy to the straight-up mandarin oranges floating in clouds of sweet white Cool Whip.

Back then, the adults focused on cribbage tournaments—which Sephie and I won one year because everyone else was too drunk to play, and boy, had we been proud—or backgammon rallies, with the occasional game of volleyball. They'd talk about college, which was where many of them had met, or the war, which most of them had protested. Many of them toked on the pot that Dad cultivated in the little greenhouse off his studio, and they got loose, and they laughed, and then somewhere along the line they decided they should all start having sex with each other.

I remember the year it started. I was maybe nine, and Dad disappeared into his and Mom's bedroom with a woman named Kristi. She was married to someone else back then, I can't remember his name,

I just knew that she made me sad. She was one of those people who laughed too loud and hung on Dad like a tree monkey and carried herself like she lived in the smallest corner of her body.

I had a crush on a boy named James that summer. His parents had brought him to the party, where James told me I had strong legs. That was the nicest thing anyone had ever said to me at that point in my life. He and I and some other kids whispered about what Kristi and Dad did on Mom and Dad's waterbed, but mostly, we didn't think a whole lot about it.

The next summer, though, other husbands took other men's wives away, and then two summers back, one guy took Mom into a room, and after that, no one brought their kids anymore. The grown-ups didn't pretend to want to play cribbage, either. They mostly kept to the big barn, which had been outfitted with garage sale pillows recased with glorious Arabian-style cases that Mom had sewn from scraps.

It was a fun place to play, though like the basement, we technically weren't supposed to go in there.

Sephie and I were powerless to resist the barn, though. We never entered through the front door, which was secured with a combination lock that only Dad knew how to open. We'd sneak through a hole in the attached silo. This required crawling through sticky spiderwebs to reach the old chute hole in the silo's base, squirming inside, and then using the chinks in the cinder block to propel ourselves up and up, twenty feet.

It was worth it every time, because the inside of that barn looked like a movie set. It smelled like salt and sweat and musk and powdery incense, but you could roll from one end to the other on a bed of pillows. I didn't think about what was done on the pillows.

"Craig!" Mom bounced out of the house and wrapped Mr. Frais in a hug. "What are you and Mary Lou doing here?"

Mary Lou took some of that hug from her husband. "It's been too long. We ran into Ray at Lake George, and he mentioned your party tonight. Hope we're welcome?"

"Of course," Mom said, taking the bottle of wine and box of potato chips Mary Lou offered her. "Always."

"How are you and Persephone?" Mr. Frais asked me when Mom and Mary Lou took off toward the house.

"Fine." I pointed to where Sephie stood behind the card table groaning under its load of liquor bottles, their amber warmth glinting in the afternoon sun. It was a cloudless day, which was good from my perspective as it kept the adults outdoors longer. "She's bartending today."

Mr. Frais chuckled. "Isn't she a bit young for that?"

The honest concern in his voice woke up something desperate in me. "Mr. Frais, the parties aren't like you remember."

He shaded his eyes so he could see me more clearly. "What's that?"

The front door slammed. Mary Lou and Mom walked out, Mom's arm looped through Mary Lou's, and she looked happier than I'd seen her in months. "Nothing. It just gets a little wild here."

His smile faltered.

I dialed it down. "Nothing you can't handle, though! Can I get you a drink?"

"It's early for me to start drinking, but thank you."

I don't know why that made my eyes feel hot, but it did and I didn't like it. "I better get to work. I need to finish setting up the lawn chairs."

Mr. Frais watched me with a bemused expression as I jogged down the hill and toward Dad's studio, which was a refurbished granary. It consisted of three rooms: Dad's front brainstorm room, his back workroom, and the second-level storage room. Only his back room, where he did the actual sculpting, was heated. The brainstorm room was all chalkboard. When Dad was really cooking, he'd hold four different colors of chalk at once, scribbling furiously, sketching and scratching out his next project, outlining measurements. In the winter, it was so cold in there that he puffed clouds of white while the chalk dust flew. It looked like he was creating art in outer space.

The workroom housed his metal-cutting, bending, and welding tools, and we could only enter there with eye gear and permission, but Dad didn't mind if we played around on the second level, a half floor where he kept a bed and some books and where the lawn chairs and card tables were stored. I pulled open the screen door and started up the wooden stairs leading to that level.

The burnished aggression of metal dust had settled on everything.

I located the spare lawn chairs behind the bed, which looked like it'd been recently slept in. Had Dad had a guest? I threaded my hand through the plastic webbing of as many as I could carry, leaving my other hand free to hold the steep wooden railing. I made my way down the steps, carefully. There was something sacred about this studio. It was the one place Dad seemed not exactly *happy* but at least like he didn't mind wearing his own skin for a few hours. He even sometimes played hide-and-seek with Sephie and me down here; at least, he had when we were little. I couldn't remember the number of times I'd fallen asleep to the click-clicking sound of his end sander. And the stuff he created here? If you never believed in magic before, you would once you saw his sculptures.

"Give you a hand with those?"

The back of my neck tightened. Four more cars had driven up as I'd made my way down the hill, but I hadn't recognized any of the drivers. I turned, even though I knew the voice. "Sergeant Bauer?"

He stepped through the studio door. Dad had drawn a three-headed dog across the chalkboard immediately behind the sergeant. In a bizarre coincidence of space, its two-dimensional leash lined up perfectly with Bauer's hand, like he'd brought a service dog from the underworld.

"Not here. Here I'm Aramis."

Unspeakable Things

I didn't understand what he meant by *hear—eye-mare-amiss*. He must have gotten that from my face, because he started laughing, a wheezy-bag sound. "That's my first name. Aramis. It was my great-grandpa's name."

I nodded, but I hadn't hopped off the bottom step. Aramis was my favorite of the Three Musketeers. I didn't like his name on Bauer.

The sergeant made no move to take the lawn chairs from my hands, despite his offer. Rather, he seemed to be studying me, spending extra time on my neck. I returned the favor, ogling the silver chain holding his dog tags peeking out of his collar, even though being stuck in here with him gave me the identical stomach-up feeling as riding the Zipper at the Town & Country Fair. He was out of uniform, his white T-shirt a sharp contrast against his tan and muscled arms.

He wore jean shorts, so short that the bottom of his pockets hung out. He was barefoot. He'd also rubbed something in his hair that smelled and looked like Vaseline. He'd combed the same hair jelly into his mustache but hadn't fully blended in a chunk by the corner of his fat red lips. His eyes were bloodshot.

"Sergeant Bauer, what are you doing down here?"

He made an angry sound. "Aramis, I said. You call me Sergeant Bauer and this'll be the shortest party in the history of Stearns County. I'm not much older than you, you know. I graduated with your dad."

He took a step closer, and I recoiled. Any smile fell off his too-red lips. "You scared of me?" he asked.

"No," I blurted, stepping down onto the cement floor to prove it. On even ground, he towered a foot above me. I glared up at him. I thought he was going to sneer, but a look of surprise crossed his face instead. It gave me a pump of courage. "Did my dad tell you that the two boys who were attacked both came from the Hollow and that maybe you should have extra patrols there?"

He stared down his nose at me. "Yeah."

He was lying—a tickle in my chest told me that—but I wasn't sure which part he was being untruthful about, that Dad had told him or that it was *only* two boys from the Hollow.

My mouth felt chalky, but I shoved out a ball of words anyhow. "I need to get these chairs back up to the house."

I hurried out of the studio before Bauer could respond. I wanted to walk out backward so I could keep an eye on him, but I was too afraid of what I'd see.

CHAPTER 26

Forty-three cars lined our driveway, filled in wide spots on the lawn, and were tucked in the field across the road. They were white, black, red, green. From the sky, it would look like Chiclets scattered by a giant child. I'd walked between the cars, counting them, letting my fingers trail over their cooling metal as the sun set and the long grass licked my knees.

There were people at the party I'd never seen before, people who I could tell were wondering if the stories were true. They mowed through the tables of potato salad, pickles, and desserts, navigated the extension cords hooked up to bubbling slow cookers, syrupy thick with cocktail wieners swimming in BBQ sauce and pulled pork and bright-orange cheese sauce.

I'd tasted all of it, everything, to make sure I hadn't missed a flavor. My stomach hurt, but I'd kept returning to that salad layered like a hot dish, with a base of deliciously crunchy head lettuce and on top of that salty bits of bacon, mayonnaise, tomato chunks, bright-green sweet peas that burst in my mouth, the whole works covered in another layer of mayonnaise, and on top of that, more bacon and shredded cheddar cheese. I'd gone back four times for seconds, pretending I was cleaning up a bit of paper or moving around a cookie plate so that I could scoop more of that salad onto my plate.

Once people were done eating, Kristi removed her clothes. It was always her who started, boobs low and big nippled, pointing toward her triangle bush, her eyes defiant. I stared the first few years she did it. She wanted to announce that it was okay to be naked here, that she was free, that this was how these parties went.

That's when Mr. and Mrs. Frais left. No one but me seemed to notice.

Soon other women began stripping, though some of them required a little one-on-one attention from Dad. I don't know how he talked those respectable women into taking their clothes off, could never figure out how he swung it, even though I swore at every party that I'd listen to what he said to them. Probably I got distracted by the food every time, because I'd turn around and then a handful more ladies were naked, and then a handful more. The men would lose their shirts, but they hung on to their shorts usually. Then they'd all begin playing croquet or lawn darts naked (women) or mostly naked (men), and there would be no help cleaning anything up, and everyone would eventually head to the barn like dogs in heat.

It wasn't full dark, but most people had already disappeared into that building. Warbly Indian music snaked out of it. I'd peeked through one of the cracks in the barn last year. It was hard to look away, but it was harder to keep staring. I wasn't going to look again.

"Help me clean out the slow cookers," Sephie commanded. Before Mom had careened toward the barn on some guy's arm, she'd ordered us to put away all the food. Sephie had taken that to mean she was in charge.

I shook my head. "I'll walk the trails and make sure no one tossed cups."

Sephie was having none of it. "You're welcome to do that after the potluck is taken care of. No way am I doing all this alone." She'd actually donned one of Mom's aprons after her bartending gig dried up. She apparently thought it gave her the power to tell the world what to do.

At least it meant she wasn't flirting with the old guy anymore. He was nearly Dad's age, and they'd been laughing too loud at anything the other said all afternoon and night. It gave me the barfs.

I eyeballed the tremendous potluck mess, glops of spilled food that the cats lapped at, crusted pans that would need to be washed and returned to their owners, forks and cups and plates stacked dangerously high. "The adults should help."

Sephie hoisted a slow cooker, not bothering to answer me.

"Fine," I said. "I'll help clean up the food and gather the garbage, but then that's it. Mom didn't even say we had to do that much. It's not like we made this mess."

Sephie still didn't respond. She was acting so grown-up, looked so mature in that apron, in addition to spending a whole afternoon bartending. I hoped she didn't think she was the boss of me.

"I'm going inside to grab trash bags," I said reluctantly.

Some stragglers had started playing instruments down by the bonfire. Mandolin music stroked the warm night air, and the smell of woodsmoke was comforting, but I was sure the rest of the party was in the barn. That's why I was surprised to hear people in the house when I stepped into the sunporch. I paused, tuning my ears. Whoever was inside was in the living room and so hadn't spotted me yet. When I heard the slur in their words, I realized I didn't need to worry.

"Naw, it's just boy shit. They're all trouble, those Hollow boys."

I perked up. Aramis was speaking. *Aramis like the stinky cologne*, I mentally corrected, *not like my favorite Musketeer*. I tiptoed toward the pantry to grab the black trash bags, sticking near the wall, hoping I could escape without being seen. The sweet skunk smell of marijuana smoke was strong, even two rooms over.

"You think they're all lying? For attention?" That was an unfamiliar voice.

"You said they're friends." My dad.

"Neighbors, anyhow," Aramis corrected. "More or less. Clamchik, Milchman, that Kleppert kid. They all live in the Hollow."

Clam, Teddy. That Kleppert kid.

An icy weight plummeted from my head to my stomach, freezing everything in its path. Were they talking about boys who'd been molested? Clam, puppy-haired Teddy, plus either Randy or Jim Kleppert, the first one a fourth grader and the other in sixth grade. Had they all been attacked? The salad that had been so delicious began to foam and bubble in my stomach, pushing acid toward the back of my throat. I'd shared Halloween candy with those kids.

"But yeah, I think it's bullshit what they're telling us," Aramis continued. "None of them can identify the guy; they all say he wore a mask. Their physical descriptions don't square, either. The perp is tall and strong in one, short and wiry in another."

"Paper says there were only two boys," the stranger said.

"Paper doesn't know everything."

Another pause, then the stranger said, "I heard they were sexually assaulted."

I could hear Aramis's shrug through the wall, then a sharp intake as he sucked on a joint. He spoke around a mouthful of smoke. "Somebody messed up that Clamchik kid, poked him in the butt, but the other two didn't have any marks. I think it was some hazing gone wrong that they're too afraid to talk about, boys trying out what it's okay to stick in and what's not, and it got out of hand."

"You stopped by Gary Godlin's last week," Dad said, almost an accusation, but he was so high that it sounded whiny. "I passed his house on my way to town and spotted your cruiser."

"Goblin lives out here?" The stranger's voice. "Man, I wondered what happened to him."

"Next house going north," Dad said.

Goblin. Godlin. It had been the similarity between the words, not his villainous face, that had earned him the nickname.

"Had to," Aramis said. "You know his stepdad used to rape him like it was a hobby, like it was softball or some shit that he had to do every Tuesday and Thursday?"

"Damn," Dad said. His voice had changed.

"Got sent away for it; died in prison. Whenever something funny goes on around town, I check on Goblin. Stopped by Connelly's house, too, the band teacher? Pure fruit. There's a few other stops I made for protocol, and they turned up nothing. I'm telling you, the boys are lying for some sorta attention. You know how Hollow boys are. No dad around, a mom who smokes in front of the television and chows down Twinkies all day."

Bauer didn't seem interested at all in catching the man responsible. I thought again of what he and Dad were hiding.

I heard one of the men take a hit and start coughing, first through his nose as he tried to save the smoke and then full throated when he couldn't contain it.

"Hey, be glad you have girls, Donny," Aramis said, followed by a clapping sound like he was smacking a watermelon. The coughing subsided. "Those boys do some weird shit. Speaking of, what happened to your youngest's neck? Looks like you collared her."

"Born that way," Dad grunted.

"She's pretty, even with that scar," the strange man said. It sent a jolt right up my spine how grody he sounded, like he was auditioning for some over-the-top pirate role.

"Damn pretty," Dad agreed, his tone fierce but also false, laid over his brittle ego. "How much would you pay for her?"

Aramis laughed, and the other man copied him, and I could tell they both thought Dad was joking and it was one of those things that Dad wouldn't even remember saying tomorrow, but those laughs still rammed their fists into my queasy belly and I ran outside, gulped in the inky night air, and that was too much, there wasn't even room for that, and I ran around the side of the house and upchucked my guts. Buckets of stomach-stew sailed out of my mouth, bitter acid with chunks of peas and weenies steaming on the lawn. The puke ejected so forcefully that I choked as I vomited.

When I was done, I went searching for Sephie. The messy potluck tables were exactly as I'd left them. She must have seen me come out, for sure heard me puking, but she didn't like throw-up, and so I wasn't surprised she hadn't rushed over to hold my hair. I couldn't locate her on the trails, either, or around the bonfire, so I ran to the cars to count them. The field grass was sharp as I wove in and out of the vehicles, peering in the windows, feeling the sweet dew gather on my calves, shivering under the cold eye of the mustard moon.

I couldn't find Sephie. Where was Sephie?

CHAPTER 27

May 28, 1983, late!

Dear Jin:

How are you? Good, I hope. I'm fine, mostly. I might have an idea who's attacking boys from my school, but I have to dig around some more. I know from the TV that when a criminal gets as brazen as this guy, he's losing his mind. If somebody doesn't stop him soon . . .

I'm really enjoying Nellie Bly's Trust It or Don't. Sometimes I think it's the only thing keeping me from going bonkers. I read one the other night about heliotropes. Do you know what they are? They're plants that always find the sun. I want to be a heliotrope. Just joshing!

I'd sure like a visit from you. Can you come here?

XOXOXO,

Cassie

CHAPTER 28

The next morning, I tiptoed down the stairs and around the sticky red Solo cups and the paper plates crusted with food, the overflowing ashtrays and sour beer bottles. I'd cleaned outdoors but not inside. I wasn't a saint.

I'd stuffed my pajamas, tomorrow's clothes, my *Nellie Bly's Trust It or Don't*, and Lynn's present into my backpack. The gift I'd wrapped was dime-size, a delicate metal moonrise dangling from a silver chain, so precious to me, so special, that I hadn't yet removed it from its box. Jin had sent it to me for Christmas the year before last, and I'd had to lie to her the couple times she'd asked if I'd worn it.

When I heard someone rustling in the kitchen, I almost scurried back to my room to wait them out. It'd make me late for Lynn's party, though. It was an all-day party! We were meeting at the roller rink, then heading to Lynn's for a sleepover. Mom had already okayed me going. It'd looked windy outside when I rose early, and so I'd budgeted an extra fifteen minutes for the bike ride to town. I couldn't waste that time hiding from a partygoer. I squared my shoulders and soldiered into the kitchen, hoping it was someone relatively sober who was rooting around for breakfast.

"Mom?"

She was kneading dough, flattening it and then wrapping the edges toward the middle until it was a ball again, striking it with the pad of her hand. She'd mixed the dough yesterday and stored it in the fridge so she could bake cinnamon rolls for everyone who slept over. I should have known she'd be up this early taking care of the meal.

For my mom, food was love.

"Morning." She didn't glance up, but if she had, I bet her eyes would have been sad behind her owl glasses. Her skin was gray-dusted, her hair pulled back in a greasy ponytail. A wormy blue vein pulsed on the back of each hand as she kneaded the dough.

"Morning. I'm heading to Lynn's."

When Mom finally looked at me, I saw I'd guessed wrong. Her eyes weren't sad. They were ghostly, big scary windows on an abandoned house. Looking into them gave me chest pains.

Mom didn't respond.

"How's Sephie?" I asked impulsively. Last night I'd looked everywhere, including her room, until I was so tired I'd walked into a tree. I hadn't checked her bedroom again before I came down the stairs this morning. I told myself it was because I didn't want to wake her up.

Mom blinked. "Fine. Why?"

"No big deal." I shrugged. "I'm staying over tonight at Lynn's. I already told you, and you already said you were cool with it."

She went back to her rhythmic kneading. I tugged on the loops of my backpack. I could see parts of her scalp through her thinning hair as she pushed at the dough. I wondered if she felt as pretty as Kristi, or the other women who Dad slept with right in front of her. I moved toward the door but stopped with my hand on the knob, turning back to face her. "You could get a divorce."

She opened her mouth to laugh, I think, but rock-heavy words tumbled out instead. "It's not that easy."

I'd already used five minutes of the fifteen I'd budgeted for biking against the wind. "Can I try?" I pointed at the dough.

"Wash your hands first."

I obliged. There were three cigarette butts in the sink. Mom hated smoking and loved her kitchen. I chucked them into the garbage and rinsed out the sink before lathering up my hands with the homemade basil soap Mom made every summer before her herbs bolted. I rinsed them, wiped them, and then took the miniature ball of dough she'd pinched off. I mimicked her movements but couldn't get my dough uniformly flat like hers.

She nudged the rolling pin toward me. "You need to work it."

I floured the length of the wooden pin before poising it dead center on my dough ball, leaning into the dowel handles to push the dough upper left, then upper right, then toward me left, toward me right. It flattened like Play-Doh, cracking at the edges. I folded it back into a square.

It smelled clean and solid. Flour, milk, sugar, eggs, yeast, salt.

"See how it's sticky? Toss on some more flour and keep kneading until it's smooth." Mom punched her dough ball, pushing a loose hair from her eye with the flat outside of her thumb.

I dunked my hand into the flour's velvet, letting it sift through my fingers.

"Don't play with it."

I rolled my eyes. "You know the store sells cinnamon rolls, right?"

Her voice was sharp. "You know they're expensive and full of chemicals, right?"

I scooped a small handful of flour and sprinkled it over the top of my dough ball and then ran my hand up and down the rolling pin. "If you divorced him, we'd have more money. He doesn't hardly sell any sculptures. He eats and drinks a lot. Mostly you pay the bills."

Her lips tightened. She snatched the rolling pin from me and used it to flatten her dough until it was the height of cardboard laid flat. She dropped yellow pats of butter onto it, then sprinkled that with brown sugar and raisins. She began rolling from the end nearest her, keeping it tight.

"I love him," she finally said. There was a tinge of defeat in her words.

I sensed an opening. "Of course you do, Mom. So do I." I wasn't sure if that last part was true, but she wanted to hear it. "We don't have to stop *loving* him. I just think life would be easier if he wasn't around."

"There's a lot you don't know about life." She slid the chef's knife from the storage block, the whisk of metal leaving wood a crisp note slicing through the humid air. She cut her dough roll into twenty-four perfect pieces, which she tucked into a greased metal pan, side by side, roll side up.

"Well, just think about it, that's all I'm saying."

"I will."

I believed her because I wanted it to be true.

"I better head out," I said.

"You're biking?" She sounded surprised.

"Yup."

"I can drive you."

I smiled. "Really?"

"Sure."

CHAPTER 29

The roller rink was housed in the basement of the Lilydale Laundr-O-Mat. The laundromat stayed open all year, but the rink closed tight in the winter. Spring and fall it had limited hours, but come summer, it was open from 10:00 a.m. to 10:00 p.m. seven days a week. Mom had let me choose the radio station on the drive so I could hear what song was number one this week.

"Flashdance!"

Man, would I love to see that movie. Maybe Gabriel and I could check it out together.

Mom had also driven past the post office so I could drop off my letter for Jin. When we arrived at the rink, though, she hadn't wanted to come inside because of how she looked. I'd scooped up my backpack and traipsed down the cement stairs alone.

The beat of "Angel Is the Centerfold" thumped against my feet as I descended into the basement. It took me a moment to adjust from the bright morning to the dark cellar, even with the help of strobe lights.

"Cassie, over here."

I turned left, toward the front counter, and blinked twice before I made out Lynn's mom. She was a plump woman, with a grand head of blonde hair wisped back with two tortoiseshell combs.

"Hi, Mrs. Strahan."

"The other girls are on the rink."

I counted four skaters, all but one that I recognized, whirring around under the disco ball, laughing and holding hands in one long chain.

"What size?" the man behind the counter asked. *Mad* magazine lay open on the counter under his elbows. I recognized the issue from a kid on the bus passing it around.

"Six, I think."

He grabbed a pair of white leather roller skates from a cubby, the number six stenciled in black marker on their heel. They were scuffed, their shoelaces frayed at the ends. They clinked when he set them on the countertop. "Two dollars."

My heart seized, and my cheeks grew hot. I spoke reflexively. "That's okay, I don't like to skate."

"Really?" Mrs. Strahan asked. The way she said it reminded me of how Mrs. Oleson talked to Laura on *Little House on the Prairie*. "I thought *all* girls liked to skate."

I'd been staring at the floor but risked a glance at her face. It was smooth, expressionless, but her eyes glittered. I opened my mouth to speak, but only a gurgle came out. I hadn't brought any money. I hadn't known I'd need it.

"You want these or not?"

"I'll pay for her," Mrs. Strahan said, unlatching her pocketbook. She slid a twenty toward him.

I couldn't reach for the skates. My hands were glued to my sides.

"How are your parents?" Mrs. Strahan asked while he made change.

"Fine."

She wanted to ask something else, but I spoke more quickly than her. "Dad is still making his sculptures and Mom is teaching full-time in Kimball. Sephie is doing well, too, thanks for asking." I finally scooped up the roller skates and speed-walked toward the skating floor.

I liked to skate. I really did.

"I am too sure!" Andrea exclaimed.

I pulled my sleeping bag tighter. All five of us—Lynn, Heidi, Barb, Andrea, and me—were huddled between the couch and the TV in Lynn's wood-paneled basement. It wasn't really a basement, though, so I wasn't afraid of it like Dad's basement. Lynn's had windows up high, plush carpeting, and paneled walls and held as many toys as a store. She and her little sister had their bedrooms down here, but her parents had Tanya sleeping upstairs tonight so that we had this whole floor to ourselves.

Andrea was Lynn's cousin, the girl I hadn't recognized on the skating floor. Andrea attended school in Kimball, same place Mom taught English but in a different grade. She'd haughtily informed us that her trendy hairstyle would find our tiny town sometime soon. It was longer and feathered in front but short and tight to her scalp in back, with a leftover braid, like a rope tossed down her neck to rescue some tiny mouse caught in her shirt. I marveled at the courage it would take to wear your hair that different.

They were talking about Evie.

"No, it's true!" Lynn said, trying to convince Andrea. "She goes to the playground all by herself. It's her and sometimes a few farm kids show up. They have *playtime*."

Heidi jumped in. She'd crimped her hair exactly as Lynn had. "I biked by and saw it. Evie's mom knits on their front porch and watches from her house across the playground. Creeper peeper."

"But not the real Peeping Tom!" Barb squealed. She was in seventh grade with me, Lynn, and Heidi, but I didn't know her very well. She was a town kid, like Lynn and Heidi.

Lynn's mom had picked up three Jimmy's pepperoni pizzas for us and two liters of 7UP, which we'd wolfed down while *The Secret of NIMH* played on the VCR. I kept trying to watch it, but everyone else wanted to talk, so I eventually gave up. Lynn said we'd watch *Swamp Thing* later, and I hoped she meant we'd actually pay attention to it.

"I heard you saw the Peeping Tom," Barb said to Lynn. "Like, laid eyes on his wee-wee."

The giggles were fierce. As the last girl to the party, I still hadn't found where I fit. I wasn't built to be the quiet one, but Barb had taken the role of funny. That was usually my bit, but she'd arrived first. That left me mostly lurking in the background, but Lynn had liked my present the best, so that was something. My necklace was around her neck. It was so pretty.

Lynn hugged herself. "I think so. I heard a knocking." She pointed toward the small basement window. If there was a fire, we'd barely be able to squeeze out of it. "Tanya and I were watching TV. I thought maybe it was Colby, from next door?"

This sent a thrill through the crowd, at least the four of us from Lilydale. Colby was a high schooler, the star of the baseball team, and he resembled David Hasselhoff if you squinted.

"I pulled aside the curtain, and it looked like someone was holding a water balloon out there, really close to the window? It was nighttime, so I couldn't really see clearly. But the balloon squirted, and I screamed, and my dad ran downstairs. I told him what I saw and he charged out there, but he didn't see anyone. He called the police. They took a report."

It felt good to know someone that something had *happened* to, to be privy to her secret. "That must have been scary," I said.

Lynn tossed her hair over her shoulder. "I guess. Hey, your parents still have those parties? My parents said freaky sex stuff happens there."

My cheeks burned.

Heidi hopped on. "Yeah, maybe your dad is the Peeping Tom!"

"He's not!"

"Jeez, Cassie, Heidi's kidding," Lynn said, sounding truly shocked. "Lay off. I just wanted to know about the parties is all."

"They have people over sometimes. Just like you have people over right now." *Except not like that at all.* "Hey, I sat next to Evie in the lunchroom the last week of school. She was making flyers for her playdates!"

Saying that out loud, turning the heat back to Evie, made something slither-bump between my heart and stomach. Besides not being here to defend herself, I thought she was genuinely nice. The last day of school, I'd overheard Mr. Kinchelhoe tell her that she wrote with a flair and flourish all her own. Evie had swallowed that like it belonged to her and went right back to whatever she was working on. Then, later that day, I was walking behind her as she told a fifth grader in outdated bell-bottoms that he wore them with "a flair and a flourish" all his own.

I liked that a whole lot about Evie, how she passed on her treasures.

"That's crazy," Andrea said, shaking her head. "But you almost can't blame her, what with all the kidnapping happening here."

Lynn bristled. "It's not *all* the kidnapping. It's just some of the Hollow boys getting too rough, that's what my dad says."

That's what Sergeant Bauer had said last night, too. The last thing I was gonna do was tell these girls he'd been at my house, though, that one of those freaky sex parties had taken place last night.

"That's not what *my* dad says," Andrea countered. "He says there's something bad happening here."

Us four Lilydale kids exchanged glances. The Peeping Tom, Dad's parties, Chester the Molester, the curfew siren—it was gross, but it was *our* gross.

"It's not dangerous at all," Lynn said, raising her chin. "I go out after curfew all the time. I even had a cigarette with Colby two nights ago, way after nine thirty."

"No way!" Barb exclaimed.

A trill of excitement bubbled up in my belly, and I hesitated with my cup of 7UP halfway to my mouth. "What was it like?"

Lynn shrugged. "Gnarly. But I think Colby's going to kiss me."

We all paused to drink that in. Being kissed by a high school boy. *Imagine.* I took a swallow of my pop, certain it was what champagne tasted like.

"Anyhow," Lynn finished, "my dad says that Connelly is a homo, and he's probably the peeper showing his ding dong to girls."

The 7UP went down too fast, the carbonation burning my nose. "That doesn't make any sense," I said. "If he's a homo, why would he go to girls' windows?"

Lynn turned on me. "Then it's probably someone who goes to your dad's parties. Some sex maniac."

Everyone was staring at me. I was stuck to the carpet with no idea what to say. It had been stupid to come here. I'd even wiped out while roller-skating and burned the skin right off both knees. I considered calling Mom to pick me up early, but then Lynn'd never invite me back.

"Hey, I know!" Heidi said, saving me. "Let's go peep on the peeper!"

Barb flinched. "What do you mean?"

Lynn put it together first. "Yeah! Let's go spy on Mr. Connelly!"

I glanced at the VCR clock. It was 8:27 p.m. "Do we have time to get back before curfew?"

"Better hope we do," Lynn said wickedly. "Or Chester the Molester might nab you."

CHAPTER 30

The sun was dropping into the plate of the earth, the dusk velvet against our skin. Town had a different tenor than the country, less wild and frog song, more muffled slamming of doors and distant conversations, almost like sound came at us through a tunnel. I felt hugged to know there were so many people around, to see lights on in houses and know people were there, living safe lives, watching TV and eating popcorn and being *normal*, ready to offer us a cup of sugar if we needed it. I breathed in the delicious scent of someone's grill and settled into my limbs. It felt so good to be out in the night with other people.

"I can't believe we're doing this!" Lynn trilled.

"My dad's going to kill me," Andrea said.

Our gang of five kept to the alleyways. We stayed close to garbage cans, flattened ourselves against the sides of garages à la *Charlie's Angels*, even pointed our fingers like fake guns. When our laughter grew too loud, Lynn would shush us.

"His house is over there," Lynn said, pointing across the open expanse of Mill Street toward the back of a towering white house with black shutters. "He still lives with his *parents*."

I knew Connelly hadn't done anything wrong. It wasn't in him.

"Oh gawd, shoot me if I'm still living with my mom and dad after high school," Heidi said.

It was almost full dark. A dark-colored car, maybe green, turned down Mill Street with its headlights on. We squealed and dove behind a lilac bush.

"Connelly is my favorite teacher," I confessed as the other girls' warm bodies pressed into mine, a human coat against the toothless cool of a May night. It was the first time I'd dropped the Mr. when saying his name.

Lynn rolled her eyes; I could hear it in the tone of her voice. "He's fine. Don't you think he dresses a little too fruity, though?"

"I like how he dresses," Barb said.

My heart swelled, and her courage gave me mine. "I'll run to his house and touch it."

The sharp intakes of breath told me I'd said the right thing. The five of us were joined in that moment, girls impossibly strong against the world. Nothing could hurt us.

"You sure?" Lynn asked.

"You don't have to do it," Andrea said, but her eyes gleaming in the reflection of a yard light told me otherwise.

"You're so brave," Barb said, squeezing my hand.

"I have a better idea." Lynn surveyed the distance from our hiding place to the imposing white house like a general mapping a combat mission. "Rather than only touch his house, grab one of the flowers near the door. That'll be your battle prize."

"Okay."

I stood and flexed my legs, gauging the distance. A wind rustled the treetops. The irritated leaves sounded like hands rubbing together. I could still smell the scent of a charcoal grill. I glanced left and then right. A peppering of lights twinkled inside the houses, reassuring. The Connelly house was dark. An owl hooted, low and lonely. Goose bumps tickled the whole length of me. I knew I was smiling, or at least that my teeth were visible. I'd never felt so *in my body*.

"Now!" Lynn whispered.

I took off. Tiny pebbles skittered across the street as I kicked them free, my tennies pumping fast, making a soft *clomp clomp* as they pounded across Mill Street. Connelly's house seemed to swell as I neared it. A car rumbled past the end of the road and my pulse leaped, but there was no stopping me. My right foot landed on the trimmed grass of Connelly's yard. The earth felt alive under my feet.

The owl questioned again, and I kept running.

A light flicked on inside the Connelly house. I heard the lilac bush shriek behind me, but I couldn't stop, not when the flowers were only feet away. The wind picked up on the treetops, shivering down the bark, that dry, rasping skin-on-skin sound even louder. I was almost there. I reached out, toward the flowers—peonies, I thought, but they weren't. It was a rosebush, its stems studded with wicked spikes.

The curfew siren's keening started as my hands curled around the stem, its thorns puncturing my flesh. Sweat broke out along my brow, and I pushed through the pain to twist that rose off its base. No way was I going back empty-handed. I thought I heard yelling, but it was impossible to separate from the shriek of the siren, which was rising to a terrifying crescendo.

eeeeeeeEEEEEEEEE

The pricks of the rose grew hot, and the flower melded with my hand. I risked a glance inside Connelly's window even though I was so exposed, even though I had to perch on my tippy-toes to see in and it would slow down my escape. I'm not sure what made me do it. Maybe some movement on the inside caught my attention, or my curiosity was simply too loud, or I wanted more to embellish my story with.

I expected to see Connelly dipping into his fridge, wearing a robe.

Or sitting at the kitchen table with his dad, talking about his mom recently home from the hospital, because hadn't Mrs. Puglisi said she'd had a heart attack?

That would have made sense.

But Clam inside that house, Mr. Connelly's hands on his shoulders?

That didn't fit in my head.

I blinked at it once, twice.

I couldn't see either of their faces, not clearly, at least, that's what I told myself.

Then I turned and ran back to the lilac bush, the siren a magnetic force that pushed me toward safety. All four girls patted me on the back when I reached them, invited me into their exultant bubble, and we ran as one back to Lynn's house, hot blood dripping from my fingertips and onto the rosebud.

CHAPTER 31

I didn't tell.

I couldn't, not on Mr. Connelly.

When they asked, I said I hadn't seen anyone in the kitchen.

Not a single person.

I'd kept my hand mostly hidden at the party, rinsing it off as soon as we made it back to Lynn's. I had to wash the blood off the rose stem, too. The puncture marks were deep, so they didn't bleed much after the first spurt. Mom spotted them as soon she picked me up in the morning.

"What happened?"

"I plucked a rose," I said, cradling my hand to my chest. "Thought it was a peony."

She studied me for a moment, her tired eyes darting to the Strahan house and then back to me. She'd dropped Sephie off at summer school before swinging by to pick me up. She sighed and then put the van into first gear. We didn't talk until we reached home, where she marched me to the bathroom and pulled a bottle of hydrogen peroxide and a pot of homemade salve out of the cupboard.

"Not a good week for my girls."

I didn't cry when she doused the three perfect circles in my palm with the peroxide, not even when it sank deep into my bones, jarring them, before bubbling back to the surface, pink from my marrow. I didn't flinch when she grabbed my fingers, gently, and held them under a stream of warm water that pooled in the holes. I did sigh when she opened the pot of salve, the texture of Vaseline, a murky amber color that smelled like road tar and herbs.

She filled in the holes with the salve and it healed me, hunting the pain up my arm, herding it back toward the openings and out of my body. She wrapped gauze three times around my hand and patted me on the arm. I wanted to tell her so bad what I'd seen last night. She'd know what to do. I had my mouth open to rat out Mr. Connelly when she surprised me.

"The trick of life," she said, "is that you can't hold the pain for too long. The magic, either."

It was the first time she'd reminded me of Jin, and I hugged her then, snuggling into the warm crook of her neck like I used to do when I was little. Mom stiffened, but she didn't push me away.

That's how Dad found us.

He was in a mood. It preceded him into a room, liquid and dangerous. "I suppose this means we're not butchering the rest of the chickens today."

I kept my groan to myself. There shouldn't be any more chickens to butcher, not this season, but sometimes after a party, Dad needed to *clear things out*. More paths in the woods, farm cats driven up the road and dropped off, bags of garbage hauled to the dump, the laying hens culled.

Mom's voice sounded strained. "Her hand has to heal before she can get it wet."

Dad frowned. He'd brought the hatchet with him into the house, and it looked angry and out of place. "I'll find dry work for her, then. Come on, Cassie. We'll clear a trail."

I glanced at Mom, hoping she'd volunteer to join us or, better yet, stand up for me and tell him I needed to rest for a day. She turned away. I trudged upstairs to change into work clothes before heading into the muggy morning. All evidence of Saturday's party was gone. I wanted to ask Dad what sort of mood Sephie had been in before she left for summer school this morning, but he and I didn't talk like that. He jabbed his finger toward a mound of sticks. He wanted it brought to the burn pile.

I obeyed, hauling the twigs and then returning for more, gathering the oak and elm branches he was hacking off a copse of old trees, enough so he could take a chain saw to their bases without being poked. Lugging branches was slow going with only one hand, but I warmed to the work as the lemon sun stretched across the sky. It was way better than butchering, even if Dad smelled like chicken soup when he perspired. He'd removed his shirt, and I could see rivulets of sweat rolling off him. The blue bandanna tied around his head kept it from dripping in his eyes, but it coursed down his back, hanging in droplets from his armpit hair when he hefted logs as big as his torso.

We worked as the sun crawled its hot eye to the top of the world and poured lava down upon us. He finally let me break for water at eleven. I drank from the hose, not minding the gassy flavor. I ran it over my head, down my back, swallowed icy liquid the color of quicksilver. When I was cooled off, I returned to our work site but couldn't find Dad. He wasn't on the back trail, either.

It was too hot to search the rest of the property. I wrung out the hem of my clothes one-handed so I wouldn't drip hose water and walked into the house to ask Mom if she knew where he was. I was careful not to bang the screen door and stood in the porch for a moment to listen. I figured I'd find Mom in the kitchen getting the week's baking done, but she might be working on one of the sewing projects she took to stretch her teaching salary.

"No one."

I stood straight, my ears at attention. Unbelievably, Dad was on the phone.

"I don't want to discuss price." His voice grew agitated. "No."

A pause on his end of the line, then he spoke again, his voice strung like razor wire. "In the basement. You think I'm stupid?"

I was trapped between stepping forward and going back. Before I could make up my mind, the phone crashed down and Dad stormed into the porch, his eyes on fire, his hands clenched into fists. "How much of that did you hear?"

I opened my mouth and then closed it.

"Never mind. Let's get back to work."

I followed him, numb. I spotted Mom in the chicken coop as we passed, going in with a pitchfork and some fresh hay. She was cleaning it completely, the worst job in the world. The chickens would scream and flap their wings, scaring up dried chicken poop and hay dust. She'd have to haul out the dry as well as the wet hay, soggiest under the waterer and around the food, where the hens pooped as they ate. It smelled like tempera paint in there, but dirtier. Usually, cleaning it out was me and Sephie's job. Mom must be doing it because of my hand.

I hung my head.

Dad didn't acknowledge Mom as we passed, didn't speak as we worked. I felt invisible to him, which was the best way to be, in my book. I was thinking about Lynn's bedroom. She had a lock, and she was safe in there. She got to sleep on top of her mattress, not under it or in her closet.

I wanted that.

It was dangerous to talk to Dad when he was like this, though. He wore his anger like knives, and you didn't want them aimed at you. There was a sweet spot when he first started drinking where he'd drop that armor. It was a small window, maybe half an hour where he forgot everything he'd been cheated of. He'd talk about trips we'd take or how he was immortal because he had me and Sephie and he loved us. I could make him laugh in that window. His eyes would crinkle up and his mouth would open so wide I could see the spaces left by the teeth they'd pulled in high school because his mom couldn't afford to fill the cavities. I puffed up to twice my size when I got him to smile.

We weren't in that honey hole now, but it must live somewhere inside him, always. It didn't matter if I hit it, anyhow. I'd made up my mind. I would demand the same safety as Lynn, no matter Dad's mood. I set my shoulders and cleared my throat.

"I want a lock on my bedroom door."

Dad paused only long enough to sneer before swinging his ax into the tree. The smell of pine oozed out, the lone fir in a line of hardwoods. "If I wanted to get into your room, I'd just break it down."

I fell into the cotton of myself, shrinking. "It's my room."

He swung the ax again, lacerating the wood. He would push back that jungle, inserting trails, forcing sight lines, hacking off low branches that wept garnet sap. He would remove any lick of wild jungle from our woods, one tree at a time, and put up trip wires that would let him know if his territory had been breached. He walked this world fully barricaded inside himself, and we were all his enemies. Me, Mom, Sephie, the bramble and brush.

The ax rose and fell, rose and fell, mashing leaves and bright, earthy pulp alike, the wet wood resisting and then finally giving in to his relentless punishment.

I never brought up the lock again.

CHAPTER 32

I hadn't known I was going to visit Frank until Dad, Mom, and I took our lunch break under the basswood tree, but the impulse felt right the second it appeared. We needed to investigate what was happening to the Hollow boys. Nobody should have to live in fear all the time, not even boys from the wrong side of the tracks. I wolfed down my food and excused myself to use the bathroom. Mom and Dad would be done eating soon, but if I called Frank immediately, I could see if he was free before Dad tromped inside.

I ran to my room to grab Frank's number and charged down the stairs, taking the bottom three all at once. I slipped the phone from the handset and dialed the four digits. I had a straight view of Dad from here. He leaned over to kiss Mom, all the dirty dishes balanced in one hand. He was being cranky with me, but at least now he was lovey-dovey with her.

"Hello?"

"Hi, Frank! It's Cassie. Hey, do you want to go biking today?"

"Can't. I have chores."

"How about tomorrow?"

Dad stopped kissing Mom and began striding toward the house, chewing up the lawn with his wide steps.

Frank was taking too long to answer.

"My parents don't want me to go out at night," he finally said.

The screen door squawked. Dad stepped into the sunporch.

"It wouldn't be at night. It'd be during the day."

"Maybe . . ."

Four more seconds and Dad would be standing in the kitchen, glaring at me, asking who I was talking to, telling me I couldn't go as soon as he knew it was a boy.

"Great! I'll stop by tomorrow and we can work out the details." I slammed the phone into the handset just as Dad appeared.

"Who was that?"

"Mr. Connelly asked me to help sell popcorn for the band trip," I lied, sort of. "Can I go tomorrow?"

He studied me, sniffing the air. "If you get your chores done first."

"I'll get up early for that. Thanks, Dad!" I whisked around him before he changed his mind. "I better get back to work. Meet you by the trail."

"Stop."

My skin grew itchy. I turned to face him. He was inspecting me, his eyes sharp. "We've done enough work for the day."

I stood in his crosshairs, not speaking.

"You rinse off and do the dishes. Your mom and I are running to the liquor store. We'll pick up your sister on our way back." There was nothing on the surface of his words, but a monster raged below.

I nodded. Something must have happened at the party, something even worse than the usual stuff. Dad grabbed a shirt and the VW keys. He stepped back into the sunshine and took Mom's hand. It wasn't until the van pulled off the driveway that my skin stopped prickling.

That's when I realized I had the house to myself! That hardly ever happened. I hurried through the dishes, wondering if I'd have time to drink sun tea and read the *Flowers in the Attic* book I'd finally gotten to the top of the library waiting list for.

I scratched at a mosquito bite and sniffed my armpit. It'd been a couple days since I'd showered. I figured I'd better take care of that first. I ran into my room to grab my favorite white sundress, the one with the red and navy-blue detail at the hem. I always brought clothes into the shower with me. In television shows, I saw girls walk from the bathroom to their bedroom wearing just a towel. This wasn't the kind of house where you could do that.

Inside the bathroom, I locked the door even though I was the only one home. A leaf was sticking out of my hair. I tugged it loose, tossed it into the garbage, and undid my hair ties before freeing my braids. Our water was so hard that I needed to brush my hair before the shower because there'd be no getting a comb through it wet.

I dropped onto the toilet to pee, letting my shorts and underpants slide to my ankles. I checked my underwear for a spot of blood like I always did. Nothing but the shadow of a good old-fashioned skid mark toward the rear. I pointed my toes and my bottoms fell to the floor. I slid out of my Coca-Cola T-shirt and padded toward the shower.

The faucets squawked when I turned them, and the gassy smell of hard water crowded my nostrils. When the temperature was just south of warm, I stepped in, letting the water spatter my face before sticking my head underneath, holding my wounded hand out on the other side of the shower door. The water drummed on my neck. I'd created a protected spot over my boobs. I cupped them with my good hand to feel if they'd grown. The boys on the bus said more than a handful was a waste, but I didn't know whose hand they were talking about.

I eyed Mom's black-handled razor. She'd forbidden me from shaving until high school. She said there was no hurry to grow up and that my body naturally had hair, and that's about when I'd stopped listening. Sephie had started shaving last summer, and her legs were curvy and creamy perfect. Maybe I could just shave mine up high, where Mom wouldn't even notice as long as she never saw me in a swimsuit. She hardly ever took us swimming anyways.

I gripped the razor. The first sweep of the blade was highly satisfying. It carved a clean path right through my long, dark thigh hair. Within minutes, I had a whole quarter of a leg clean-shaven. It would be crazy to stop.

I leaned over to have a go at the rest.

That's when I heard the chopper overhead. My stomach dropped. There was an army base by St. Cloud, but they never came out this far. I hoped the helicopter in these parts didn't mean another boy had been attacked, a boy who lived nearby.

A boy like Frank.

I shook my head. Frank was safe. We were country kids.

I positioned the shaver head over my left ankle's outer knob. I pushed in and swicked, just like I'd done with my thigh. I was two inches up my calf before the blood started, a shock of red against newly skinned muscle. It didn't hurt until the water hit it, and then it was the purest pain I'd ever experienced. I jumped out of the water stream. Blood gushed from my ankle. The razor held a ribbon of flesh as long as my pinkie finger. I tapped the shaver on the side of the tub until the skin came loose and washed down the drain. The blood was still flowing, a violent red at my ankle, shark-water pink as it neared the drain.

Why wasn't it stopping?

I began to worry I'd bleed out and Dad would find me naked in the shower. I twisted off the faucets and leaned as far out of the tub as I could until my fingers just barely grazed the edge of the toilet paper. I managed to pull it toward me, close enough to grab a wad that I shoved at my ankle. Jeez Louise did I wish Sephie were here so I could ask her what to do. I might need a blood transfusion before the hour was out.

Sephie.

I still didn't know where she'd gone the night of the party.

CHAPTER 33

"Sephie?"

She hadn't wanted to talk yesterday afternoon when Mom and Dad brought her back after their liquor-store run. Said she had to study. Expressed zero interest in my shaving trauma. Closed herself in her room until suppertime, came down to eat and clean up, and then straight back she went.

I'd had the worst dreams in my closet afterward, all haunted woods and grabbing hands. I couldn't stand another night of that and set my alarm so I'd be up today same time as her. I stood outside the bathroom, hands on hips, my voice low because Mom and Dad were still asleep. I heard water running, and then the sound of her spitting.

"What?" she finally said.

"How's summer school?"

She yanked open the door. Her face was bulgy with sleep. "I told you yesterday. It's fine."

"I'm biking with Frank today. Maybe we can stop by the school and say hi to you."

She tossed a shoulder. "Whatever."

I reached toward her but stopped short of touching her. "Where did you go the night of Dad's party?"

There it was, finally said out loud. Her eyes slid sideways. I didn't know what I saw in them. Guilt? Fear? She walked toward the bathroom mirror, and I followed. "I went to bed."

"No, you didn't. I checked there. Then I walked all the trails."

She pulled a brush through her long hair, watching herself in the mirror. Her lips appeared swollen, the bags under her eyes dark as bruises. "Did you come back to my room after you walked the trails?"

"No."

The shutters dropped from her face, and she was suddenly my Sephie again. "Then you just missed me, silly! I was on the trails myself, checking for garbage, and then I went to bed."

I searched her argument for a hole but couldn't find one. That didn't change the fact that she was straight-up lying. "I think one of the farm cats had a litter. Want to help me look for them later?"

"Sure. Maybe." She began closing the door on me. "I need some privacy, Cass. I have to get ready."

I stood at the closed door for a full minute, staring at the painted wood, wondering where my sister had gone. She still hadn't even asked about my bandaged hand. A little solid part of me broke loose.

"I don't think your dad likes me," I said.

Frank was puffing up a hill on his Hutch BMX, the prettiest bike I'd ever seen. If a dragon-slaying knight rode a no-speed, it'd be a Hutch with that sparkling chrome frame, the jack of spades wedged through the spokes making it sound like a roulette wheel as he biked. He told me his parents had bought it so he didn't feel so bad about moving out to the boondocks. I thought that was a fair deal, even though the bike wasn't made for the monster hill you had to labor up to enter Lilydale, no matter which direction you were coming from.

"He acts like that with everyone," Frank said, standing to pedal, the last resort of the person about to walk their bike.

"Your mom seemed happy to see me."

Frank dismounted and steered his bike to the side of the tar, his face flushed by the early-afternoon sun. I'd caught him and his dad on a lunch break from working in the field. His dad hadn't wanted Frank to leave with me, but his mom had insisted. She'd doubled down when I explained I needed help selling popcorn for next year's band trip.

"You sure care a lot about what other people think of you," Frank said, panting.

I hopped off my own bike and walked behind him. I was careful to protect my hand, though thanks to the magic salve, the punctures had already scabbed over. I addressed the storm of cowlicks on the back of Frank's head. "Why won't your parents let you out at night?"

He stopped and turned to look at me square. "You can't be serious."

We'd almost made it to the top of the hill. Stearns County was spread out like a quilt on each side of us, farmhouses and barns planted in the middle of square patches of corn and soybeans, Lake Corona in the distance, sloughs and creeks curving through the fabric. There's about a hundred shades of green in a Minnesota summer, light like celery, deep like emeralds. You wouldn't think one color could have so many different flavors.

I puffed up defensively. "If you mean the boys who were attacked, you don't need to worry. They're part of some Hollow hazing gone wrong." I realized I was mimicking Sergeant Bauer's words. I didn't like that, so I tried again. "Or they're not, and you and me can find out what's happening. Like the A-Team would."

"Hollow hazing?"

I sped up so I could walk alongside him. The flowery smell of blooming trees tickled my nose. "The Hollow is the neighborhood on the other side of the train tracks. It's where the—" I stopped myself from saying "bad kids," just. "It's where some of the rougher boys hang out."

Frank shrugged and stepped closer to me as a car zoomed past, kicking up gravel from the opposite shoulder. "Whatever it is, my mom doesn't want any part of it. She read in the paper that kids aren't supposed to be out at night. And anyhow, boys are weird in your town."

"It's your town now, too." A surge of heat rushed my chest. The deerflies we'd been outrunning caught up to us, hovering near our heads. "What do you mean, 'weird'?"

"Some of them remind me of werewolves. Like they got bit, and now they're turning." He threw his head back and howled.

"Stop it!" I said, but I was laughing. "Hey, wasn't it the same in your town? With boys being taken?"

He shrugged. "I suppose. My parents were fighting a lot then. That's mostly what I noticed."

I stopped.

He went another three feet before he stopped. "What?" he asked, turning to stare at me, squinting against the sun.

"You just told me something about your family." Dad would be so angry if I ever did that, ever spilled something real about our home life.

"Yeah?" he asked, waiting for me to explain.

Rather than answer him, I let that warmth move over my skin, that feeling of a thread connecting me to him. Frank had shared something with me. I'd do the same. "Hey, you know the band teacher, Mr. Connelly?"

"Yeah?" Frank said again. He hadn't gotten back on his bike, even though we were at the top of the hill.

"Two nights ago, I stopped by his place with some friends. I spotted Clam inside his house. The kid who was attacked?"

Frank made a low whistle. "You think Connelly attacked him?"

It'd crossed my mind. But hearing that thought come out of Frank's mouth, past lips that didn't know how awesome and friendly and *good*

Mr. Connelly was, it sounded bananas. "Naw," I said. "I think he was probably trying to help Clam. Maybe get him to join band."

I was grateful Frank didn't question that, because while I didn't believe Mr. Connelly would attack Clam and then invite him into his house, I also didn't believe Clam had stopped over to talk about his classes. It was something I'd need to ask Clam about directly. Maybe we'd track him down today.

We hopped back on our bikes and raced down the other side of the hill, yodeling as we glided into town. It had taken us thirty-three minutes to bike the four miles. Not a record, but not the worst ever.

"Is that Evie?" Frank was standing on his pedals, coasting, hip cocked to one side. He pointed his head toward Van der Queen Park.

I shaded my face. "Looks like."

Two other kids played nearby, one swinging next to Evie and the other on the slide. I didn't know if they were together on purpose or had simply found themselves at the park at the same time. "The other two girls are going to be in your grade in the fall. I can't remember their names."

"No boys out," he observed.

"It's early," I said, just to say something. "Take a right here. That white house is Mr. Connelly's."

Frank shot me a look.

"I want to check in about the popcorn sales. You remember me talking about that."

Because I had the popcorn brochure including the order form, there wasn't really a reason for us to stop by Mr. Connelly's. I guess I needed to see him in the light was all. I hadn't thought to call ahead, though, and so when another guy stepped outside of Mr. Connelly's back door, right next to those savage rosebushes, and Mr. Connelly gave him a hug before sending him on his way, I blushed as if I'd just walked into Mr. Connelly's own bedroom uninvited.

Mr. Connelly still wore a smile as his friend drove away and his eyes landed on mine. "Cassandra?"

"Hi, Mr. Connelly!" I hollered before biking up his driveway. "This is my friend Frank." My voice was too loud.

Mr. Connelly stood there like it was the most normal thing in the world that I was here with a stranger and yelling at him.

"Nice to meet you, Frank," Mr. Connelly said when Frank dismounted and walked up the sidewalk. "That's a beautiful bike you have there."

Frank puffed up like a bird in a bath. "Thank you."

Mr. Connelly smiled. "And what school do you go to?"

"Lilydale come fall," I said, inserting myself back into the conversation. "But he was there for a couple days last week."

Mr. Connelly held out his hand. "I'd love for you to join band."

A loud scratching noise came from inside Connelly's house, and his eyes flashed. He retracted his hand. "That's my cat. She's supposed to be on a diet, but she makes my life miserable if I don't feed her."

I kept a smile pinned on. That hadn't sounded like a cat. I wanted to ask Mr. Connelly about Clam, but I couldn't, not without explaining that I was a no-good spy who'd peeped on him.

"Would you like to come in for some water?" Mr. Connelly asked, stepping aside. He sounded concerned.

I held up the brochure that I'd tucked into my waistband. "Can't! We have popcorn to sell."

I could see into the hallway behind him. I was surprised to catch a view of crowded knickknacks stuffed on tables and shelves built just for them, red-cheeked ceramic creatures. It was a glimpse of a fussy house, built for walking through rather than living in, with lots to dust. There was a metronome at the end of the hallway, ticktocking back and forth. *Click click. Click click.*

I pointed at it. "Do you always keep your metronome going?"

He glanced over his shoulder, a rueful smile on his face when he turned back. "Once a music teacher, always a music teacher, even in the summer. But no, I don't always have it on. Just warming it up for Gabriel's lesson. He should be by any minute."

I gasped audibly. *Gabriel.* I'm sure my crush was written on my face in blinking neon.

"I remember you were thinking about taking lessons here, too. The offer still stands, Cassandra."

I wanted to hug him right there for not asking me why I'd just gone full-on nerd. "I'll think on it," I said, as if it were an option. "Will you tell Gabriel hi from me?"

"Of course," he said, smiling. A cloud scudded over the sun, and suddenly I couldn't see his eyes. "And if you two aren't coming in, you should get to work selling that popcorn, because you don't want to be out after dark. Not these days."

CHAPTER 34

We hit twenty-three Lilydale houses. Fourteen of them had no one home, another seven had claimed to already have bought popcorn from someone else, and two placed orders for the caramel corn–cheddar corn–plain corn blend. Knocking on strangers' doors hadn't gotten any easier. Felt like asking for a handout. I was about ready to call it done when Frank asked about eating.

"I'm hungry. What d'you have in your backpack?"

For the first time, I felt much older than him. "Peanut butter sandwiches and apples."

"Can we have a picnic?"

The sun was pulsing, pushing at two o'clock, curling my baby hairs with its hot breath. "Let's go down by the creek. There's a shortcut over here." I steered into a wooded area on the west perimeter of town. The paved road to my left led to Crow River Park in a roundabout way, but the path through the woods led directly to the creek. Lilydale Elementary and Middle School held its May Day Play Day picnic there every year. We weren't allowed to swim at that picnic, but today was so hot that it'd take a herd of horses to keep me out of the water.

Tree-greened sunrays dappled the forest floor as I bounced along the rutted path through the woods. We were in an enchanted land, a thicket hiding trolls and mushroom fairies, princes and queens. I thought of joking that the My Time lady's bathtub was around here somewhere, but it seemed like too much work. The creek was a thread of mercury that I caught glimpses of, but the scent of moving water hit me before a full view did, and I yahooed.

Frank echoed the yell. "That water is going to feel so good!"

I dumped my bike and backpack on the riverbank and flew over the shore reeds and into the creek. The water came to the bottom of my shorts, deliciously cool, catching and reflecting the sun. My feet dug into the sand. I played my good hand through the current, glancing behind me for Frank.

A huge splash exploded next to me.

"Oh my god!" I yelled, laughing.

Frank broke the surface and spouted water out of his mouth like a dolphin fountain.

"You cannonballed!"

"You better believe I did," he said, flipping so he was belly-up and facing the sun. He waved his arms and legs lazily, the slow current pulling him away.

I splashed some water toward his feet. "Goofball. You're lucky you didn't scrape the bottom."

"I did." He held up a foot, and I saw a river rock had scored it, slicing in. Blood flowed spidery down his puckered white foot. "Worth it."

I shook my head; then a thought exploded in me. "We should be blood brothers!"

He twisted his foot so he could peer at it, no mean feat while he was balancing in the water. "Where would your blood come from?"

I thought of the contents of my backpack. "I packed a Swiss Army knife."

His eyes widened. "You'd cut yourself?"

"That's how you're supposed to do it." I squinted up toward the sun. "Or I could pick a fresh scab."

189

He fell back into the water, ladling his hands across the surface. A lock of wet hair had fallen across his forehead. "Can you be blood brothers with scab blood?"

"Blood is blood," I said defensively. I waded toward him, using his shoulder to balance so I could pick a corner of the shaving scab that had dried a Morse code line up the outside of my ankle. The skin underneath was a startling white, then flushed with blood.

He brought his foot to my shin. I *think* we managed to touch our blood spots together before tipping over. We came back up, splashing. I'd kept my punctured hand raised above water, though it probably would have been fine getting wet.

"That means we're friends forever," I said.

He nodded solemnly, his brown hair water-slicked to his face, his big sea eyes wide and innocent. "Better than friends. *Blood brothers.*"

"Frank," I said, before I lost my courage, "what would you do if you found out your dad was a criminal?"

Frank cocked his head. "What kind of criminal?"

"Someone who hurts people."

"I'd turn him in," Frank said, no hesitation.

Something brushed against my leg, and I jumped. "I'm going to move our bikes to the beach and set up lunch."

I trudged toward the shore, grabbing a tuft of tall grass on the bank and using it to pull myself up. I blame the height of the grass for not being able to see Clam until we were nearly eye to eye.

My breath froze in my throat.

His posture was predatory, his eyes the same. His bearing reminded me exactly of being trapped in the instrument room with him, except this time I wasn't alone. I had Frank.

"Are you swimming in our river, country mouse?"

I almost couldn't hear him over the pounding of my heartbeat. "It's a public river."

Ricky Tink and Wayne Johnson appeared at his shoulders. Ricky was wearing even more bandages than usual. His warts must sweat in the summer. Wayne was smirking.

"How do you feel about public *nudity*?" Clam asked. At least it looked like Clam, but just like in the band room, it wasn't really him. I thought of what Frank had said about the boys here being like were-wolves. Were Ricky and Wayne changed, too?

"I saw you at Mr. Connelly's the other night," I said, the words coming out fast.

Ricky and Wayne did a double take.

"What?" Clam said. "That's stupid."

He was so confident, I wondered if I'd imagined it. But I hadn't. He'd been there. I'd seen only the side of his face, but it'd been Clam for sure. "What were you doing there?"

Something clenched behind his eyes. "I said I wasn't there."

"What'd he look like, Clam?" I asked. "The man who attacked you."

Wayne gasped. Clam was looking at me like he'd already killed me every which way but Wednesday and was deciding what to do with my bones.

I stepped back from the force of Clam's rage. My heart was trying to beat its way out of my chest. I searched for the pulse at my neck, genuinely afraid I was going to die of a heart attack.

"That scar of yours," Clam said, pointing at it. "Was it because someone tried to hang you?"

"You know she was born with it," Ricky said.

Ricky sounded normal, like he was standing up for me. Relief flooded my body.

Frank stood up in the water behind me. "Cassie?"

"Well now, who's your friend?" Clam walked to the side of the bank and held out his hand, a regular ol' gentleman.

"Don't take it," I yelled. I wanted to turn and help Frank myself, but no way was I showing my back to Wayne and Ricky until I was sure whose side they were sticking on.

"Holy shit, lookit this bike!" Ricky strode over to Frank's BMX. He tipped it up and straddled it, raising the front wheel in a mock wheelie. "Yee-haw!"

"Hey, that's mine!" Frank launched himself out of the water and toward Ricky but stopped just shy of him, like Ricky was surrounded by a force field. One of Ricky's Band-Aids had come loose, and it was hanging over Frank's handlebar.

Wayne hooted. Clam stepped closer to me and put his finger on my scar, tracing it. His touch burned. He had something green in his teeth and smelled chicken soupy, like my dad after a hard day's work.

"Are you like your sister?" he asked.

"What?" I spat the word.

Clam chuckled. It was a dirty, scraping sound. "I'm wondering if you're like Sephie. If you like chips like she does. Her favorite brand is *Free-to-Lay*."

Ricky and Wayne matched his laugh.

"Yeah!" Wayne said. "Sephie is easy like Sunday morning!"

A coldness overcame me, beginning at my feet and crawling like sludge through my veins. Something about their laugh, their words, made me achingly lonely, fear replaced with desolation. I couldn't escape them, there was no way. I was a girl against three boys, and I had Frank to protect to boot. My brain told me to go to sleep, to get whatever was gonna happen over with quick. I might have rolled if Clam hadn't flicked my left breast.

"Musta been a mosquito there." Clam flicked again. "Looks like it bit you!"

Ricky and Wayne were crowding in, I saw it out of the corners of my eyes, but I didn't care, not anymore. I'd let Clam touch my neck, but his hand on my boob was too personal. I could feel the poison of it leaching into my skin, then my muscles, and if I didn't pour it all back on him, it'd set up permanently in my bones.

I launched myself at Clam, yelling and scratching and kicking, my limbs moving so fast that they were a blur even to me. I felt his flesh collecting under my fingernails, and it spurred me to fight harder. Someone grabbed me at the waist and I got lucky, connecting my elbow with his jaw.

I was dropped, and I turned to see it was Wayne who'd grabbed me, his eyes wide, his hand to his bleeding mouth. I turned back to Clam, spitting, and saw the same expression of disbelief plastered on his face. Their surprised expressions would have been comical if I weren't so terrified.

"Run, Frank!"

He was staring at me from the riverbank, slack-jawed, appearing closer to five years than eleven, but he was a smart kid at any age, and he jumped on his chrome BMX and speed-pedaled ahead of me, up the hill and out of the woods. I grabbed my backpack and flew onto my own bike, pedaling like my life depended on it, biking away from the horrible things Clam and Wayne were yelling that they'd do to me when they caught me.

CHAPTER 35

"You fought like Isis!"

I'd caught an episode of the show at my grandparents' two summers ago. Beautiful science teacher Andrea Thomas discovered the Tutmose amulet on an Egyptian dig. When she exposed it to the sunlight and invoked Isis, she was endowed with magical powers. It was good TV.

"But your hand's bleeding," he finished.

I glanced down at my handlebars. The gauze over my punctured hand was speckled with red. "That's not my blood."

Frank barked a laugh. "You really gave him the what for."

The adrenaline was fading, leaving a gray sensation. I risked my first glance behind. Clam, Wayne, and Ricky hadn't followed. My knees went wobbly as I released the last of my fight juice. "Let's turn on the gravel."

"Sure thing," Frank said. "Man, you went at him. Why'd you fight so hard?"

"Let's sell at a few of these houses," I said, steering my bike into the first driveway off the tar. I didn't want to talk about what had happened at the creek like Frank did. I felt pride and shame, and I didn't know where to store that.

"Okay." Frank was as chipper as a kid at the DQ. He stayed that way as we meandered our way home, biking down occasional driveways, catching farmers on their way to the barn or housewives hanging the laundry. I made five more sales before I was ready to talk.

"You were right about the boys here being werewolves."

"I told you!" We were a mile from Frank's house, two miles from mine, on a side road my bus passed by but never went down. We'd agreed to stop at one more house before going our separate ways for the day.

"They've been bit," Frank continued, "and now they want to bite you. I tried to tell my dad, but he said that's just how boys are."

"You're not like that," I said.

Frank shrugged and pedaled ahead. "There's only one house down here," he called back. "It doesn't look like anyone's home. Want to check it out?"

I caught up and then passed him down the driveway. The place used to be a farm, it looked like, the layout the same as my parents' place and Frank's. It held a crumbling barn, a silo covered in vines, and a red outbuilding that was maintained and probably used as a workshop. I didn't see a car in the driveway, but the house could have been blocking it. I biked farther, hearing the comfortable crunch of Frank's tires behind me.

I was fully around the house before I spotted the police cruiser. I braked so fast that my back tire skidded to the side.

"Whoa! Porky Pig," Frank said, biking up next to me.

A screen door banged, and I whirled toward the house. My tongue grew thick in my mouth. "Sergeant Bauer. I didn't know you lived here."

He was bleary-eyed, a mug of something in his hand. He ran his fingers through his hair, scraped them down the stubble on his cheek. "Renting. A little trouble at home."

Heidi's parents had gotten divorced a few years ago, back when her, Lynn, and I still hung out. Heidi's dad had rented a room at the Purple Saucer Motel in the Hollow. He stayed there for six months and then disappeared.

"I'm sorry to hear that," I said.

He grunted. "What are you doing here?"

I yanked the brochure out of my bag. I wished I hadn't brought it, that I hadn't biked down this driveway. I wasn't going to spill anything about Ricky, Wayne, or Clam's behavior by the creek, and I knew Frank wouldn't, either. Those were the unspoken rules. "Selling popcorn for band."

He kept his stare on my face rather than the brochure. "I'm buying from Liz."

His daughter in Sephie's grade. "Sorry to bother you."

His smile surprised me. It seemed genuine, but that didn't fit his demeanor. "That's fine. Nice to see you."

He hadn't even peeked at Frank the whole visit, not that I'd seen. I steered my bike around and pedaled out of his driveway, not bothering to say goodbye.

When we were out of earshot, I spoke. "I think your dad is wrong, Frank. I don't think it's just how boys are. I think it's something to do with Lilydale."

The clicking of the playing card against Frank's spokes and our tires chewing gravel were the only noises for so long that I thought he hadn't heard me. Finally, he said, "I think so, too. Hey, that guy's farmhouse looked like mine. Think he has a creepy dirt basement, too?"

I suddenly didn't want to go home. I tried to keep the desperation out of my voice. "Do you have to go straight back to your place right now?"

"Yeah."

I could see his house ahead on the right, deposited like a game piece on the board-flatness of the prairie. "We could stop by Goblin's."

"Who?"

"Goblin! That guy who lives on the corner between you and me."

"The one with the green car?"

"That's him." I was thinking quick. "He's a person of interest in the attacks, I heard Sergeant Bauer say it. Maybe we can see what's turning Lilydale boys into werewolves."

"We can't trespass."

"We won't. We'll sorta skirt around the edges." I risked a glance. Frank's mouth was set in a line. I wondered what his parents had told him about Goblin.

"I don't wanna," he said.

"You chicken?"

His chin quivered. Sometimes I forgot he was only ten. "I'm no chicken. Race you there!"

He took off in a flash. I chugged those pedals to catch up with him. "Slow it down," I hollered. "We have to come up quiet."

"He's probably at work," Frank yelled back at me, but he eased up. I pulled ahead. "Follow my lead."

All the farms in this grid had been constructed the same—identical layout, including the houses, barns, and outbuilding, tree shield surrounding each, fields beyond. Goblin's house was more exposed than most, but he still had a good copse of trees protecting the west side, catawampus from where the wild strawberries grew. I led Frank in that direction, walking my bike through the ditch. It was swampy since the rain, and once I was in the tall grass, it smelled like peat. I'd have to check myself for ticks later.

"Leave your bike here," I whispered, setting mine down to demonstrate. On their sides, our bikes would be invisible in this tall grass. I held a fist in the air. "This sign means stop." I opened the fist and waved my fingers. "This means go."

Frank made a smart salute. I dropped to my belly with a smile on my face, army crawling along the spongy earth, careful not to rustle the grass too much. The swamp gave way to a stunted forest, and we made a dash for a cluster of oaks. We were within a hundred yards of Goblin's house. I held up the fist, and Frank stopped immediately. I swallowed my giggle along with the clover dust air. We were really good at this.

I scanned the perimeter. Goblin's house was a run-down version of my own, Sergeant Bauer's, and Frank's. Goblin had recently fried something, and underneath that, I caught a whiff of sourness. He owned a few head of cattle. They were kicking and lowing in the field behind the red barn. He'd converted an old shed to a garage. Its door was open, but because of the angle and the shade, I couldn't tell if Goblin's car was parked in it or not. I searched the windows of his house, at least the main floor ones. His basement windows were blacked out. I didn't know what I expected to spot. I was just happy to have gotten farther onto his property than Sephie had, to feel my heart thudding pleasantly on a warm summer day.

"I don't think—" was as far as I got in my sentence before the vise grip closed on my neck. Fear popped like a bitter berry between my teeth.

"What are you kids doing on my property?"

Goblin held me and Frank by the neck, pushing our faces into the earth. His accent was coarse, pure backcountry Minnesotan. If he had to string together more than five words, we'd hear the "I seen it" and "can you borrow me some" that my parents said were the signs of ignorance.

"Let us go!" I hollered, except my voice was strangled.

"I'll let ya go." He released us so quickly that my head shot up. Frank rolled over and scurried to hide behind me. Goblin's dog, a growly looking mutt, watched us both, his hackles raised. The right side of his face was swollen.

I stared from Goblin to his dog and back again, feeling more busted than scared. I got to my feet, my legs shaking. "You had no right to grab us."

"Well now, you had no right to be on my property." He smiled. His feed cap shaded his eyes, but his mouth was wide and open. He was missing teeth.

"We wanted to pet your dog." Frank stood and offered his hand to Goblin's mutt.

Goblin laughed, and it sounded for-real friendly this time. My shoulders inched down from my ears. We *had* been trespassing. Maybe he wouldn't tell.

"No one wants to pet Cliffy. He's an old mutt."

I pointed at his swollen head. "What happened?"

The laugh sizzled away like water in hot bacon grease. "None of your business." He squinted. "You're Donny's girl."

I didn't think that needed answering. "We have to go."

Goblin looked at Frank. "And you're the new boy, just up the road, aren't ya? Your dad a farmer?"

There was something grabby in his words, but his smile was back. He tipped his head so I could see one of his eyes, dark and glittering.

"We really have to be going." This time, instead of waiting for permission, I grabbed Frank's hand and backed away.

I worried that Goblin would stop us, but he just watched from under his brim.

"Don't come back," he finally grumbled. "My dog don't like strangers. I can't be responsible if he catches you next time."

CHAPTER 36

I biked Frank back to his house. It was the least I could do after the danger I'd put him in. He walked into his house without saying goodbye. My bike ride home was miserable, made more terrible by the drizzle that turned to a downpour by the time I hit the driveway. What a monumentally crappy day. And just when I thought it couldn't get any worse, I found Dad waiting for me in front of the house.

"Where've you been?" His shirt was off. He stood under the awning, but raindrops glistened on his chest hair. Mom was nowhere to be seen.

"I told you. Selling popcorn."

His eyes narrowed. "Let me see."

"I don't actually have popcorn." I leaned my bike against the house, hugging my elbows when my hands were free. "I take orders now and deliver later."

"Did you get any orders?" His voice was deadly gentle.

"Yeah." I yanked my backpack off my shoulders and pulled out the brochure, grateful that I'd sold some. "See?"

He kept his malachite eyes trained on me. "You look scraped up."

The lie tumbled out. "Goblin's dog chased me when I was biking, and I wiped out."

Dad's eyes grew hooded and then cleared. "When?"

"Just now. Dang dog. But it didn't get me." Better the mutt take the heat. Dad already didn't like him.

Dad seemed to swallow that story, because he changed the subject. "We're going to town."

"You and Mom?" His stillness was alarming. Had Goblin called after all and told on me for trespassing? Did Dad know the dog story was a lie?

"You and me. I have some shopping to do. We can grab Sephie on our way back."

My eyelid twitched. I didn't want to drive to town with Dad in this mood, but I didn't see a way out. I cleared my throat. "Let me put my bike away first."

It was a tense drive. The only bright spot was that Dad had put a shirt on, though he hadn't changed out of his holey jean shorts. The road raced by underneath the VW van, visible through the hole in the passenger-side floor, its grays and blacks accented by a gash of white when Dad veered too far to the right.

Even with Dad's mood, I always found the road passing under me exhilarating. It reminded me I could go anywhere when I got older, explore bottomless blue-green oceans, climb icy snow-capped mountains, drink tea with monks. The irony of being reminded of the size of the world through a hole in the floor of a rusted-out van was not lost on me.

We pulled into town without saying a single word to each other until Dad hit the first stop sign. "I'll drop you off at the library."

My blood fizzed with joy. I'd finished *Flowers in the Attic* last night. "Thanks!"

"You'll have half an hour."

"What're you going to do?"

His knuckles grew white on the steering wheel. "I have a meeting."

"With who?"

"With none of your business."

I hopped out of the van in front of the library, situated in the center of downtown Lilydale. I slammed the door closed behind me, only mildly unsettled at the idea of Dad at a meeting. Thirty minutes later to the second, I stood outside the library clutching four new hardcovers. I held them like treasure because they were. The rain had stopped, but the sidewalks were worm soup. I stood there for ten minutes, but no Dad.

I shifted my weight from foot to foot. A little girl exited the Ben Franklin across the street, gripping her dad's pinkie finger with one hand and a Jolly Rancher Stix in the other. I could tell what flavor it was because of her corpse-green lips. Stix were the popular candy now, and a lot of kids ate them on the bus, either green apple or fire flavored. I'd wanted so bad to taste them, but I was no beggar. I squeezed my books tighter. I wished I'd brought money with me. There were so few candies I'd gotten to taste. Sephie and I liked lemon drops and root beer barrels and bridge mix only because that's what our grandparents had out when we visited.

The girl and her dad walked down the street. When it came time to cross, he picked her up, but he moved too fast and she dropped her candy. The bright green fell into a rivulet of water heading toward a storm drain. She screamed, but he wouldn't let her retrieve it. They disappeared around a corner.

I found myself walking toward the dropped candy. A feverish need to taste it had overtaken me. I forced myself to step past it, toward the Ben Franklin door, my eyes trained on the sidewalk. Maybe I'd find some money that someone dropped. I'd only need a quarter. *Or maybe I could go in the store, and a fresh, slick stick of candy would slide right into my pocket, and I could take it home with me, savor it in my closet along with one of my new books.*

I had the cool Ben Franklin door handle in my hand, my stomach churning from the fish smell of rain-swollen worms, ready to step in and get some candy one way or another, when the door to Little John's opened, emitting raucous noise and a thick plume of cigarette smoke.

Dad stepped out, Sergeant Bauer behind him. The sergeant was wearing street clothes. They shook hands and clapped each other on the shoulder; then Dad marched toward our van parked on the opposite end of the street. I charged back to stand in front of the library, which is where Dad found me.

That night, when I heard the sharp snip of him clipping his nails followed more quickly than ever by his step on that bottom stair, I knew it was my fault. I'd brought bad luck all day, first with Clam at the river, then Goblin. It made sense Dad would follow. But he didn't know that my writing was preventing him from reaching the top of the stairs.

He tried to make it past the sixth step, farther than he'd ever gotten, but my pencil flew across my journal and every word pushed him back, spinning a word web thick as a brick wall.

Cassie's— Believe It or Don't!

THE GIRL WHO SURVIVED A SHARK ATTACK!

TEN-YEAR-OLD BETTINA HOGGINS WAS SWIMMING IN THE TASMAN SEA WITH HER FAMILY WHEN A GREAT WHITE SHARK GRABBED HER BY THE ANKLE AND BEGAN TO PULL HER OUT TO SEA. BETTINA'S MOTHER GRABBED HER DAUGHTER'S WRIST AND WOULD NOT LET HER GO. THE SHARK GAVE UP, AND BETTINA LIVED TO SWIM ANOTHER DAY.

When I penned the last word, I tasted sweat on my top lip from the exertion of writing it. The house was silent. Dad stayed on that sixth step for years, it felt like, before my words finally worked. He shambled back down the stairs and to his room. I could feel each of his footfalls like the heartbeat of the house.

I made up my mind then and there that tomorrow, I'd tell Mom what was happening.

Dad had said that we should never tell what happened at our house, that no one in the outside world would understand, that tattling would be the worst thing we could do to him.

But Mom wasn't in the outside world.

She was family.

CHAPTER 37

I woke up in the closet with a crick in my neck. A flutter ran along my wrists. Maybe I would get to return to sleeping *on* my bed tonight. Maybe after I told Mom that Dad had been coming up the stairs after she fell asleep, that would be enough for her to leave him! I shot out of the closet, tore through the fuzzy morning air, and nearly ran into Sephie outside my door.

"What're you doing?" I asked.

She rolled her eyes. "Getting ready for summer school, dummy."

"Are Mom and Dad up yet?"

"Yup." She headed down the stairs. "They're packing."

The flutter gave way to a hollow feeling. "For what?"

I had my answer when I hit the bottom step and turned into the kitchen. Mom was shoving a toothbrush into her overnight bag, which was already stuffed with clothes. "We're going on a trip!"

Dad appeared from the direction of their bedroom holding a folded T-shirt. "Found it! Will this fit?"

"You bet, love," Mom said, grabbing the shirt from him and cramming it into the bag.

I shook my head to clear the cobwebs. "Where are we going?"

Dad grinned at me. "Just me and your mom. We're driving up to Duluth. Jim Kendum is having a party. You remember the Kendums?"

I wiped sleep out of my eyes. Mom and Dad had never taken a trip without us.

"Are they the ones with the motorcycles?" Sephie asked.

"You bet!" Dad said.

"Who'll take care of us?" I asked. Fear was warring with relief. No Dad, but also no Mom.

"Sephie's old enough to watch you both," Dad assured me.

Mom's eyes narrowed, but she didn't argue.

Sephie stood next to me. Our shoulders were touching. She smelled freshly showered, and I smelled crusty. "When are you coming back?" she asked.

Dad shrugged, his tone teasing. "Maybe never."

"Donny." Mom playfully punched his shoulder and then grabbed his hand. "We'll be back early tomorrow. It's a short trip. We decided we need a vacation is all. You can roast a chicken for supper tonight. No parties. Sephie, you're on your own for getting to summer school. I called the Gomezes, and they said you could call there if you are in trouble."

Sephie grabbed my hand. We were mirror reflections of our parents.

We all turned toward the open kitchen window at the sound of tires coming down the gravel from the direction of the Gomezes', and I wondered if they were coming right now to check on us. Or maybe it was super-early mail delivery and I was getting another package from Aunt Jin! My heart leaped at the first bright spot of the confusing morning but plummeted when the green car crested the rise and appeared in our driveway.

Goblin.

CHAPTER 38

I was sure I was about to get in the worst trouble of my life.

We stepped outside as a family.

Dad had tied one of his sculptures to the top of the van, a blue-and-yellow tulip the size of a kayak. I thought we must have looked like the Joads taking off for California, with our misfit van all packed up and my parents dressed in their frayed best. I didn't think Goblin would get that reference. He didn't strike me as the type of guy who'd read *The Grapes of Wrath*, or any book for that matter.

"Gary," Dad said when Goblin pulled up and stepped out of his car without turning it off. Dad's stiff posture told me he liked Goblin on his property even less than he liked him at the liquor store. That was one thing we agreed on.

Goblin lifted his feed cap off his head almost high enough for me to get a peek at what was underneath and then tugged it back to where it'd started. The bill shaded his face, but his tight-slice mouth and big lumpy nose were visible, just like yesterday. So was the wormy snake tattoo at his neck and squirming down his arm. "I'm looking for my hound."

Dad had moved so he stood in front of me and Sephie. I had to crane my neck to see around him, surprised that Goblin's first words weren't to rat me out.

Dad still hadn't answered, so Goblin repeated his question.

"My dog. You seen it?"

"No," Dad finally said. "But it's within my rights to shoot strays. I have kids to protect."

Those words were loaded, and Goblin knew it.

"My dog ain't a stray."

Dad sneered. "Then you know where he is?"

I wondered how Dad knew it was a male dog, or maybe he was just guessing? But then I had the most awful thought that turned me inside out, bones to the sun. Had Dad gone and killed Goblin's dog because I said he'd chased me?

"I'm looking for it, I told you." Goblin stared off toward his place. It was a speck across the rolling cornfield. If I ran as fast as I could, I could be there in under fifteen minutes, winded. "You heard about that boy being hurt?"

The abrupt subject change caused Mom to stiffen and wrap her arms around me and Sephie.

"More than one boy," Dad said. "It's in the papers."

Goblin shook his head. "Naw, this is a new boy. Mark Clamchik."

My shoulders slumped in relief. "That was a couple weekends ago."

Goblin made a wheezing noise, and I realized he was laughing. The sound made a cold sweat break out across my back.

"He got attacked again."

I flinched.

"Donny," Mom said, releasing us to grab Dad's shirt.

Dad pushed her away and stepped forward until only five feet separated him from Goblin. "I want you off my property."

Goblin hadn't expected that, judging by how long it took him to answer. "Not very neighborly," he finally said. "This going to be like high school, when you and Rammy Bauer come at me?"

Dad stood his ground, quiet.

Goblin must have sensed the same thing he had in the liquor store, because he made that identical *cuk-cuk-cuk* of a sound in the back of his throat, like something small was knocking to get out of his voice box. He spat a wad of snoose before sliding back inside his car and slamming the door.

He didn't do the civilized backup onto the belly of the driveway so he could leave facing forward. Instead, he chunked down the gearshift on his steering wheel, slamming it into reverse, and tore out so hot that I smelled burning rubber.

"I have a phone call to make," Dad said to Mom, "and then we'll leave for Duluth."

CHAPTER 39

Frank biked over the hill of my driveway like the sun rising. It's dorky, but that's how happy I felt. I had a friend coming to my house to see *me* and only me. Even when Lynn and I were hanging out, she hardly came over, but here was Frank cruising toward my house like he wanted to be here.

I pumped my hand waving at him, not even bothering to hide how excited I was.

I cupped my hands around my mouth. "Hurry up, Frank!" I yelled. "These birthday invitations aren't going to make themselves!"

That was the ruse I'd used to get his mom to let him bike with me two days in a row, that I'd needed help making invitations for my party on Friday. I didn't know if Frank was still sore about yesterday, but he'd agreed to come once his mom okayed it.

My birthday party would be held at Lake Corona Park. Besides the one-story metal slide that deposited you right into the deep water, the park had a dock and a raft with two diving levels. Mom said it'd be fine to hold my party there, but we hadn't discussed invitations, and then I'd forgotten to ask before they skipped town. I decided to make my own and then bike them directly to everyone's mailboxes. I'd invite exactly the same people as had been at Lynn's party, plus Frank and minus Andrea because no way could I bike to Kimball.

Frank held his hands toward the sky and coasted down the second half of the driveway. The morning sun glinted off his glorious BMX. He whooped as he flew down, his longish hair flying straight behind him. When it was almost too late to stop, he braked, screeching up loose rocks onto my legs. His cheeks were ruddy and his smile ferocious.

"How about them apples?" he asked, out of breath.

"Those are nice apples," I agreed. "Now come on into the living room so we can get started."

He let his bike drop onto the edge of Mom's flower bed. I'd have said something, but it was only on the rock perimeter. Meander rubbed against one of his legs and Bimbo the other. He stopped to pet both. "I'm *already* working."

"Petting kitties?"

"Naw." He stood and shielded his eyes from the sun, pointing toward his farm, which we could see blinks of through the tree line. "I'm starting tomorrow in the field. My dad said he'll pay me three dollars an hour to pick rocks."

"That's three times what I make for babysitting for half the work!"

His chin drew back into his neck. "You ever pick rocks? They're heavy."

"Whatever." I was mathing it as I walked into the house, Frank on my heels. In ten hours, I could make $30. One week, $150! "Do you think he needs more help?"

He shrugged. "Maybe."

I could tell he didn't much care about my finances. "If you help me get a job picking rocks, I'll let you join my kitty clinic."

"Does it pay?"

"Not a red cent." I led him into the dining room. "Hey, sorry about yesterday, about getting you in trouble with Goblin."

"It's fine." Frank nodded as if that settled it. He pointed at the dining room table, where I'd laid out the art materials. "You're going to make the invitations from scratch?"

"*We* are. Starting with one for you." I beamed as I held up a white sheet of paper. "What do you want it to say?"

"When's your party again?"

"Friday." I'd told him when I called him this morning.

He slid his hands into the rear pockets of his cutoffs. "Nuh-uh. No can do. I have to work."

His words were casual, but my cheeks burned. I'd actually already made an invitation for him. It was hidden under the pile of construction paper so I could surprise him with it like magic. "Friday's my actual birthday."

"That's cool," he said, dropping into a chair. "Save me some cake."

I sat next to him. I'd laid out glitter, glue, sequins, yarn, a hole puncher, and the construction paper. We began cutting out colored circles, hearts, squares, whatever seemed fun. I wrote the party information on the inside, and Frank glued on the decorations.

This close, I noticed he had eyes like a girl, with long lashes. I liked the warmth of him next to me. We leaned into each other, swapping silly knock-knock jokes. We grew so comfortable that Frank told me about his friends back in Rochester and how much he missed them. I spilled about Sephie acting weird since December and that I was going to be a writer when I grew up. He announced he was going to join the United States Air Force. I bragged about the Apple IIe computer I'd learned programming on last fall, and he topped me by telling me about the Oregon Trail game his old school had.

It was so easy, talking to him.

"Your mom and dad gonna drive these into town?" he asked when the last invitation was inside its homemade envelope.

"They're on vacation."

He pretended to fall backward in shock, but the surprise on his face was real. "Your parents left you and your sister home alone?"

I crossed my arms. "Yeah. So what?" I knew what. I didn't want him to say it, though. I didn't want to be the odd-duck family anymore.

"When are they getting back?"

"Early tomorrow. We're supposed to call your mom and dad if we have an emergency."

"Huh." He seemed to think about it. "You have any ice cream?"

"You shouldn't eat processed food." I didn't mean to sound so harsh.

He scratched his scalp. It was loud. *Scritch scritch.* "I should probably go."

I wished I could take back my words. "Hey, I'll bike with you. I should head to town and drop all these off, anyhow. You want to come into Lilydale?"

"I dunno."

"We could drive by my friend Gabriel's house." I'd dreamed of creating an invitation for him, but in the end, I hadn't. If Gabriel happened to spot us bike by, though, and asked me what I was up to, I could casually invite him to my birthday.

"Gabriel the dentist's kid?"

I swallowed my spit too fast and started coughing. "You know him?"

"Yeah, my dad does, anyhow. He's farming some of the land they own. He a friend of yours?"

"Sorta." No way was I biking by Gabriel's house now. "On second thought, I think I'll just stick these in the mail. We have stamps."

"Okay," Frank said.

He followed me into the kitchen, and I poured us each a glass of pink-gold rhubarb-ade. When I slid the jug back into the refrigerator, Frank pointed toward the ceiling.

"We have one of those holes in our house, too. For the heat to go up."

I gulped the honey-sweetened drink, my eyes watering at its tartness. "Same here. That's my room up there. Hey, you know what would be so cool?"

"What?"

"If we were tall enough to see the top of the refrigerator without standing on our tippy-toes. I can't wait until I'm big like that. Imagine being that tall."

He rolled his eyes. "You'll grow, you know."

I pinched his arm, but not hard. "No shit, Sherlock."

"Then keep digging, Watson."

I giggled. I hadn't heard that one. It must have been something they said in Rochester.

"I should get home," Frank said.

"I'll bike with you."

We both stared at Goblin's house when we passed it. There was no sign of movement, but then there rarely was. Frank's mom and dad were having ice cream drinks when we showed up. Mrs. Gomez was quick to swear that they normally never drank during the day and was embarrassed we'd caught them, but the girls were down for a late nap and tomorrow they'd start fieldwork in earnest and you only lived once.

I loved her.

My grandparents used to end a hard workday with a Brandy Alexander or a Grasshopper, and they'd let me and Sephie have a sip. That's what I thought hard liquor tasted like until I snuck a sip of Dad's whiskey a few years later and realized actual booze tasted like gasoline.

Mr. Gomez set his drink down and insisted on driving me home, even though Frank and I had been hanging out all day without supervision. I told Mr. Gomez that he didn't have to do it, but Mrs. Gomez told me I was fighting a losing battle because Mr. Gomez believed in being a gentleman and I might as well get it done and over with.

The ride was uncomfortable, just like when he'd driven me home from babysitting. At least there was no mob of crows coming at his truck this time. We discussed the weather. It looked like it would rain again. I thought about him and Mrs. Gomez being the people we should call if there was an emergency.

That's when the question burbled out of me. "Why'd you guys move here?"

I watched myself ask it in the reflection of my side mirror. I wished I could take it back. It was too personal.

Mr. Gomez shifted his toothpick from one side of his mouth to the other. He smelled like the outdoors. His gray T-shirt was stained at the armpits and covered in dirt. He took the turn past Goblin's house, not bothering to signal. I didn't think he was gonna answer me.

"Wanted my kids to grow up on land we owned, like I did," he finally said.

I had another personal question waiting right behind that one. "Frank said you moved here earlier than the rest of them. Didn't you miss them?"

He removed his toothpick at this question and looked at it, one hand still on the steering wheel. "Sometimes a break is nice."

It was clear he meant from conversation with me, and so I held my tongue rather than ask the other questions that were burning into it like Cinnamon Discs.

CHAPTER 40

I should have guessed when Sephie didn't want to watch *Real People* and known for a fact when she pooh-poohed the CBS Wednesday Night Movie showing of *Young Frankenstein*.

"I've already seen it. Twice." She was in the bathroom slathering on mascara. "But you can watch TV all you want. I'm going to have *actual* fun."

"How?"

Mom and Dad had left us no money. After Mr. Gomez dropped off me and my bike, I'd held my first kitty clinic of the year waiting for Sephie to return from summer school. After she showed up, we cooked supper, ditching all the vegetables and baking the chicken whole, slathered in salt and butter. Then we'd cleaned up the kitchen so we wouldn't land in trouble if they arrived home early.

What else was left to do but watch TV?

Sephie's mouth formed a perfect O as she lengthened her eyelashes, scraping them along the black-tarred brush. When she was done, she blinked rapidly like a cartoon girl bunny. "Inviting friends over," she said.

"What? You don't have any friends."

I hadn't meant it mean, but her eyes grew all damp. If one of those salty globs dropped, that mascara was done for.

"Shows what you know!" she said.

Her reaction surprised me. I'd only been stating fact. "I'm sorry. It's just you never talk about anyone, or have anyone over." I thought of Clam's comment about her being a Frito-Lay, and my mouth grew starchy. "Are girls or boys coming over?"

She shrugged and dropped the mascara into a wax-paper sandwich bag along with her Bonne Bell cherry lip gloss and blue eye shadow. "You don't have to hang with us. Just stay out of the way."

The air grew thicker. "Sephie, you know Mom and Dad wouldn't want boys here."

She unbuttoned her top button as she strolled past me and toward the stairs. "They won't know."

"They will if I tell them."

She whipped around and bunched up my collar in her fist, just like in the movies. "If you tell them," she hissed, "I'll tell the whole world you sleep in the closet, that you won't even leave your room at night because you're afraid of monsters. I'll make sure *Gabriel* knows."

Her unexpected rage jolted me. Of all the people who'd said mean things to me, I'd never expected it from Sephie.

"I don't care who you have over," I said, jerking free and stomping off toward the living room. I made sure she didn't see me wipe my eyes. "They better not bother me when I'm watching TV."

When a car pulled in the driveway, I kept my face trained on the television, not even glancing out the window when the vehicle left a few minutes later. I thought for one excited second that whoever was supposed to come over had changed their mind, but then I heard Sephie opening the door and laughing too loud at some boy's noise. Whoever was here must have been too young to drive. I strained to hear if I could recognize the voice, but the Frankenstein monster was moaning too loud. I situated myself on the recliner so I appeared focused yet casual.

My throat tightened when Wayne and Ricky appeared in the living room entry, their cologne preceding them in a sweet, boggy cloud. They'd dressed themselves up, wearing button-down shirts and jeans even though it'd been a hot day, and our house had gone approximately the temperature of middle earth since we'd used the oven. Wayne had a bruise on his chin, maybe from where I'd accidentally clocked him by the creek. Both boys looked small in my dad's house, out of place.

Ricky spoke first. "Whatcha watching?"

I was prepared to glare at him for making me feel on display in my own house, hyperconscious of everything—the shabbiness of the furniture, how small our television was, my body—but his hunched shoulders told me he was just as uncomfortable as me. "*Young Frankenstein.*"

"I've never seen it," Ricky said.

I let the glare fly. There's stupid and then there's *stupid*.

"Cassie, entertain Ricky, won't you?" Sephie said as she showed up behind the boys, her voice as brittle as her face. "I'm going to show Wayne my room."

"Yes, dear Cassie," Wayne said, copying Sephie's stuffy delivery, "please do entertain our Ricky. He likes to be scratched behind the balls."

Wayne sniggered as Sephie punched him. Ricky had the decency to blush.

"Come on, you burnout," Sephie said, pulling Wayne away. "They're just kids, you know."

"Wayne is only one year older than me!" I hollered, but they weren't listening. Wayne had his arm slunk around Sephie, and she had her hand shoved in his back pants pocket, and I wanted to cry when I thought about what they'd do up in Sephie's room. It's not like I thought she'd still be playing willowacks with me every day. I just wasn't sure when she'd gone from zero to easy.

"Don't think I'll be macking with you," I told Ricky, too mad to even glance his way.

The movie was at the spot where the villagers storm Frankenstein's castle, which gave me an excuse to stare at the television until my pulse calmed down. By the time the scene was over, I'd grown curious. Ricky hadn't uttered a word since he'd sat. I could see him out of the corner of my eye, perched on the edge of Dad's chair, his hands on his knees like he was at church.

"You can relax, you know. I don't bite."

Ricky glanced at his Band-Aids. He reminded me a little bit of Albert, the boy the Ingalls adopted in *Little House on the Prairie*. He was nervous and dimpled and might be cute if he weren't in my living room with his warty fingers.

"Why'd you come, anyhow?"

He lifted one shoulder and then let it drop. "Wayne said it'd be a good time."

"You always do what Wayne says?" I felt big talking to him. Like I could push as far as I wanted. The power surprised me.

That one-shoulder shrug again. "He's my best friend."

I felt myself grow bigger, meaner. "He hardly ever talks to you on the bus. It looks like he and Clam are the ones that are best friends."

Ricky blinked hard at the television.

I dove full in. "Did Clam really get attacked again?"

Ricky jerked back like I'd slapped him, and my sudden shame turned my mouth sour.

He tried to look at me, but his eyes couldn't quite lift that high. "I guess. Most of us boys in the Hollow been chased, at least."

The television went to commercial. The first ad was for Chiffon margarine. Mother Nature sat in a wooded glen, telling a fairy tale to a bear and a raccoon. It was normally one of my favorites, but I didn't have the stomach for it. "What do you mean?"

He looked at me dead on this time. He resembled Albert more than ever.

"It's gross," he warned.

"You don't have to tell me," I said. I meant it. I'd tried mean on for size and didn't like it at all.

He reached over to run his fingers across the paperbacks that filled the living room shelves. "Sure are a lot of books."

I glanced around. I'd grown so used to them that I hardly noticed them anymore. "We're a reading family." I'd heard Dad say that to a grocery checkout lady once. She'd complimented him on how smart I was, reaching over to massage his arm.

Ricky scratched the side of his nose. "We don't have any books in my house."

I hadn't ever been in a house with a library like we had, so him not owning any books didn't surprise me one bit.

"None," he continued. "Not even any my mom read to me when I was a kid. Or my stepmom."

"Your parents are divorced?"

"Yup. My mom left my dad."

I leaned in. "How'd you get her to do that?"

"Huh?"

My heartbeat had slowed. "How'd you get her to leave him?"

He looked at me like I'd just pooped from my ears. "She ran away. I was in third grade. Haven't seen her since."

"Oh." It hadn't occurred to me that a mom would leave her kids, just a dad.

He was massaging one of his Band-Aids like it would release a magic genie. "It happened the same to me as to Clam and some of the other Hollow boys. Clam was by the creek, smoking, when he was caught the first time. Teddy Milchman, too, I think. Me, I couldn't take the yelling in my house anymore and so I ran outside to get away. Some guy grabbed me right by the entrance to the park where we found you and that kid with the nice bike yesterday."

He ducked his eyes. "Sorry about that. We were just having some fun. We wouldn't have hurt you." Something played behind his eyes, and he laughed. "Not like you beat up Clam, anyhow. You got a good crack in on Wayne, too."

I considered asking if Clam was all right but didn't want to seem like I cared. "Who grabbed you?"

Ricky's face went the color of paper. "The guy wore a mask. He grabbed for my pockets. I thought he was trying to rob me, but then he squeezed my johnson. I kicked him as mean as I could, but he just squeezed me harder, rubbing me up against his front. Made some growl noise, and then let me go." Ricky scratched the back of his neck. "I wasn't taken into a car, not like Clam both times or Teddy. They were driven somewhere and dropped off when he was done."

I felt green and wobbly. "Did you tell the police?"

"Naw."

"Why not?"

"You tell me," he said, the first flash of anger I'd seen on him.

My face blazed by way of answer. I could recall Bauer's words at the party verbatim. *Naw, it's just boy shit. They're all trouble, those Hollow boys.* Cops didn't believe kids, not kids from that side of the tracks.

"That's what I thought," he said, reading my expression.

The movie came back on. We watched it for a few minutes before Ricky spoke again. "There's another reason I came out here. Besides being Wayne's friend, I mean."

I flinched. We'd been getting along fine, and now he was gonna muck it up.

"I heard your dad's a welder," he said.

That threw me for a loop. "He was. He makes sculptures now."

Ricky began to make a repetitive gesture with his thumbs and pointer fingers, rubbing them together as if he held a tiny crystal ball between each. "I know. I want to be a welder, though. Do you think he could teach me?"

"You came out here to see if my dad would teach you how to weld?"

"Yeah!" he sat up, more excited than I'd ever seen him. "Art welding or real welding. Anything to help me get into college."

"Have Sephie ask him, then." I had zero interest in explaining to Dad who Ricky was or that he'd been by our house.

"Okay, if you think it'll help." He was watching television again, but I could see a cape of seriousness dropping over his face. "Hey, we all know how Sephie is, but you don't have to be that way."

My words were frosty. "How *is* she?"

"You know."

I did. It made me feel alone. "How long has she been like this?"

Ricky scratched his nose again. "Not very long. Since this winter? But she's mowing through the summer-school boys quick. Pretty much every kid in the Hollow's had a crack at her."

I felt that loneliness again, that deep ache like my heart had gone rotten at its roots. Something thumped against the ceiling overhead, and then giggling. "Does everyone know about her?"

"I dunno. She did her rounds on the top tier before she made it down to us. You know how boys are."

"Not all boys. Not Gabriel." Or Frank, though Ricky wouldn't recognize the name.

Ricky hooted in agreement. "Yeah, Gabriel would never go for your sister."

I felt a cocktail of smugness and shame. I didn't want to talk about Sephie anymore. "What did the guy who grabbed you look like? I mean, other than the mask?"

Ricky's tone was offhand. "It's for sure Connelly."

The air in my lungs froze. "What?"

"Yeah, we're all positive it's Connelly. Chester the Molester is as queer as a three-dollar bill."

I flew to my feet, ready to kick him out of the house. "Even if he is, that doesn't mean he attacks boys!"

Ricky shook his head. "It's not that. It's the metronome he brings with him when he attacks. Teddy and Clam heard it same as me. A clicking like an old clock while he's touching you, the sound just about worse than what he's doing with his hands. Click. Click. Click."

CHAPTER 41

June 1, 1983
Dear Jin:
   Please come visit. I need you.
   Sincerely,
   Cassie

CHAPTER 42

I woke up to a tangerine-cream sky, the smell of buckwheat waffles, and a sitcom family. Wayne and Ricky'd left before midnight, and then Mom and Dad had returned sometime after that but before the sun had risen. Mom had waffles prepared for Sephie and me when we came down. Dad was smiling, drinking his coffee, and making plans. Sephie picked up on the mood right away and free-fell into it, bringing her sweetest self to the table.

Not me. I was hunched over my plate of maple syrup–drenched waffle, suspicious. "Why is everyone in such a good mood?"

Dad laughed and honest-to-god ruffled my hair. "Guess your mom and I needed a vacation, Cass. You girls good while we were away?"

I shoved a forkful into my mouth and glared at wide-eyed Sephie. Her silence pleaded with me to keep the peace. She spoke before I could. "We finished all our chores. I made sure I was at class on time yesterday and stayed until the end."

Mom beamed. "That's wonderful! Your dad can drive you in today." She looked like she'd lost at least five bad years on that trip. Grudgingly, I lightened up a fraction.

"I got my chores done, too."

"How are your kitties doing?" Dad asked. He never asked about my kitty clinics.

"Good," I said, reaching across the table to grab the glass jug of milk. "Meander had her kittens somewhere, but I haven't found them yet. Bimbo has another eye infection, but I rinsed it out with eyebright tea."

"That's my girl," Dad said, and I sat taller. "How're your grades, Sephie?"

"In summer school?" Her fork was halfway to her mouth. "Umm, I don't know. I could probably study harder."

"I'll help!" I offered. It was a reflex.

"Thanks," Sephie said, her gratitude genuine.

I smiled back. With her sleep-fuzzed hair and happy eyes, she resembled my sister again. Maybe she hadn't become as awful as I'd thought. I dug into my food with new energy. The home-tapped syrup wasn't nearly as good as the Log Cabin they served on pancake day at school, but it was better than dry old eggs by a mile.

"I'm thinking of for sure getting a summer job, too," Sephie said tentatively. "To save up for college."

Dad nodded agreeably. "That's a wonderful idea. Peg, what do you think?"

Mom seemed to be rolling the idea around. "Where would you work?"

Sephie wiped at a drip of syrup on her chin. "I haven't decided. Maybe waitressing?"

"We can pick up applications when I bring you into school," Dad offered.

It felt like the whole house was floating on bubbles. Things were fine. Better than fine! Something good had happened on Mom and Dad's vacation, and it had shifted them, shifted the whole world. Maybe they'd attended an exorcism. I didn't care, as long as it kept up.

It wasn't the first good time we'd had. Whenever we traveled, packing up the chuggy old VW van, Dad grew happy, and when he was in good spirits, life was the best. Maybe this time he'd hold on to his joy permanently, a jar of fireflies that he could keep alive forever.

I didn't even mind that Sephie and him got ready for town while Mom and I had to slip on our cruddy work clothes and head to the garden. I normally hated working outside before the dew was burned off. Wet shoes were the worst, and the weeds and dirt stuck to my fingers and worked their way under my nails. But this foggy, muggy morning, Mom was humming, and I would get to spend the day with her.

"I made party invitations yesterday."

She cocked her head like she wasn't sure what I was talking about at first. "Oh, that's right! Your birthday is tomorrow. What kind of cake do you want?"

"Devil's food with chocolate frosting. And vanilla ice cream on the side." I was pushing it, but on our birthday, we were allowed.

Mom laughed. It sounded like a calliope. "I can manage that. How many kids will be coming?"

"I invited three."

She smiled, and I could have snuggled under that love like a blanket. For the first time in a long time, I felt like my life had hope. I had a best friend. I'd stood up for myself at the river. My family was being relatively normal.

The harsh shrill of our telephone disrupted the air. Both Mom and I paused, but then continued.

"Did you make the invitations for a lunchtime party?"

"Yep," I said. "How much weeding do we have to do today?"

Mom laughed again, but it was dryer than the previous laugh. "All of it."

I was going to whine about Sephie not having to help, but I didn't want to wreck the magic fizz we were floating in. A car rumbled in the distance. A red-winged blackbird trilled from the direction of Goblin's house. Red-winged blackbirds loved swampy land.

Mom moved over a row and clapped her hands. "Look at all this lovely spinach! We can eat it for supper. That and fried chicken. You won't mind having it again? I've been craving it ever since we butchered."

"Peg."

I hadn't heard Dad come up behind us. Mom must not have, either, because she whipped around, holding her garden spade out like a weapon. "Donny. What is it?"

At first, I thought he was standing in a shimmer of the fog hugging the low spots this early in the morning, but then I realized he was all-over white.

"Donny?" Mom repeated, dropping her spade to rush to him. She placed her hand on his chest, and when he didn't respond, she wove her arms around his waist. "What happened?"

He didn't return her embrace. "Another boy's been abducted, but this time, he hasn't been brought back."

I felt a cramp in my belly, like maybe I'd finally gotten my period. "Who?"

Dad didn't look at me, just stared a thousand miles away over Mom's shoulder. She pulled back. "Who was it, Donny?"

"Gabriel Wellstone. The dentist's son."

My blood turned to sludge.

If Gabriel had been kidnapped, it was my fault.

My fault.

I'd let down my guard this morning. I'd been powerfully selfish, forgetting everything Ricky had told me last night, that kids were still getting attacked out there. My family had acted normal for a few hours this morning, they'd offered a tiny slice of okay, and I'd let myself care about nothing else.

Dad sounded as far away as I felt. "That was Bauer on the phone. He said they arrested the band teacher. Connelly."

Nononono. I ran toward my bike. I couldn't breathe, couldn't see, couldn't feel. I was a nerve in motion. I grabbed the backpack that hung off my handlebar and tossed it over my shoulder.

"Cassie!" Mom hollered, but she didn't try to stop me.

I took off toward Sergeant Bauer's house, pedaling so fast that the road argued below my tires. Bauer needed to know what only a kid could see: it wasn't the Hollow connecting all the hurt boys.

It was that they all rode bus twenty-four.

CHAPTER 43

My brain raced after my body, churning to catch up. I couldn't slow down for it, though. I tore around the corner past Goblin's, then by Frank's place, careening down Sergeant Bauer's road.

I had to tell him about the bus route.

Once he knew, he could find Gabriel and bring him home. The sun was warming the treetops when I skidded into Bauer's driveway.

"Sergeant Bauer!" I yelled, biking toward his house. "Are you home?"

I hopped off the bike with the wheels still spinning and raced to his screen door, pounding its wooden edge with both fists. The police car was parked in his driveway. He must have had the day off, or he had worked the night shift. I yanked open the screen door and stepped into his sunporch to wallop directly on his front door.

When there was no answer, I put my hands on each side of my face and peered in, hollering for him. His kitchen was directly off the porch. At the rear of his kitchen was an open door, its black pitch telling me it led to his basement. Every cell in my body was sure it was a dirt basement, wet and smelly, exactly like the one underneath my own house, just like Frank had guessed.

"Hey, little girl with the forever necklace."

I jumped so high that I left my skin behind. Sergeant Bauer had been sitting on the screened-in porch all along, hadn't reacted when I'd pounded on one door, then the other, hadn't moved from behind the unpacked boxes stacked nearly to its ceiling. He lumbered toward me, slowly, navigating the boxes but with something more, something invisible, weighing him down. I backed out of his porch, through the creaking screen door, stumbling down his front steps toward my bike.

He followed me outside, stepping off his porch as the sun hit his yard. He looked a hundred years older than he had when Frank and I'd been here selling popcorn. His jowls were bristled, his skin gray as old deli meat.

"Your dad send you over?" he asked. His voice sounded like it'd spent the night in a rock tumbler. "He say I called?"

"I came by myself." I backed up all the way to my bike.

"You know, that stuff we do at your place, it's totally legal. Grown-up stuff, that's all." He was slurring his words. "No need to tell anyone about that."

"I know." I was aware of every hair on my body.

"Even if you told anyone, they wouldn't believe you, not since you stole that Cawl girl's lipstick. No one trusts a thief."

I nodded. I was panting.

"Your dad tell you about Gabriel, yeah?" He rubbed his protruding belly. His shabby button-front shirt was completely open. "They've brought in the big boys now. Gonna take over my town, rip it apart piece by piece now that it's a rich kid who's been taken. Ride in on their high horses and tell us everything we're doing wrong."

I cleared my throat. "I need to tell you something, Sergeant Bauer."

I pitched my voice loud enough to carry across the driveway even though my heart was beating so rapid-fire that I thought it'd turn into a hummingbird and fly out of my mouth. "All three boys who were attacked ride my bus. Clam, Teddy, and now Gabriel. Plus some of the other Hollow boys who were molested but didn't tell anyone. They all ride bus twenty-four."

Sergeant Bauer covered his eyes, almost like he wanted to play hide-and-seek, and then ran his hand over the top of his head. "I know."

The floor fell out of my stomach. "What're you gonna do about it?"

"I'm gonna do my goddamned job, that's what I'm gonna do, as long as that's okay with you, Ms. Priss." He abruptly raised his hand and stamped his foot like he was shooing a mangy mutt out of his yard. The motion pulled out the dog tags from the open front of his shirt, and they clicked against each other. "Now git, you little lipstick-stealing thief!"

The sound of his dog tags made me so scared I saw stars.

Because I suddenly knew who was attacking the boys and why he'd gotten away with it for so long, just as sure as I knew that Bauer hadn't told anyone about all the victims riding bus twenty-four.

Ricky had good as told me when he described the sound Chester the Molester made when he was attacking: *a clicking like an old clock while he's touching you, the sound just about worse than what he's doing with his hands.*

Click. Click. Click.

CHAPTER 44

I lunged for my handlebar grips, righted my bike, and sped down the driveway, my head full of swarming bees. I didn't look behind me as I biked away. I wouldn't give Bauer the satisfaction. I cruised past Goblin's, sticking to the north side rather than heading toward my house. Goblin's dog was still nowhere in sight. I thought it likely my dad had murdered him.

I didn't have a destination in mind.

I was killing time to give Bauer a chance to leave.

Because I now knew he was the one molesting boys, had known it the second his dog tags had escaped his open shirt and made their metal noise at me.

Last night, Ricky's words had itched something in the back of my head, but I knew what it was for sure now that I'd heard that sound on Bauer. It was the same sound I'd heard when I caught him thrusting over Kristi at Dad's party.

His dog tags.

Click click, click click, as he did his bad thing.

I waited ten minutes before turning around to bike back to Bauer's. I'd hide in the ditch if I saw him coming out, but I didn't need to worry. The police car was gone from his yard. He couldn't have gone into work in the condition he was in. Could he? I wanted to peek in his windows but was too scared. His house seemed to be watching me, all except for the basement windows, which had been blindfolded by something that resembled tinfoil.

The sun began to crisp the back of my neck, so I pedaled toward a drainage ditch. I tipped my bike on the gravel road and slid down the embankment to sit on the metal mouth of the drainage tube, dipping my feet into the tepid water. Pin-legged water bugs skated across the surface. A mud turtle sunned itself in a mossy spot. When I judged it to be near twelve, I stood, scaring the turtle *plop* into the water.

Gabriel had been kidnapped.

The sweetest boy I'd ever met.

I tried not to feed that idea even though it was blobby and starving. Gabriel must be so scared. He was probably crying for his mom, and no one could hear him. I knew I would be. I climbed back to the road and took off on my bike toward Lilydale.

I was a mile out when I spotted my first army truck, followed by state police vehicles. When I hit town, I saw a poster stapled to the electric pole near the Mobil gas station. Gabriel's face smiled at me. MISSING. I turned away. A second one appeared just up the street in front of the Ben Franklin. MISSING.

The Farmers and Suppliers State Bank sign blinked its message:

BRING GABRIEL HOME. CANDLELIT VIGIL TONIGHT AT 7:00 P.M.

I braked in front of that sign. I'd tried to keep moving, but I couldn't escape the despair any longer. It landed on my shoulders like a strong-clawed buzzard. That's when I noticed there were no kids on the street, only adults shuffling like zombies. I needed to find Mr. Connelly and tell him about Bauer. No one else would believe me, but Connelly might.

I spotted the picketers before I ever saw his house.

I didn't recognize any of the people. Their signs were angry, scary.

FREE GABRIEL. GOD HATES SINNERS.

They were pacing in front of Mr. Connelly's home, back and forth, back and forth, six of them, all of them older. Watching them hate on someone they didn't even know made me angry. I took off toward Van der Queen Park, flicking the bird at the picketers.

I found Evie swinging, same place I'd seen her last time I biked past. I jerked my handlebars so I could jump the curb, pedaling through the grass to reach the playground equipment.

"Hey, Evie," I called so I wouldn't surprise her.

She turned, her face calm, like she'd been expecting me. "Hey."

I swung a leg over my seat so I balanced on one side while I coasted toward her. When I reached her, I dropped my bike into the pea rock and fell into the swing next to her. "You heard about Gabriel?" I asked.

Evie spread her hands to indicate the park, her fox nose and sharp little teeth glinting in the sun. "Everyone has."

"They know who's hurting the boys?" A quiver had snuck into my voice.

Evie launched her legs in front of her to begin swinging again. "Not who, but they do know where. All the boys got attacked near the swimming hole at the creek. The police asked around and found that a black car has been there a lot, but then they found out that so has a blue car and a green car and a silver car. The boys don't know anything except they think it's Mr. Connelly."

Acid burned the back of my throat. "Did he confess?"

She shrugged. "Your guess is as good as mine."

"I don't think he did it." I started to pump my legs to get my swing to move, my voice tentative. "I have an idea of who might have."

Evie didn't seem impressed. She pumped harder. Her words caught up to me when our swings passed. "Then you should go to the police."

I thought of Bauer, his words slurred. *Even if you told anyone, they wouldn't believe you, not since you stole that Cawl girl's lipstick. No one trusts a thief.* "They won't care."

Evie was swinging so high she looked like she could taste the sun. At her peak, she was nearly level with the top of the slide. "Then you'll have to do it on your own," she called out. "That's how it is with anything important."

She leaped off the swing, soaring with her back arched. She hit the ground like a cat and walked toward a blue duffel bag near where she'd landed.

"What do you have in there?"

"Dolls," she said. "Want to play?"

I stopped pumping so I could see better.

"I'm too old to play with dolls," I said.

"If you say so." Evie pulled out a Cabbage Patch doll, a Raggedy Ann and Andy, and four Barbie doll knockoffs that had seen better days. Then she tugged out a plastic carrying case and snapped it open to reveal all sorts of tiny outfits, including go-go boots and heels.

I flew off my own swing and stepped closer.

I dropped to the ground next to her. "Can I dress up the one with brown hair?"

"Sure." She handed her over.

We played with those dolls for over an hour. It seemed like a baby thing to do, but I couldn't get enough of it.

"Does your mom let you play out here all day?" I asked.

Evie pointed toward a tan-colored house in the middle of a street of ramblers hugging the park. "She watches from the window."

I couldn't believe I'd ever thought Evie was fox-faced. Sure, she had a pointy nose and sharp little teeth, but there were worse things.

"Hey," I said, digging into my backpack. I found the invitation I'd made for Frank and yanked it out of its envelope so it didn't have another kid's name on it. I handed it to Evie. "I'm having a birthday party. Do you want to come?"

Evie glanced at the invitation. "Thanks, but no."

She didn't use any excuses, just said it simple and straight, handing my humiliation right back to me, thanks but no thanks. It took me a minute to figure out what to do with that. I finally swallowed it. "Well, if you change your mind, it's noon tomorrow at the Lake Corona Community Park." I didn't know if that was true, if we'd still get to have parties now that the army was here and Gabriel was gone. "There'll be lunch and cake and swimming."

"Thanks," she said again. She wasn't going to come.

"I better be going."

"Okay," Evie said. She didn't look up from her playing.

I slung my backpack over my shoulder and hopped back on my bike. I didn't realize I was returning to Connelly's house until I was in front of it. The picketers had left. I biked right up to his door and knocked. I had no plans what to say because I figured he wasn't home. I almost fell off my seat when he answered.

"Mr. Connelly!"

He looked like he hadn't eaten, slept, or shaved since Frank and I had visited.

He stared at me like he didn't recognize me, then looked over my shoulder, right and left. "You shouldn't be here."

His vacant gaze scared me. I lost my nerve to tell him about Bauer, at least right away. I'd need to work up to it. "I wanted to let you know how my popcorn sales are going."

A flare like annoyance crossed his face. "You shouldn't be seen with me. I'm a dangerous man. Haven't you heard?"

"I saw Clam here the other night," I said, stared down at my feet. And that's when I realized why I'd biked here. I needed Connelly to tell me that my eyes had deceived me, that of course he hadn't invited Clam into his kitchen, not when all this horror was happening to Lilydale boys.

"I hired him to do yard work," Connelly said, his voice brittle. Then he closed the door in my face.

I biked home, something hard settling in me.

CHAPTER 45

I'd gone to bed a kid, but I woke up a teenager.

An honest-to-god thirteen-year-old. I felt different, I was sure of it. The sun was shining, the birds were chirping, and I could almost pretend that the world wasn't collapsing around me, could almost stay ahead of the gray dread that nipped at my heels. I got to eat cornflakes, milk, and bananas for breakfast. Name-brand cornflakes Mom had bought special for me.

I played with the cats until it was time to leave.

"Ready for your birthday?" Mom asked when I found her loading up the van.

"I was born ready for my birthday."

Mom didn't laugh at the joke. I don't think she got it, or maybe there wasn't much worth laughing about today. She'd made the cake and bought the ice cream, though, plus the Kellogg's Corn Flakes, sliced ham and cheese, white bread, mustard, and potato chips. The perishables were on ice in a cooler that she shoved in the back of the van.

Sephie was at summer school. Dad wasn't around, not that I'd seen. It was only Mom and me in that van, heading toward Lake Corona early.

"Tell me again how many people you invited," Mom asked.

"Three."

She flipped down the van's visor to shield her face from the sun. "Nice day for it."

"Thanks for having it."

She nodded. Her hair was tied in a ponytail, and she was wearing coral-colored shorts and a matching shirt that she'd sewn herself. Her one pair of sandals didn't match the summer set, but they were in good shape. Lynn and her mom probably wouldn't even notice.

She flicked me a look. "What are you staring at?"

"Nothing. You look nice." I brushed imaginary dirt off my knees. She'd never noticed that I'd shaved. She also hadn't asked about my bike ride yesterday, and I hadn't offered. "What was Rammy Bauer like when he was younger?"

She looked over at me again, sharper this time. "You mean Mr. Bauer?"

"Goblin called him Rammy."

She frowned. I saw new lines carved between her eyebrows and alongside her mouth. "He was fine. Well, nice enough."

"Why did you two break up?"

Mom brushed a lock of hair behind her ear. "It was a high school thing. Not meant to last. Your dad's always been the man for me."

"Did Mr. Bauer get into trouble in high school?"

She chuckled at this. It was a papery sound. "I suppose he did. Fights and the like. But everyone deserves a second chance, don't you think?"

"Everyone?"

"Sure. Take our new neighbors." She leaned her head toward Frank's house as we passed. "Mr. Gomez went to jail."

"No way."

"Yep. Aramis told us, but he won't say what for."

"Mom, I think Mr. Bauer—"

"Is upset about the boys getting hurt? I'm sure he is. And he's doing everything in his power to find Gabriel."

I watched the hillocks roll past, my scar tightening like a rope at my throat. The gravel gave way to tar. Mom wasn't going to listen to me about Sergeant Bauer. I opened my mouth to make my case, but a whole different set of words tumbled out. "I'm afraid of Dad."

The car jerked forward as her foot spasmed against the gas. "You and your imagination. Stop being so dramatic."

My heart was about crashing out of my chest. I pressed my lips together. I was going to get this out, finally. "He always says gross stuff."

Her hands tightened on the wheel. "Not this again."

She wasn't hearing me, had never been able to hear me, but I desperately hoped that if I ordered the words exactly right, like I had the nights my writing stopped Dad from coming up the stairs, I could make her understand. "Why do we have to live with him?"

"I told you. I love him. He's a good husband."

I shook my head. "No, he isn't."

"There's so much you don't know."

I looked out the window again. Cabins were zooming past. The park was just ahead. I supposed there *was* a lot I didn't know. For starters, I didn't know what to do with the hot little rock that settled in my belly every time Mom shut me up like that. I didn't know what to do with a dad who hunted me and Sephie. I didn't know what to do with my fear that he was now helping Sergeant Bauer stalk boys, or at least looking the other way as Sergeant Bauer did.

"Hey, is that Lynn's vehicle?" Mom pointed toward the far end of the parking lot we'd pulled into. "They're here early!"

She eased the van next to the silver sedan, and we both got out. We balanced the dry goods on top of the cooler and lugged the heavy blue-and-white box between us down the hill and toward the public picnic tables. Lynn and her mom had already saved us the best one, the one under the oak tree. I couldn't let go of the cooler to wave, but I hollered as soon as we were close. "Hi, Lynn!"

She glanced at her mom and then me. Her mom said something to her, and then Lynn ran up to us. "Let me help you with that."

"Thank you," Mom said. Her expression was strained.

"Angie," she said when we reached the picnic table, "how are you?"

"I'm well, thank you. And you?" Mrs. Strahan wore a white sundress with blue trim and three gold buttons on each shoulder. Her white sandals matched perfectly.

"I'm well," Mom said.

They began unpacking, making small talk. It was stilted at first, but as Lynn and I walked toward the playground, I saw Mom begin to relax. Maybe that's how I'd get her to leave Dad. She'd see how nice it could be to hang out with normal people.

"You want to go swimming?" I asked Lynn. "Or should we wait until Barb and Heidi get here?"

Lynn tossed me an *are you for real* look. "I don't think Heidi or Barb are coming."

I planted a fake smile on my face. "It *was* short notice."

"It's not that," Lynn said. "Didn't you hear Gabriel is missing?"

"Yeah," I said.

"You should have canceled your party. That's what my mom said."

I was suddenly so angry that I could kick a tree. "Why'd you come?"

Lynn shrugged and hopped on the merry-go-round. "Because you came to mine."

We played some more, quietly, doing stupid toddler stuff like swinging and sliding, our mood gloomy. If you could hold a funeral on a pea rock playground, that's what this felt like.

"If we're not going to swim, we might as well eat," I finally said.

"Okay."

We began trudging back toward the picnic table. There was so much food. It'd be embarrassing to eat with only four of us. I was trying to figure out a way to escape my own birthday party when I spotted a car that looked like Heidi's drive up. Heidi's mom stepped out and jogged down the hill toward the picnic table. Her face was all wound up, like sweatpants after they'd gotten their string caught in the dryer wheel.

"Heidi came after all!" I said, exulted. But the excitement died because Heidi was nowhere to be seen, and since when do moms run? Lynn and I reached the picnic table at the same time as Heidi's mom.

"They caught him!" Heidi's mom cried, winded. "They caught the man who took Gabriel!"

I skidded to a stop, my heart soaring. *Gabriel!*

Mom and Mrs. Strahan jumped to their feet. Mrs. Strahan spoke. "The molester? They caught him? Did they find Gabriel? Is he alive?"

Heidi's mom was leaning over at the waist, her right hand pressed into the bare skin above her knee, her left waving in the air to let us know she needed to catch her breath. "They caught the pervert staring in Becky Anderson's backyard window, and they think he's the same man who took Gabriel."

"Who was it?" Mom asked.

"Arnold Fierro."

Mom grabbed the side of the picnic table. Mrs. Strahan had to help her sit down.

"The Shaklee salesman?" Mrs. Strahan asked, fanning Mom.

"That's the one. He claimed he was stopping by on a sales call, but he was caught with his face up against that poor girl's window, his hand in his pants."

Lynn and I exchanged a look. The Peeping Tom!

"What about Gabriel?" Mrs. Strahan repeated, asking the question that was on all our minds.

"No word on him, but it's only a matter of time. They're questioning Arnold at the police station as we speak."

I should have been elated, and I was glad, believe you me.

Only my gut was telling me the police had the wrong guy, at least when it came to who was attacking the boys. I didn't know Arnold Fierro, but he for sure wasn't Sergeant Bauer.

But I ate my birthday cake, and I opened my one present—my very own Magic 8 Ball, still new and in the box—and I helped Mom pack up, and I wondered why I felt so uneasy when I should probably be happy. Mom talked a mile a minute on the ride home, and she never did that. She was so relieved.

I wondered if she'd worried, like me, that Sergeant Bauer had been the one molesting boys, along with Dad's help.

I nodded at everything she said.

I didn't tell her it was all wrong, Gabriel wasn't safe, the predator was still out there, even when we drove past our mailbox, crested the rise in our yard, and spotted the police cruiser snug in our driveway.

CHAPTER 46

I didn't recognize the officer talking to Sephie and Dad. His car said STATE TROOPER. Dad had his arm around Sephie, the picture of a protective father.

"There they are!" Sephie pointed toward me and Mom as we got out of the van, unnecessarily, I thought.

I stopped shy of the police car, on high alert. The officer held his hand out to me. "Hello. I'm Officer Kent. You're Peggy and Cassandra?"

I didn't take his hand, but Mom did.

"Is this about Gabriel?" The words thudded against my teeth.

The officer glanced warily at Dad. "In a way."

"He wants to know what we know about Mr. Godlin," Dad said.

Officer Kent tried not to look at my neck scar while he talked. "As I was just telling your father and sister, we're checking out any leads we have in the disappearance of Gabriel Wellstone. Gary Godlin is a person of interest. Have any of you seen anything unusual happening over there?"

"But you caught the man who took Gabriel," I said, feeling like a big, dumb vegetable, like saying it would make it true even though I knew it wasn't. "We heard it at the park. The molester was peeking in Becky Anderson's window."

"Arnold Fierro," Mom confirmed, slipping Dad a strange look.

Officer Kent stood up straighter, his hand resting casually on his weapon. "We have made an arrest. Just being thorough. Can you offer any information on Mr. Godlin? Has he had people over that you know of? Any unusual sounds coming from his property?"

"He doesn't have anyone over," I said.

The officer nodded encouragingly.

"He always scared me," Sephie offered.

The officer chuckled grimly. "I'm afraid that's not probable cause to search his house a second time."

Words and images spun in my brain. The Peeping Tom had been arrested. Gabriel was still missing. Sergeant Bauer's dog tags had made that noise, but the police thought Goblin was connected. Bauer's words at the party came back to me: *You know Goblin's stepdad used to rape him like it was a hobby, like it was softball or some shit that he had to do every Tuesday and Thursday?*

"What's 'probable cause' mean, exactly?" I asked.

"The police have to have a good reason to enter your house," Dad said, his voice frosty. It sounded like a warning, but I didn't know if it was directed at me or the officer. "They can't harass you."

"That's right. If you've seen anything suspicious at all, that might help."

I wanted to cry out. If you think it's Goblin, go look *golookgolookgolook.*

And then go to Sergeant Bauer's house.

I cleared my throat, making room for the only words I could form. "If you'd met Gabriel, you wouldn't stop until you found him. If you knew him, you'd look inside every house in Stearns County. He's someone important."

The officer removed his hat. He looked serious. "I have a son Gabriel's age."

That glimpse of kindness almost convinced me to talk, to spill everything I knew, about all the boys being on my bus route, that the bus went right by where Bauer was staying, that the attacks must have started about the same time Bauer was kicked out of his own house, Bauer, whose dog tags made that clicking sound when he was excited, that same sound that Ricky said the man who attacked them made. I was even going to tell him about Dad and how our situation wasn't urgent like Gabriel's, but if they had extra time, could they see if my dad was helping Bauer to do something with boys and basements and also please save me and Sephie before my dad came up those stairs?

I opened my mouth.

Officer Kent raised an eyebrow. *I'll listen,* it said.

Dad and Mom both tensed.

The words were there on the edge of my lips, bitter pills that I was desperate to spit out, but I couldn't. I snapped my mouth shut. It wouldn't be any use. Bauer had told me the police already knew all the boys were on my bus route. Bauer *was* the police. Besides, Dad had told me and Sephie a hundred times that the worst thing we could do was tell. I swallowed all that like a mouthful of poison, my eyes on my feet.

Officer Kent was probably watching me, I didn't know. I couldn't peel my stare off the ground until he spoke.

"Call if you see anything," he finally said. I looked up, and our eyes connected. "If we get so much as a peep, we can go in and look for your friend."

Dad stepped in front of me, reaching for the card Officer Kent was offering. I saw he'd been holding Sephie so tight that he'd left finger marks on her bare shoulder.

The officer's eyes lingered on me a moment, and then he slid into his cruiser and drove away.

CHAPTER 47

Dad started drinking as soon as the officer drove away, his mood black as tar. I wanted to scream at him, tell him he had no right to take up all the attention, every minute of every day of my life, that other people had feelings and worries and needs, too, thank you very much.

But I didn't say a word.

I found Mom in the kitchen, poring through her cookbooks. My muscles were shivery, my skin too tight. I wanted so bad to not think anymore. It was too early to go to sleep. "I'm going to my room to read."

"I need help with supper."

It was four in the afternoon. "Now?"

"Yep. Get Sephie."

"Can't we have leftovers? We hardly ate any of the food at my party."

Her lips thinned. "You've earned yourself an extra chore for talking back. Go pick eggs."

I almost reminded her it was my birthday. *Almost.* "All right."

I sent Sephie to the kitchen before stomping outside. The sun was too bright, the cicadas too loud, the air too humid. Inside the chicken coop, the burring hens irritated me. I gathered four warm brown eggs. As soon as I held them, I knew I wanted nothing more than to pitch them at the side of Dad's studio.

I walked down the hill, glancing back at the house only once. Dad would have his butt in his chair for the rest of the day. Me, Mom, and Seph would wait on him, bringing him dinner, cleaning up after him, even though he hardly brought in any money. We'd squash down our own feelings and experiences to create the maximum amount of space for his stories of how terrible his life was.

We'd do it today, we'd do it tomorrow, we'd do it forever.

I muttered a swear word as I chucked each of those four eggs at the back side (I wasn't stupid) of the studio, one cracked egg for each cracked person in this family. Their mucousy orange slid down the side of the studio. I drew a hitched breath and wiped my face.

Happy birthday, Cassie.

I was headed back toward the house when I decided to step into the granary. I hadn't been inside since I'd run into Sergeant Bauer there at the party. He'd seemed very familiar with the layout. I yanked open the front door. The three-headed dog drawing was still up on the chalkboard.

I crawled up the steep wooden stairs to the bed that had looked slept in.

It still did. *Penthouse* and *Easyriders* magazines lay on the table next to it, along with an ashtray full of roaches and a single slip of paper. The information written on it was organized into three columns: first names on the far left, numbers and ounces in the middle, and dollar amounts in the far right. Some of the dollar amounts had a line through them, some didn't. The first names matched up with some of the party regulars. Dad must have been selling them weed or shrooms, except the handwriting on the sheet wasn't his.

I shoved the paper into my back pocket and shambled to the house.

CHAPTER 48

"I'm going to work," Mom declared after supper.

Dad was too lit to argue.

"I thought all your grading was in," I asked.

"Of course it is," Mom said absentmindedly. "But I forgot to bring my plants home for the summer."

Sephie and I both glanced out the window. The sun was low in the sky, turning the air lavender. It was unusual for Mom to go to work at this time, but she had keys.

"When will you be back?" Sephie asked.

"Late," Mom said, kissing the top of Dad's head. He pulled her in for a mouth kiss. Her shoulders tensed up like chicken wings, but she let him finish before grabbing her purse and heading out.

It took Dad another hour to slip into pass-out drunk, lying back against his recliner, mouth open, spit glistening on his bottom lip. That left me in control of the television. *The Empire Strikes Back* was showing. It'd be my first chance to see it. Every single kid in the world but me and Sephie had viewed it at the movie theater three years ago. I'd had to pretend I knew what they were referring to when they made *pewpew* noises and talked about the dark side.

"I'll make popcorn," I told Sephie when she appeared. She'd been in her room or on the phone since Mom had left.

"I'm going out."

"What?" I tore my eyes off the television. Sephie's hair was curled as pretty as Farrah Fawcett's. I could see the outline of her nipples through her tight T-shirt. "Who with?"

"Wayne and Chaco."

"Did Dad say it was okay?"

She grimaced at him. "I'll be back before he wakes up."

"What about Mom?" I was frantic. I didn't want to be alone in the house with Dad.

"I'll sneak back in. She won't even know I left."

"Sephie, please," I begged.

She frowned at me like she was thinking about it, but then headlights flashed off the wall. "It'll be okay, Cassie. Go to bed early. He won't bother you."

I watched her go, my mouth hanging open. The NBC Friday Night at the Movies opener appeared on the screen, all fireworks and snappy music. The peacock flashed its pretty feathers above a golden "NBC." I glanced at Dad. The spit was beginning to dry.

"Tonight, on NBC Friday Night at the Movies . . ."

The words thrilled me. I returned my attention to the television. I was going to get to watch *The Empire Strikes Back*! Either Mom or Sephie would get home before Dad woke up. If they didn't, I'd just do what Sephie said and go to bed early.

I tamped down the clammy twisting in my belly.

Everything would be fine.

CHAPTER 49

I was sitting so far forward on the couch that a feather would have knocked me off. Luke and Darth Vader were battling in the bowels of Cloud City, their lightsabers crashing and screaming against each other, Luke's blue dragging up underneath Vader's red. It was the best thing I'd ever seen in my life, the whole movie.

"That's not real fighting."

I swallowed hard. My eyes were hot from going too long without blinking. I didn't want to tear my attention away from the screen, but Dad wouldn't be ignored. "It's *The Empire Strikes Back*, Dad. I think you'd like it."

"I don't *like* fighting, Cassie. I had to kill men when I fought. It's not play. Do you know that?"

I braved a glance. He hadn't moved, hadn't even licked the crusty white spit off his mouth. Only his eyes were open, hunting on me. "I know, Dad. Real fighting isn't fun."

His laugh was ugly. "Not in Vietnam, it's not."

Dad's drunk had stages. One of the worst was when he talked about his parents, the same story over and over again. He blamed his mother for him getting drafted. Sometimes after that he'd sink lower, talking about getting beaten by his stepdad, purple bruises that his stepdad would keep punching until Dad's skin split, but only sometimes would he go that dark. And even more rarely, he'd skid into a monologue about how he was magic and could control the wind and the rain and make animals understand him.

We were past all those stages of drunk.

I glanced back at the screen. Vader was sawing at Luke, forcing him backward down an impossibly tiny catwalk leading to an emergency platform. Dad had woken up mean. I knew I should go to bed.

"Do you want to watch this movie with me?" I asked. "Everyone has seen it."

My eyes flicked in his direction. He'd finally licked his lip but caught only part of the white crust.

"Do you think you're a woman yet?" he asked.

I stood.

He sat up, his tone gone wheedling. "Now, sit down. I didn't mean anything. I was just wondering when you'd gotten so uppity, telling me what to do."

"I'm tired, Dad. I'm going to bed." I shot one last mournful gaze at the television. Luke was cornered. There was no way out.

I walked away. My legs were stiff.

I paused at the bottom of the stairs, listening.

I heard a creak, the sound of Dad closing his recliner. My throat sealed up.

I had an impulse to run out the front door, but the stairs were closer. I dashed up them, whipping open my bedroom door and slamming it closed, leaning all my weight against it.

When I heard the bottom step complain under his weight, I moaned. I should have gone with Mom, should have forced Sephie not to leave me alone, even if it meant I had to ride in the back of a car with a stranger. Dad was going to get me, *he was finally going to get me*, and it wouldn't work to hide under my mattress or in my closet. My eyes darted around my room. I had a bed, a dresser, and homemade bookshelves.

The dresser was the only object I could move.

The second stair creaked, tentatively.

"Cassie, I'll watch the show with you," he called up, his voice low.

Gabriel was a boy who would have yelled at my dad. He was the only one. Except Frank. And maybe Mr. Connelly. Plus Aunt Jin would for sure rescue me. But the last three weren't here, and Gabriel was gone forever; I'd known it the minute my dad said he'd been kidnapped and not returned. No one was going to save me. The movies and the books and the shows were all pretend. Sometimes, maybe lots of times, kids got hurt really bad, and that's all there was. The terror-shock of the truth hit me like a slap, burning and freezing at the same time.

Dad stepped on the third stair, and then the fourth, and then the fifth, spider-quick. A rope tightened around my lungs. I rushed to the far side of the dresser, wedging myself between it and the wall. I brought my knees to my chest and pushed quietly, steadily. If he heard me moving the dresser, he would hurry to my door.

I'd been quiet, but I must have made enough noise that I didn't hear him take those last few steps, didn't know he stood on the landing until I heard its characteristic whine. My heartbeat shredded my rib cage. The dresser gave way, shrieking the last six inches across the floor. I leaned against it, trying to modulate my breath.

I needed to say something, to acknowledge the dresser's screech. "I'm tired. I want to sleep."

Dad's voice was just outside my door. "You don't want to watch TV with your dad?"

I bit down on my scream, my stomach thumping at the back of my mouth. Mom could drive up any moment. Or Sephie. Or maybe the dresser in front of the door would keep him out. I was panting like a scared dog. I tried to take sips of air, but that only elevated the panic. I glanced at the grate in my floor. I couldn't fit down it, no way. I was about to make for the window, to rip the screen away and leap off the roof, when I heard a shuffling on the other side of the door.

"Well, I guess I'll go watch it alone." Almost a whisper, but just loud enough that I could hear.

I heard him shuffle down the stairs.

I slid to the floor.

Eventually, I fell asleep. I may have remained in that spot until sunrise if the weeping hadn't woken me.

CHAPTER 50

The crying was soft.

So soft.

A lost child's cry. It had woven through my dreams, convincing me my own baby needed saving, waking my brain before my body. I didn't move a muscle, trying to orient myself to the strange familiar sound. I was jammed between my dresser and my shelves. The house was dead silent but for the crying. My digital clock radio told me I'd been asleep for no more than twenty minutes. Were Mom or Sephie home?

My ears strained as far as they could, disoriented. Was it Gabriel weeping? I stood, giving the pins and needles in both legs time to back off. I could stay in my room, safe, or I could sneak out and see who was crying. But what if it was a trick? What if Dad was on the other side of the doorway, waiting?

The weeping sounded like it was coming from the kitchen, though. I tiptoed to the hole in my floor and knelt.

Not the kitchen.

The sound was emanating from the pantry.

Or the basement.

My guts turned to jellymeat.

I counted backward from ten. I knew I couldn't remain in my room. I was just hoping something would stop me from leaving. When nothing did, I got to my feet again, my knees groaning, and pushed the dresser back more quietly than it had originally moved. My doorknob protested when I turned it, its screech ringing across the house. I stopped and listened. The crying was still audible.

I yanked the door open. The vinegary smell of my own sweat pierced my nostrils.

You gotta do this, Cassie. You gotta.

The landing between me and the stairs was clear, unless Dad was lurking around the corner. I took the chance and charged across the expanse. No hand grabbed me. I darted down the stairs before the monster had a chance to catch up, careened around the corner, and then another corner and then one more, until I stood in the pantry.

With my dad.

He was butt on the floor, leaning against the wall, sobbing brokenly.

I tried to swallow past my heart. Maybe he hadn't seen me. I began backing away.

He made no move. He appeared miserable, what I could see of him, the kitchen moon pooling near his feet, his face swollen and melting. I'd never seen him cry before. I couldn't leave him.

"Dad? Are you okay?"

A sob escaped him. I took a tentative step forward. He didn't lunge off the ground toward me.

"Dad?"

His voice sounded like it was coming from far away. "What are you doing up?"

I said the first thing that came into my head. "I couldn't sleep."

He nodded as if he'd expected that, running his hand across his face. "I need to teach you the trick."

He didn't say it creepy. I could smell the liquor pouring off him in waves, but he wasn't hunting me, not right at this moment. I took a deeper breath. "What trick?"

He sat up straighter, garbling his words. "Whenever you can't sleep, take five deep breaths, pulling them all the way into your toes and holding them until you can't stand it. Then you stretch everything, even your little finger. Even the hair in your ears."

I smiled at this, though he wasn't looking at me. That was something he used to say to us when we were younger. *I love even the hair in your ears.*

Eww! We'd say. *It's full of wax!*

I still love it because I love you.

"Then hold your eyes halfway closed to the count of twenty-five, then all the way closed to the count of one hundred. Think you can do that?"

A big tear globe was swelling up in my right eye. I nodded.

"Good," Dad said. He pushed himself off the ground but started to tip. He got it on his second try. "You don't need me, then. I think I'll go for a walk."

He pointed toward the basement door. "Don't go in there. Basements are where men hide their secrets."

Cassie's Believe It or Don't!

COUNTRY GIRL
SURVIVES AN ENCOUNTER
WITH A MONSTER!

CASSANDRA MCDOWELL OF
LILYDALE, MINNESOTA, IS THE
ONLY TEENAGER ON RECORD TO
SURVIVE AN ENCOUNTER WITH
THE RARE DONNYMONSTER.
THE EVIL CREATURE LED HER TO
BELIEVE HE WASN'T DANGEROUS,
BUT CASSANDRA (MOSTLY) WASN'T
FOOLED. SHE LIVES TO FIGHT
ANOTHER DAY!

CHAPTER 51

I was nervous to head downstairs Saturday morning, but I shouldn't have been. Dad was quiet but not mean. Mom seemed more serene than she'd been in a while. Sephie had a secret smile on her face. We did our chores. Dad even stopped to tell me that I shouldn't worry, that Gabriel was probably already home. We cleared a trail, laid mulch in the garden, mowed.

When it was time for supper, we were all tired but seemed to be listening to the same song. That was one thing my family was exceptional at—treating each day like it was its own, disconnected from the day before. Yesterday was a *bad* day. This so far was a *good* day.

I even started to doubt the bad feeling I still carried. Gabriel proba-bly *was* home. I should bike over to his house first thing in the morning.

Life was too short to wait to tell him I loved him.

Deciding that felt like the sun had come out after a monthlong eclipse. I could breathe again. We ate leftover cake and ice cream for dessert, plopped in front of the television, watching *The Love Boat*.

"Hey, babe," Dad said to Mom, who was sitting at the foot of his chair eating her dish of vanilla ice cream. "I forgot to tell you that I sold a piece."

She spun around. "Don! That's fantastic. Which one?"

"It's a concept right now. A giant turtle. A guy in New York wants me to make it for him."

Mom's light dimmed. "Is it a paying gig?"

Dad chuckled and rubbed her back. "Don't worry. He's giving me a thousand dollars down to cover materials."

"Probably Sephie's braces money can come out of that, too," I said. I'd let the ice cream melt into the rich chocolate birthday cake, turning it damp and sweet.

"Yeah! Of course," he said. "Sephie, how would you like that? Your dad's art buying you the best smile in the county?"

She beamed, her perfectly fine (to me) buckers on full display. "That would be so awesome, Dad."

"How about you, Cass? What extravagance would you like with all the money that's going to come in?"

I held up my plate. "More cake!"

Everyone laughed. The room was loose and happy, so much so that when Dad suggested another swinging party to celebrate that they'd caught Chester the Molester, my stomach barely even tumbled. The television broke to commercial, and I turned to Mom and Dad because I'd thought of something better than cake to spend the money on: I wanted a subscription to *Mad* magazine. They hadn't yet bought me a birthday present. I hadn't asked for one because the party had seemed like plenty, but if they were handing out gifts . . .

My mouth was opening to toss out my pitch when I saw the color drain from Mom's face like someone had pulled her plug. She was staring at the television. When I looked back, Gabriel's mom was on the screen. She was sobbing.

At first, I thought she was happy weeping. *They DID find Gabriel!* But she wasn't joyful. She was broken.

"This has to stop," she said, tears streaming down her face as the ABC News microphone was pushed toward her mouth. The words on the bottom of the screen told us it was a breaking news report. "We have to save our boys."

"What's happening?" Sephie asked.

"Sshhh." Dad turned up the volume. Sergeant Bauer was now on-screen. I recognized the Dairy Queen in the background. The ABC News people were in Lilydale.

"Another Lilydale boy was assaulted this afternoon," Sergeant Bauer said, grim and forceful. "This leads us to believe that the man we have in custody for misdemeanor trespass is not the same person who abducted Gabriel Wellstone on the evening of June 1, as we'd hoped. Lilydale and its surrounding area are under complete lockdown. No children are allowed outside unsupervised."

Sephie grabbed my ankle and was holding it so tight that the skin was turning purple around her grip. My cake had morphed into sawdust in my mouth. I spit it onto my plate.

"We have two people of interest in the case," Sergeant Bauer continued, adjusting his police cap as if it hurt him. "We're following up on both."

"Connelly and Godlin," Dad said too quickly.

"It's not Mr. Connelly," I said, swiveling to glare at Dad. I poured all my anger in his direction, but it was anger tainted with fear, because I didn't think it could be Sergeant Bauer, not anymore, not if another boy had been taken. Sergeant Bauer would have been working all day long with the other police in town. Wouldn't he?

Dad pointed at the television. "You could ask your friend. Looks like he's the latest victim."

I flinched. I didn't want to see what he was referring to, but my face was pulled toward the screen. A newscaster had appeared. The banner on the bottom of the screen read, FOURTH CONFIRMED ATTACK IN LILYDALE. The newscaster stood on the road that ran in front of a familiar house.

Wayne Johnson's.

Sephie sucked in her breath.

The singing of frogs was the only sound other than the far-off rumble of a car. The vehicle grew nearer, its tenor changing as its tires hit the gravel. It kept coming. I expected it to drive past, I think we all did, but then its headlights turned toward our house, pinning us in our living room.

CHAPTER 52

"Aunt Jin!"

I used a month's worth of exclamation points to greet her, running toward her car like a bat out of hell. She leaped out and wrapped me in her gauzy, patchouli-scented arms. I was so happy to see her that I couldn't breathe normal. I kept sucking in fast baby sips of air, and it made me feel light-headed, like *boom*, time to pass out. She was just so beautiful, her hair loose and wavy, her clothes flowing.

My prayers had been answered.

"You've had quite the summer so far, baby girl," she said, murmuring as she held me, safe and tight. I pulled back just enough to look at her. She was so beautiful, so glamorous and strong. She was ten years younger than Mom, but it wasn't just that. She was so *alive*. The setting sun turned her skin tawny. Her ankle bracelets tinkled like fairies. Fireflies popped and waned in the woods, like they were signaling to her.

"Sephie too," I said, pointing. Mom, Dad, and Sephie had followed me out of the house, but I was the only one who ran up to Jin. Jin! She was here. "She needs a hug, too."

"Of course she does," Jin said. "Come on over here, princess."

Sephie walked toward us, brittle as glass.

"Are you hungry?" Mom asked.

"Starving," Jin said, smiling at her sister. "And thirsty."

She winked at Dad at this, but I was okay with that. She'd known him since she was a little girl. He was like a brother to her, always had been—I knew it from the letter of hers I'd found in his drawer.

Jin stepped away from me and Sephie, just far enough that she could turn a full circle and check out the property. "I've always loved Minnesota this time of year! Why don't you girls fill me in on what's been happening while your mom and pop set me up. Sound good, munchkins?"

I nodded and led her into the house and then the living room, where I steered her onto the couch. She sat in the middle. Sephie had gotten small and inside herself, like she always did when Jin was around, which meant I had to catch Jin up to speed all by myself. And I did—on the boys being attacked by the river, Mr. Connelly and how he hadn't done anything wrong, and Gabriel and how the police had to find him, but I didn't think they would because now Wayne had been attacked.

That's where I broke down.

"There, there now." Jin threw an arm around me. "With a friend as good as you, I know Gabriel is going to be okay."

But she *didn't* know that. When had she stopped listening to me? She was reaching up to take the drink Dad was offering her.

"Thank you, Donny. I see this is as strong as usual." She winked again. Had she always winked so much? "You still dealing?"

The line between Dad's eyebrows grew deep enough to hold a sheet of paper.

"Art, silly," she said.

I glanced at Mom. She'd taken her usual chair next to Dad's, a smaller, stiffer-looking version of his recliner. Her face was stony. I tried to remember the last time we'd seen Jin. I wrote her so much that it seemed like she was always around, but . . . had it really been a year?

Dad laughed at Jin's joke like we hadn't all just seen him flash and then hide his angry face. "Sold a big piece yesterday."

I was still watching Mom. If anything, her face grew harder.

"You finally turned him around, Peg!" Jin called out. She fake whispered to Dad along the back of her hand. "I always knew she'd be able to fix you."

Dad guffawed at this, that same exposed-throat laugh he only trotted out at his twice-a-year parties. My heart froze and then started pounding. Dad and Jin were flirting right over my head. Had they always? I glanced at Sephie. Her shoulders were drooped, her eyes wet, apologetic.

She'd known this awful thing all along.

She was sorry I had to learn it now.

I slipped into a cave deep and black inside myself. Jin wasn't going to make everything right.

No one was.

Mom stood. "I'll make sandwiches."

We sat uncomfortably while she rustled in the kitchen.

"So you like the *Nellie Bly's Trust It or Don't* I sent you?" Jin asked.

I wanted to rip the title right out of her mouth. "Yeah."

"What's this now? You've been writing me two letters a week for a year, and you're shy suddenly?"

I tried to smile, but I felt like a clown. There it was, so plain it might as well have been written across a movie screen. How could I ever have overlooked it? Jin was missing a piece of herself, that same piece that Sephie had lost back in December. I turned toward Dad, who was perched on the edge of his chair, grinning at Jin like an ape. That's all he was. A big, swinging ape who *took* and *smashed* and made us all clean it up.

A yell was building in my throat, a scream that would shame them all.

That's when Mom returned with a ham sandwich and a slice of chocolate cake on a TV tray. She kept her head down and handed it toward Jin. "Here you go."

"Thank you." Jin drained her drink and handed it to Dad. "Another, please."

Dad stood to take it, his gaze greedy. "Be right back. Then let's take our drinks down to my studio. I have something new to show you."

Jin was tucking into her sandwich but blinked like she had something in her eye. It reminded me of the trick she'd taught me for removing gunk: Grab your top eyelashes to pull your top eyelid out and over your bottom. Hold your eye closed like that, blinking the bottom lashes against your eyelid interior. It loosened whatever was stuck in there. Worked every time.

"Aunt Jin, I don't want you to go to Dad's studio," I said.

She chucked my chin. I smelled the onion from her sandwich. "Whatever you say, peanut. I can head down there after you two are asleep."

Mom winced.

I had banked everything on Jin rescuing me. She wouldn't, or couldn't. I didn't think so, but I had to be sure. "Jin, I want to come live with you this summer."

She guffawed at that, a lettuce fleck shooting out of her mouth and landing on the knee of her peasant skirt. "I don't know where I'm staying *tonight*, let alone all summer."

"You can sleep here tonight," Mom said through gritted teeth.

"Or stay here and not sleep," Jin said, coyly.

Mom nodded. It was a tight movement. "Or not sleep."

"Sephie, tell me about your summer," Aunt Jin said, turning toward my sister. Jin was already halfway done with her sandwich. She was so pretty, her brown hair cascading down her back, bright peacock feather earrings accenting her blue eyes. She was a butterfly, fast and temporary, and she was one more person who played the game by Dad's rules.

I watched her talk to Sephie, but I didn't hear what they were saying. All this time I'd thought of Aunt Jin as a hero. Well, here's something you should know: heroes are willing to pause their own lives to help you. Jin was wasn't that. She was a regular person.

"Mom, I'm sorry," I said suddenly, so loud that everyone stopped talking.

Mom had been sitting on the edge of the ottoman, hands clasped between her knees, leaning toward the three of us but disconnected. "What?"

I jumped up and ran to her, hugging her as tight as I could. "I'm so sorry."

She patted my arm. Her laugh was surprised. "What for?"

"Yeah, Cassie-bo-bassie, what for?" Aunt Jin asked, chuckling. "Where's the love for me?"

"I love you, too, Aunt Jin." And I did. But not like I loved Mom.

"More importantly, where's the love for me?" Dad asked, wandering into the room with a full drink in each hand. He offered one to Aunt Jin. She took it, sidling closer to Sephie. She patted the spot I'd vacated, and Dad dropped into it, his arm behind Jin. Mom twitched in my embrace.

"So many beautiful ladies here tonight!" Dad said. He was gregarious drunk, but there was an edge to it. "Who shall I sleep with?"

"Donny!" Jin said, faux shocked. She slapped his leg. "You shall sleep with your wife."

"You know," Dad said, his voice too loud, "there are some cultures where all the women in a family become lovers to a single man." He meant it as a joke, or at least we were all supposed to act like it was. When it came to the extra-creepy things he said, that was the agreement we'd had for as long as I could remember.

Aunt Jin leaned toward Sephie, her voice brassy and loud, their faces too close. "That reminds me of your grandpa," she said, waggling her eyebrows. "He was a good drinker, too, just like your dad."

I didn't think that was funny. I guess Mom didn't either, because she gasped, pushing me aside so she could jump to her feet.

"Jin, I think it's time for you to leave."

Jin's eyebrows shot straight up. "You have got to be shitting me, Peggy."

"Now," Mom ordered.

"You've always been able to forgive anything but the truth, haven't you?" Jin asked, standing. Her face had fisted up small and tight. "Don't talk, don't feel, and welcome the past into the present."

"You can save your therapy bullshit," Mom said. She was shaking. "My girls don't need to see you flirting with their father, that's all. They've both gotten some terrible news. If you can't respect this family, you don't need to be here."

"Hey, hey now," Dad said, his voice lazy. He grabbed Jin's hand and tried to pull her back onto the couch. "You're family. You're always welcome here."

Mom and Jin faced off. The air crackled between them. Dad could have been a booger on the ceiling for all they cared at this moment.

"Cassie, Seph, I guess I'll be going," Aunt Jin finally said. She was still glaring at Mom. She didn't move, maybe hoping we'd try to talk her into staying.

None of us did.

No one stopped her, either, when she stomped away. We all four stayed still as statues when the front door slammed. It wasn't until her car started up that Mom's shoulders slumped.

"I hope you're happy." The poison in Dad's voice startled me. He was staring at Mom with the blackest of hate.

"Not for years," she said. "Sephie, Cassie, go to bed."

Neither of us argued that it wasn't yet full dark.

Halfway up the stairs, Sephie grabbed my hand. "Sleep with me tonight. Please."

CHAPTER 53

Sephie held me in her bed. We were both shivering, me so hard that my teeth chattered.

Mom and Dad were yelling in the living room below.

"You try to fuck every woman you see!"

Dad's burry voice, a low-enough rumble that I could only hear snatches. ". . . lucky . . . past your prime . . ."

Mom yelled over him, her voice breaking. "I could leave you!"

"Sephie," I whispered, "I thought Bauer was the one attacking the boys, but I'm not so sure anymore."

"What?"

Dad's voice came through loud and clear this time. "I pay my share. Me and Bauer's side business makes twice what you do."

I raised my voice just enough to drown out Mom and Dad. "Every single boy who was attacked rides our bus. Ricky, Gabriel, Wayne, Clam, Teddy. Ricky said he heard clicking when he was grabbed, same as that clicking noise Bauer's dog tags make."

"The other night, Wayne told me it was Mr. Connelly's metronome," Sephie said, sitting up.

"If Connelly was gonna attack kids, he would never bring along a metronome," I said, wanting to believe my own words. "That's just stupid. Besides, he's not like that. Bauer is."

The moon shone in through Sephie's window, laying a strip of light across her eyes. She was piecing together scraps of a story. "Clam made the noise for me at summer school. It wasn't the sound of dog tags jangling."

Mom and Dad grew quiet below us, like they were waiting along with me.

"What did it sound like?" I asked.

She squished her eyes shut. I felt the noise more than heard it, back in her throat.

Cuk-cuk-cuk.

Like something small was trying to get out of her voice box.

Hearing it felt like my skin was being peeled off, like it hurt just to be alive.

Because I recognized that noise.

It was the same back-of-the-throat sound Goblin had made when I'd collided with him at the liquor store, and then again when he'd appeared in our driveway, arguing with Dad about his dog.

It wasn't Bauer molesting boys, hadn't ever been. The Goblin had been the one all along, and the police knew it but couldn't stop him. Dad didn't hate Goblin because he was a draft dodger, like Mom said. He hated him because monster hates monster.

"Sephie, if that's the noise, it means it's Goblin attacking the boys." The words surged out of my mouth, hot and painful. "It makes sense. He follows our bus *a lot*, and all the boys who were attacked ride bus twenty-four. Besides, we heard him make that same noise a couple times."

I could see her connecting everything she knew with what I'd just said. She shuddered. "We should tell Mom and Dad."

They were still arguing, but now they were using their civilized, educated voices to slice into each other. Dad told Mom she wasn't pretty anymore and that he could do better. Mom said Dad was a loose cannon and that he didn't really have PTSD like he claimed. They were both taking their fears out for a walk. They didn't mean it. They never did.

"They won't do anything."

"Then go to the police," Sephie said.

I rolled my eyes, even though I felt like puking. "Bauer told me no one would believe me because I got caught stealing that lip gloss."

"So we do nothing?"

I thought for a moment. "Let's run away!"

"How will that help Gabriel?"

"We'll run away to somewhere where they believe kids. I can tell them about Goblin and about Dad." I felt older than her, or more whole than her, and that realization made me feel emptier than I ever had.

I pulled her into an embrace. "Dad isn't going to change. You know that, right? He's going to keep hurting you, and he's going to come for me. Maybe if we turn him in, you can stop having sex with all those boys."

She drew back, her face as white as her sheet. "I don't have sex with *all those boys.*"

"It's okay, Sephie, I still love you."

The skin of her face moved like insects were wrestling underneath it. "You can't understand because you're not a woman."

That twisted my heart nearly free of its moorings. "Sephie, please. Come with me. We'll grab Frank, and all three of us will run away to somewhere safe."

"I can't." She lay back in bed and tugged the blankets to her neck. "Besides, there is no such place."

Mom and Dad's argument fired back up right below us.

I wanted to crawl under the covers with Sephie so bad. It'd been years since we'd slept together, months since I'd been brave enough to relax on top of a bed. I might have given in if she hadn't whispered that last sentence.

"Frank is neighbors with Goblin, isn't he?"

CHAPTER 54

Frank.

I had as good as served him up to Goblin, convincing him to ride with me to Goblin's house, letting Goblin put his hands on my one true friend. I thought back to Goblin's grabby eyes, his words massaging Frank for information.

And you're the new boy, just up the road, aren't ya? Your dad a farmer?

If Goblin was attacking the boys, then he had Gabriel in his house, and it was only a matter of time until he got my Frank because he wasn't slowing down, Goblin, not one bit, he was going to keep hurting boys until he was caught.

If I rescued Gabriel, though, he could tell the police everything, and Goblin would be arrested. Frank would be safe, and the Hollow boys wouldn't have to live in that quicksand fear anymore.

"I need to sleep in my own room," I told Sephie.

She pouted, but she let me go.

Once there, quiet as a mouse, I pulled on my sweatshirt and stuffed my backpack with a flashlight, my Swiss Army knife, *Nellie Bly's Trust It or Don't* for courage, and my new Magic 8 Ball for direction. I couldn't leave through the front door as long as Mom and Dad were still arguing. They'd see me.

I padded downstairs and took a left toward the bathroom. The window in there was normally closed because it lacked a screen. I hoisted it open, crawled out into the hot kiss of night, and slid the window closed behind me.

"Goodbye, I love you," I whispered to Mom and Sephie.

A soft touch at my ankle startled me. I let my eyes adjust and then bent down to pet the cat. "Bimbo kitty, you can't come with where I'm going."

I tiptoed to my bike, booted the kickstand, and pedaled into the soft night. The gravel gnawed at my tires. The trees murmured up at their very tops, shushering important secrets, but I couldn't make out what they were saying. I let the fireflies lead the way, dancing just ahead of me, sparkling as I passed and then dimming to nothing.

I neared Goblin's, fortifying myself with what I'd learned to survive living with Dad. *Gather your fear, stuff it down.* I lurched to a stop at the same spot where Sephie had stolen those strawberries a lifetime ago, the whoosh of wheelie gravel breaking through the nightsong.

Goblin had a light on inside his house. If his place was set up like ours, and like every other farmhouse in this county, that light was his living room. I rubbed my neck scar. The canned noise of a laugh track wafted across the night air. I couldn't tell what direction it came from, but the sound of someone watching television made me feel safer.

The gigantic lilac bush near Goblin's house would be a perfect place to hide. He would leave, or the living room light would go out, signaling he was going to bed. Then I would give him a little bit to fall asleep before sneaking into the house. If Gabriel was inside, I'd get him out. If I was wrong about Goblin, and he caught me in his house, I'd apologize just like when he'd found me trespassing the two other times.

I was heading toward the lilac when the moon glinted off something in the middle of the wild strawberry patch.

I dropped my bike and stepped toward it.

Sephie had stood in the exact spot. Whatever was catching the light of the moon had not been here when she'd eaten those berries.

I reached toward it, my hands trembling.

Because you see, I knew what it was even before I touched it.

Gabriel's paper airplane necklace.

CHAPTER 55

I felt an aching drowning torpor as I watched Goblin's house from the relative protection of the lilac bush. If I didn't follow through on this I'd be floating in that gray hopelessness forever, always a hunted child, no matter how old I got, how safe, how big, how rich.

I knew that way down deep, where the truth lived.

The sticky night air was an unwanted breath at my neck. Mosquitoes buzzed, hypnotizing me, whispering sharp lullabies. My head grew heavy, bobbing, jerking up, bobbing. That's why I didn't notice the living room light flick off or catch the soft snap of the screen door opening and closing, or register the crisp click of a car door. It was not until the vehicle fired up that my heartbeat woke me with its thudding cry of *look look look.*

I started. My eyes were scratchy with middle-sleep. I rubbed them, focusing. It was Goblin. He drove off, toward town.

I darted out of the lilac bush, across his lawn, over his porch, and to his door.

It was unlocked.

The pushback at the thought of walking through that door was a tangible force. It felt grossly improper, the warning of *wrong place wrong time shouldn't be here* crawling across my skin like an army of ticks.

Cass, sweet lass, hope your summer doesn't go too fast! I will see you around, promise.

Gabriel's paper airplane necklace rested in my back pocket. I'd felt a slip of paper when I'd shoved it in there. I yanked out the paper, holding it up to the moonlight. It was the note I'd discovered in Dad's studio. I had a guess what it was: Dad and Bauer's drug sales tally sheet. It explained why they'd been spending so much time together, why Dad had told Mom him and Bauer's "business" was earning more money than her, why Bauer had his cellar windows covered and Dad never allowed us into our own dirt basement.

They had illegal grow rooms down there.

I stepped through Goblin's door, numb.

I found myself in his dining room. It smelled dank but sweet, like rotting fruit. The living room was to my right, kitchen to my left, with a closed basement door off the kitchen. If it was like my house, the master bedroom was straight ahead down the hall, the bathroom across from that. The second floor surely housed three small rooms with sloping ceilings matching the roofline, two with closets.

But I didn't need to visit any of them.

The basement with its blacked-out windows was the only place Goblin would hide Gabriel.

Basements were where men kept their secrets.

I padded across the cracked linoleum of Goblin's cluttered, dirty kitchen.

I knew I shouldn't be there. The moon was scudding across the windows, warning me. But I couldn't leave without being sure. If I did, Goblin would get Frank, and Gabriel would never come home, and Dad would slurp me up whole and then spit out my bones so he could keep sucking on them, just like he was doing with Sephie.

So I walked toward that basement door.

Toward the smell of too-ripe peaches.

I grasped the knob and turned it, pausing at the top of the stairs. The darkness below was so complete that it devoured sound. I heard a wheezing before I realized it was me, fear shrinking my lungs. I wanted to run, but the only thing worse than going down there would be turning back and waiting for my dad to finally make it all the way up the stairs and into my bedroom.

I snapped on my flashlight, swallowing past the sharp edges in my throat.

The bright yellow made the dark worse somehow, highlighting the absolute black on its perimeter.

I shut the basement door behind me in case Goblin returned early, and I counted every step into the deep, feeling the old wood's warning creaks in my teeth. Seven stairs, and I was past halfway down, far enough to see the basement's dimensions.

My blood thudding, I played the egg yolk circle of my light over the sweating walls, across the packed dirt floor. The single room was the same size as the one below my house, a root cellar more than a basement, the musty smell caking my lips and nostrils and coating my hair.

My light ran over the murky canning jars against the far wall, found the table stacked with boxes, flashed off the single bare light bulb dangling a lonely string in the center of the room, but it kept returning to that one corner, the pulsing corner, the one with the cigarette-size gash of brightness against the dirt.

I scanned for any noise that would warn me Goblin was home, but the country wind shushed everything. Even the frogs had stopped singing. I took the last six steps, pushing through fear as thick as blister skin. When I placed my foot onto dirt packed so hard that it shone like oil, I could no longer stay above the gravedirt smell and had to swim in it like cave water.

There was no protection for children down here.

My flashlight was tugging, demanding I look closer at the slit of white in that not-right corner. The only sound was the thumping of my own heart, a dark-alley pumping more terrifying than silence. The closer I got to the corner, the worse the sugar-sour smell grew. I stumbled toward it, outside of myself, tugging my body along like a reluctant puppet.

I knew what I was looking at before I reached it, but I kept walking because

Ohnononoooooonooo

My stomach spasmed.

I grasped the wall to keep from falling. My hand met the rough, moist coolness of cement. I recoiled from the wet. My flashlight stayed focused on that white line in the dirt for several beats before my brain could remember the word

finger

A single human finger poked out of the dirt, crooked and the color of ghosts and screams.

Gabriel's finger.

I moaned.

The basement door whipped open, flooding the stairs in craven yellow light.

"Who's down there?"

I bit my tongue to keep from whimpering, blood flooding my mouth with the taste of pennies. Goblin stood thirteen steps above me, framed in the bright rectangle, his shoulders hunched. He must have parked up the road, which is why I hadn't heard him arrive, missed him entering the house, had no warning.

He would never forgive that I'd seen that finger.

I clicked off my flashlight and backed up against the damp wall. I tried to shrink into it, to become rock and dirt because you can't hurt either, but it didn't work. I stayed a girl made of quivering flesh.

"Who's down there, I said."

For a moment, an insane humming second, I considered answering him.

Just me. Cassie. I didn't mean to see anythingIwon'ttellanyonepleasel etmego.

"I know you're there. I can hear you breathing."

I ate my tears, my blood flowing acid with terror.

Goblin heard my fear.

He charged down the stairs, bringing his own flashlight to poke into the corners. Its light speared me. "Heh?"

He hadn't expected to discover me in this basement. He flicked his light to the finger near my feet, *Gabriel's finger*, then back to my face.

I tried to blink away the yellow, but it pooled in my eyes.

My feet were glued to the dirt. I could only nightmare whisper *help*.

A sound like new leather being stretched told me Goblin was smiling.

I understood then that he was rotting from the inside, a jack-o'-lantern left outdoors after a hard frost. He was a man who fed his dark, and it had grown so ravenous that only entire bodies could satisfy it.

He shuffled close and touched my wrist, almost a caress, before twisting my arm behind me. The pain was excruciating. He didn't know how to hold kids, not the right way. My skin slipped and burned under his grip and I thought of *Charlie's Angels* and Sabrina and how she always escaped, but that was TV. This was real and I was going to die and all I could do was wet myself before crying like that baby rabbit I'd released from Meander's jaws too late.

The memory gave me a burst of fight, but my arms and legs were aluminum foil to his steel.

He pulled me against his body.

He covered my eyes with his hot paw.

The other he used to squeeze my throat with something like curiosity.

That's when I heard it.

cuk-cuk-cuk

My yell flooded the basement, each word exploding like a firework: *You should have believed me.*

CHAPTER 56

My vision narrowed as Goblin crushed my neck.

Cass, sweet lass . . . I will see you around, promise.

Gabriel had honored his pledge. The kindest boy in the world had kept his word, and he'd had to die in this basement, cold, with only a monster to witness.

And I was going to join him.

I felt okay with that, drowsy almost.

The popping fireworks disappeared. Everything shaded to gray, and then ink. I was beyond speaking. Just when I thought it'd be blackness forever, my brain did the sweetest thing and threw me a going-away party.

It showed me a movie of the best parts of my life.

Sephie and me putting sunglasses on a kitty butt and laughing until she snorted and I peed a little.

Mom reading books to little Sephie and me, making all the voices.

Aunt Jin showing me how to dance with my hips.

Sephie finding three boys picking on me on the playground and pushing them down, fierce as an Amazon.

And . . . my dad? I was surprised to see him in my final movie, but there he was, loud and angry. Before I could figure out how that fit, the earth rose up to hit me, smack on the side of the face.

It should have hurt, but I could breathe again, and suddenly I was frantic for it. I sucked in air, gasping and coughing so hard I threw up. The more air I got, the wider my vision grew, expanding so I could see beyond a pinhole. The edges grew fuzzy, then saffron colored. Dad was there, his hands around Goblin's neck as Goblin's had been around mine.

Goblin was punching at him, kicking, but Dad wouldn't let him go.

Once Goblin didn't fight anymore, Dad dropped him. Goblin's chest was rising and falling, but he was out. Dad turned to me.

I saw it all in his eyes.

Mom had gone to bed.

Dad, angrier than he'd ever been, had clipped his nubby little nails.

Then, finally, he'd entered my bedroom.

But I hadn't been there.

And he'd come looking for me.

He must have spotted my bike in the ditch, charged into Goblin's house, found him choking me, and then returned the favor.

That all seemed just fine, and so I returned to the comfort of oblivion.

CHAPTER 57

I woke up in the hospital. The smell of dirt was so strong that I came to thrashing. It took me a while to stop, even when I realized where I was. Mom and Sephie were brought to my bedside, but not Dad. They had matching bags under their eyes. In fact, they looked a lot like each other. I'd never noticed it before.

Mom rushed immediately to my side. "Cassie! How are you?"

I aimed to say "you tell me," but it came out as a croak.

Mom grabbed a cup of water from my hospital tray and pivoted its straw in my direction. The cool liquid felt like live coals going down at first, but once it coated my parched throat, I couldn't get enough. Mom explained the situation as I drank. Goblin had broken my wrist when he'd twisted it, and he'd strangled me within an inch of my life. The doctors said my scar tissue saved me, which is a hoot and a half if you think about it. They said they'd need to keep me twenty-four hours for observation, but other than my wrist, my body would be just fine, they thought.

"Where's Dad?" My voice was deeper than usual, but back.

Before Mom could answer, Mrs. Wellstone showed up, right there in my hospital room. Her hair was loose and looked like it hadn't been washed in a while. When she ran over and gently held me, I could smell that I was right about that second part. I felt miserable for her, but it felt so good to be hugged.

"Thank you," she sobbed.

When I blinked, I could see that finger on the back of my eyelids. Maybe I would forever. "It was Gabriel?"

She nodded.

"You shouldn't be here," I said. I meant that she should be with him, or at least his body, but it came out wrong. Then I remembered the necklace.

"Are my pants here?" I asked Mom.

She nodded and fished them out of a skinny cabinet. She handed them over. I dug in the back pocket and felt the riffle of paper and the cool metal of Gabriel's paper airplane necklace. I handed the latter to her.

"Ohmygod." She held it as if it were made out of tissue paper.

"I found it outside Goblin's house. I think Gabriel must have thrown it out to help us find him." I wasn't sure I thought that, but I desperately wanted to say something nice about Gabriel.

She began weeping again, but softer. "Thank you for bringing my boy back to me."

Her pain was so big, but she was trying to keep it to herself so it didn't spill all over me. "I'm sorry he's gone," I said.

She nodded, rubbing her fingers over the necklace. "I want you to have this," she said, handing it back to me.

I held up my good hand. "I can't!" I didn't want to take anything from her. She'd already lost too much. Besides, the police probably needed it for evidence.

"No, please," she said. "It would mean everything to us. You know Gabriel wanted to be a pilot?"

I did.

In the end, I took the necklace, and if me ending up with that doesn't tell you that there is a grand plan for this life, then you're hopeless.

CHAPTER 58

Mrs. Wellstone and I ended up talking some more. We promised we'd keep in touch. She left, but Mom and Sephie were still haunting the corners of the room, almost like the three of us didn't know each other.

A knock at the door saved me from having to figure out what to do about that.

"Cassandra?"

I recognized Officer Kent but not the woman with him. He closed the door behind them both.

"This is Ms. Didier. She's a social worker. We'd like to talk with you."

I held Gabriel's necklace. My jeans were draped over me, the edge of the drug tally sheet showing in my back pocket. Mom moved toward me, but Officer Kent held up his hand.

"We'd like to talk with her alone, if you don't mind. We have your permission?"

Mom nodded, but she looked wretched. When she and Sephie stepped out, I caught a flash of colors in the hallway. It was Evie and Frank. Frank was holding flowers like he'd come to ask me to prom rather than was visiting me in the hospital. What a dork.

I smiled, even though I couldn't smell anything but Goblin's basement.

I was going to tell my story.

ACKNOWLEDGMENTS

It takes a dream team to assemble a book that cuts this close to home, and boy, did I get one.

First, deep and forever thanks to my agent, Jill Marsal, and my editor, Jessica Tribble, for believing in this story. It's an odd duck of a suspense novel—a thriller for adults but with a teenage protagonist, set in a flyover state—and it wouldn't have found its audience without those two. Thanks also to Jessica and Charlotte Herscher for zeroing in on the heart of the story and trimming away the distractions. (If you'd like to read the ten scintillating pages of chicken butchering they cut, shoot me an email.) Thanks to Jon for his incisive and encouraging copyediting, Kellie for her supportive proofreading, Carissa for her oversight.

Gratitude to my emotional support creatives: Shannon Baker, Johnny Shaw, and Terri Bischoff, who read early drafts and gave crucial feedback and love; Catriona McPherson, for taking me in at a low point, opening up her warm hug of a home, and shoring me up inside; Linda Joffe Hull for sage career advice; Lori Rader-Day for the title of this book and so much more, including the scream room; Susie Calkins and Nadine Nettmann for the laughs, wine, and wisdom.

To my writing group, Prose before Bros, thank you for providing a sounding board as well as a watercooler. Thank you especially to Carolyn, who's on this journey with me in so many ways.

Gratitude to my aunt Suzanna, who has waited patiently for me to find my way out of the madness: thank you for leading with courage, kindness, and humor. Zoë and Xander, I am unbearably proud of both of you, and of your compasses that point true north. Amanda, I see your strength, and it's humbling. Christine, Kellie, and Cindy, thank you for being my sisters. Looking forward to many more adventures. Tony, thank you for growing with me, standing by me, and sharing your creativity and beautiful heart.

And finally, thank you to Patrick, who opened the door to a whole new world.

ABOUT THE AUTHOR

Jess Lourey writes about secrets. She is a bestselling Agatha, Anthony, and Lefty Award–nominated author of crime fiction, magical realism, young adult, and nonfiction. She is a tenured professor of creative writing and sociology, a recipient of The Loft's Excellence in Teaching fellowship, a Psychology Today blogger, and a TEDx presenter. (Check out her TEDx Talk for the inspiration behind her first published novel.) When not leading writing workshops, reading, or spending time with her friends and family, you can find her working on her next story. Discover more at www.jessicalourey.com.